A favor for a friend had me running for my life. Maybe I was in the wrong business...

I rolled over a big rock which tore at my parka then came up against a tree trunk with a bump. Hurriedly, I rose to a crouch and got behind the tree. As I did so, I heard another shot and pieces of bark showered my left cheek. I kept moving, dodging between trees, heading downhill. I heard several more shots as I ran but none seemed to come as close as the one that had struck the tree. I didn't dare look back but I had a good guess as to the identity of my pursuer.

How the hell did he find me? I wondered. Then it struck me: he must have been waiting for me. He had taken a chance on me visiting Gabrielle, had seen me go by on my way there, then had waited for me to pass on my way back. Smart. I should have considered the possibility. I wondered how many bullets Legere's gun held. I didn't know anything about guns, but I had held it in my hand and I knew it was not full size. I had a notion that a full-size handgun might hold about twenty rounds. I knew a compact handgun would hold more than six but less than twenty. Maybe twelve? I would not have bet my life on it. He had fired about seven or eight rounds so far. Did he have an extra clip?

I kept moving down the hill. I could hear him following, bounding down the hill after me, his feet sliding in the leaves and dirt with every step. Two more shots rang out.

Justin Vincent is a San Francisco based artist who leads a secret double life as a cat burglar. He likes the freedom, money, and self-determination his unusual career provides but also increasingly feels that it is a life he fell into by accident. When a valuable painting is stolen from his lover, Valerie, Justin agrees to use his underworld contacts and knowledge of the black market to help. The search leads him to an antiquities dealer who has fallen on hard times and a mysterious European middle man. With the help of his friend Ashna, a skilled hacker, and Gabrielle, owner of an art gallery in Nice, Justin gathers clues that lead him to a mysterious chateau in the South of France and a dangerous web of secrets and lies. To escape with his life and complete his objective, Justin's skill, luck, and perseverance will be tested to their utmost limit.

KUDOS for *Old Gold Mountain*

TAYLOR JONES SAYS: In *Old Gold Mountain by* Bradley W. Wright, Justin Vincent is an artist, and an art thief. During the day, he's a successful sculptor, and by night, he's an equally successful cat burglar. When his lover, Valerie, has an important painting stolen from her house, Justin uses his skills to track down the painting. But the painting has been sold on the black market, and the search will take Justin to the limit of his skills and endurance, and he will be lucky to escape with his life. Wright combines superb character development, vivid descriptions, and fast-paced action to create an exciting and suspenseful thriller. A really great read. ~ *Taylor Jones, The Review Team of Taylor Jones & Regan Murphy*

Old Gold Mountain by Bradley W. Wright is the story of a sculptor/art thief, Justin Vincent, who has begun to have second thoughts about his secret life. As he struggles with his dilemma, his lover, Valerie, has a valuable painting stolen from her home. Even though the painting is insured, the artist is a friend of Valerie's, and he left the painting in her keeping. Too embarrassed to tell the artist that she's lost the painting, she begs Justin to use his skills and contacts in the black market art community to find the painting and get it back. The hunt takes Justin from the hills of San Francisco to Italy and then the South of France, dealing with antiquities dealers, crooked lawyers, and mafia members, barely escaping with his life, and requires the use of all his skills, his wits, and the help of a computer hacker. Not exactly your average heist. *Old Gold Mountain* is an intriguing mystery, a tense thriller, and an adventurous romp. Combining mystery, suspense, action, and exotic settings, this one will keep you on the edge of your seat all the way through. I thoroughly enjoyed it. ~ *Regan Murphy, The Review Team of Taylor Jones & Regan Murphy*

ACKNOWLEDGMENTS

I would like to thank my first readers David Hunkins and Shanti Markstrom for their valuable critiques and suggestions. I would also like to thank Lauri at Black Opal Books for taking a chance on this manuscript and my two amazing Black Opal Books editors Reyana and Faith.

OLD GOLD MOUNTAIN

BRADLEY W. WRIGHT

A Black Opal Books Publication

GENRE: MYSTERY-DETECTIVE/AMATEUR SLEUTHS/THRILLER

OLD GOLD MOUNTAIN
Copyright © 2018 by Bradly W. Wright
Cover Design by Shanti Markstrom
All cover art copyright © 2018
All Rights Reserved
Print ISBN: 978-1-62694881-5

First Publication: MARCH 2018

DEDICATION

for Shanti and Taren

CHAPTER 1

July 12 ~ December 9:

I had Hilary Hahn's recording of the Bach Partitas on the stereo. The car windows were open and the smell of the sun warmed Northern California redwood forest was intoxicating—simultaneously sweet and pungent, clean and earthy. It was a nice place for a drive but an even better place for a walk. Rounding a gentle curve, I spotted my turn off, slowed, and bumped off the edge of the pavement onto soft dirt and pine needles. The single-lane access road led straight into the forest, ending after about two hundred yards at a small dirt-and-gravel trailhead parking area. I set the brake and shut off the engine. For a moment, I just sat there, enjoying the silence and earthy smell drifting in. A glance at the clock on the dashboard reminded me I was on a schedule, though, so I rolled up the windows, climbed out of the car, and retrieved my daypack from the rear seat. Before leaving the city that morning, I had outfitted myself in typical hiker garb: cargo shorts, trail runners, T-shirt, and hooded fleece pullover in drab colors. My pack was probably a bit larger than average but not enough to attract attention. On my wrist was a recently purchased, aggressively masculine GPS watch. I wasn't much of a gadget person but the GPS unit was going to come in handy. I also had a well-used SLR camera on a shoulder strap.

It was my fourth trip to this particular spot in the last few months. I'd been taking pictures of trees and posting them to a photo sharing site, and I'd also told a few people casually that I was working on an art project about trees.

I had a pretty good hike ahead of me, so I locked the car and set off, gnawing bites of salmon jerky while I walked and snapping occasional pictures. The forest was fragrant and damp. I saw some fresh chanterelles poking up from the duff a few feet off the path but left them. After a couple of miles, I came to a diverging path, less wide, with lower branches creating an almost solid roof of foliage, and turned onto it. There was a stream paralleling this new trail and I could hear the gurgling water as I walked.

After another mile, I stopped and checked my GPS. This was the spot. I sat on a rock to rest and drank some water. A couple of minutes later I was ready. I found a space between two trees and left the path. Now I was bushwhacking through redwood forest, carefully hopping over ferns, using fallen trees as pathways. Redwood forest was not too bad when you were off-trail but you could step on a rotten log and twist an ankle if you were not careful. I had done some off-trail hiking over the last weeks to practice, and I had a good idea of how much distance I could cover in a fixed amount of time. I knew how far I needed to go and calculated it should take about an hour.

I checked my GPS regularly to make sure I was on course. After about forty-five minutes, I suddenly saw the road below which meant I had been moving faster than I thought—probably a bit amped up. I slowed and crept carefully down the slope until I was about twenty feet from the road. I had hit it almost dead on. The house was twenty yards down the road to my right so I moved across the slope until I was even with it. I had a good view, and I was well concealed in the trees, so I went ahead and changed into the clothes I had packed in my backpack: black cargo pants, long sleeved black T-shirt, black knit cap. I stowed various items in my pockets including a thin pair of black gloves and some tools. I also took a telescoping tube three inches in diameter at the widest end out of my bag and hung it by a small strap crosswise over my shoulders. I was early, as I often was, so I sat down, leaning against a tree trunk, and thought back over the series of events that had led me to this place...

ↄ/ↄↄ

It had started several months before with a job—a catering gig. I saw an ad for on-call catering help and applied via email. A few days later, they responded. I used a throwaway email address and a fake name. I had forged papers to go along with the fake name, and I was pretty sure they wouldn't ask any questions. I had done that kind of work before so I knew a lot of my co-workers would be undocumented. Like most service industry employers, large catering companies didn't worry much about identity and background checks. They would be chronically understaffed if they did. The company was called A Touch of Elegance. I went in for a brief interview, and they said they would reach out when they needed help.

My fake ID and Social Security card listed me as Dustin Cruz. I had to think of something, and that was the name that popped into my head. It was an amalgamation of the names of two friends from high school. A friend of a friend had recommended a guy, who could do the work, so I made an appointment and showed up at his apartment in West Oakland in the middle of the day on a weekday. I guess it wasn't unusual for people to forget to come up with a name before they arrived at his kitchen table. Or maybe people just assumed it was part of the service. I remember his blank stare and the smell of his filter-less cigarettes. His supplies were neatly arranged on the surface of the table which was buckled from spills and scarred with burns. Three small children were watching cartoons in the next room. One little girl kept wandering into the kitchen doorway and staring at me with huge, dark eyes. The papers were high quality and I had used them several times. Dustin was similar to my real name Justin. I went through a phase in my teens when I read a lot of old hard-boiled detective novels—Dashiell Hammett, Raymond Chandler. A piece of advice from one of those books stuck with me. It said when choosing a fake name, you should go with something that sounds like your real one. That way you will respond more naturally. It seemed to work fairly well. When I was on a temp job, I was Dustin. My real last name, Vincent, sounded nothing like Cruz, but it was what I came up with, and I stuck with it.

An email from A Touch of Elegance showed up in the inbox of my disposable account a couple of days later. It was from a manager named Fred and asked if I could do setup and help serve at a house party. The catering company mainly did private parties at people's homes which was why I had answered their ad instead of somebody else's. I didn't need the money. I was after something different: anonymous access to nice houses. I was free the night of the party so I wrote back and accepted.

The address Fred gave me when he forwarded the details the next day was up in Mill Valley, not far from

Muir Woods, off a curving road running up the lower slope of Mt. Tamalpais. When I saw the address, I had a good idea of what it would be like—quiet, wooded, and serene. Mill Valley real estate was very expensive and very exclusive. The particular area where the house was located was, if anything, even more so.

I arrived early and parked my borrowed car in the lot of a church a quarter mile down the road as instructed. They didn't want the help taking up prime parking near the house. It was a Saturday, and I was the first to arrive so the lot was empty. The long shadows of redwoods and the reddening afternoon sunlight looked good stretching across the blacktop surface of the lot and climbing up over a carved wooden sign near the street advertising Sunday Services, All Welcome.

I pushed the button to lock the car and set off walking up the hill in the eerie silence of the semi-rural Marin suburbs. A red tail hawk was circling high up above, and I heard small creatures rustling in the underbrush, hiding out under the leaves, trying not to be dinner for the raptor.

It was a good ten degrees warmer than in the city, and I had worked up a light sweat by the time I made it up to the top of the hill. The residence was what the real estate people called a "snout house" with double garage doors facing the road, a blank second story rising up among the trees, and not much more of the house visible from the front. The lot was large and sloped with plenty of forested land on either side. I guessed at probably one lower level, built into the hill, with walls of windows facing the wooded hillside and looking out over the Bay. Probably a great view. I had mapped it before coming out and I knew there was state and federal park land across the road and also on the slope below the house. A number of public hiking trails passed close to the location. There were other houses on the road but the closest was over a hundred yards away and hidden by trees.

I found some shade under a big old redwood across the road and waited. it was pleasant sitting there on a mossy boulder in the warm afternoon shade just staring at the house and letting my mind wander. I didn't spend much time in nature. I lived in the city and spent most of my time there. My childhood though, was spent in the country, and when I sat in nature my mind flowed back to that feeling of peace and silence. After about fifteen minutes, I saw the catering van coming up the road, flashing white between the trees, and walked out to meet it.

Fred, the crew manager, parked in the driveway and got out. He was a middle-aged guy with an acne-scarred face, wearing a white chef's jacket already starting to show rings of sweat under the arms. We exchanged pleasantries while he retrieved his clipboard from the van and took a minute to read over the instructions, occasionally running a worn rag from his back pocket across his forehead.

"It says we can pull into the garage and unload. The owners won't be here till later. Got a garage opener here somewhere." He dug through the console in the van and eventually came up with the opener.

The door rolled up revealing a big space all nicely finished and painted. Everything in the garage was neatly arranged—rakes, shovels, weed whacker, clippers, etc. all hung on evenly spaced hooks. At the far end and wrapping around halfway across the back wall were matching white plastic bins stacked on industrial shelving. I imagined if I started opening those bins I would find one for Christmas decorations, one for camping gear, one for extra blankets and sheets, one for cleaning products…I shuddered. Suburban living gave me the creeps. I'd lived in the country and in the city but never in the weird, limi-

nal in-between. I'm sure it's fine. I'm just not used to it.
A white Range Rover was parked beside the open spot. Fred pulled the van in, and we began unloading tables, bins of prepped food, bags of ice in coolers, and more bins of plates, silverware, napkins, table cloths. Once the van was empty Fred parked it out on the road. He came back and checked his clipboard again, running a short, callused finger along under the text as he read.

"The door should be unlocked. There's a security system. Wait here." He opened the door that led from the garage into the house, stepped up into a dim hallway, and disabled the alarm system via a panel opposite the door. He was standing between me and the keypad so that there was no angle from which I could see him entering the code. We started carrying everything inside and I saw right away that my earlier guess was correct. The short hallway opened into a soaring entry with a grand staircase leading up to the second story and also down to lower levels. It was a modified Cliff May style Northern California mansion with open plan, concrete floors, high ceilings, and lots of raw wood. The second floor ended at the midpoint of the house. The back half had a full height, peaked ceiling. Under that ceiling was an informal living room area with sofas and chairs. To the right of that was a giant open kitchen with the ubiquitous, stainless steel restaurant grade appliances. There was a wall of windows, and a balcony wrapping the entire back side of the house. The view, as I had guessed, was good. I could see the bay in the distance and the red-orange flare of low, late afternoon sunlight reflecting off the water.

As we moved back and forth between garage and kitchen carting food and equipment, I began to surreptitiously check out the art on the walls. This place was a bonanza. I saw two Rauschenberg prints, some good photos by Sherman and Leibowitz, a few big abstract paintings by unfamiliar artists, and, glimpsed through a high, open entryway to the formal dining room, a Lichtenstein lithograph.

Just as we were finishing packing all the gear in I heard the garage door open, a powerful engine purr and die, and, not long after, footsteps clacking across the polished concrete floor toward the kitchen. A small man entered, dressed casually but expensively in jeans, loafers, and a well pressed blue Oxford shirt. He was middle aged and handsome with a receding hairline, gray at the temples, and sharp features. A few steps behind him came another man, also handsome but rangy and larger boned. He was similarly dressed but with more flair and pops of bright color. He wore architectural glasses with aquamarine frames. To my surprise, I saw that he was carrying a large, brightly colored tropical bird on his wrist. I don't know much about birds. It might have been a parrot, maybe a macaw. The bird turned sideways, glaring at us with one bright eye, and raised a purple/yellow/blue wing, bobbing its head slowly up and down.

"Hello," said the first man, "Looks like you got in all right. I'm Carl, and this is Bill. And this—," He gestured to the bird. "—is the birthday girl Lucille."

Lucille let out a piercing shriek and flapped her wings. Bill walked over to a large tangle of what appeared to be driftwood suspended from the ceiling by several steel cables. Lucille carefully clambered off his wrist onto a branch. I noticed then that the floor below the hanging driftwood was covered with seeds, shells, bits of chewed plastic, and large, irregular circles of dried bird shit.

Fred stepped forward, shook Carl's hand, and they went off toward the formal dining room to go over the plan for the evening. I kept my face turned away from the home owners as much as possible, unloading bins onto the counters. Bill brushed by me, took a diet soda from the giant refrigerator, gave Lucille a pat on the head, and headed off up the grand stairway leaving me alone with the bird. *The master suite must be upstairs*, I thought. Several moments later, I jumped and almost dropped the two champagne flutes I was unloading, when the bird let out another massive shriek and shouted very clearly in a creepy, high-pitched but human-like voice, "Lucille is the birthday girl."

Carl's answer rang out from the dining room in a baby talk voice I wouldn't have expected from him. "Yes, she is, Yes, she is!"

Soon, a crew of house cleaners arrived, then more catering crew members trickled in by ones and twos. One of the cleaners set to work on hands and knees cleaning the area under Lucille's perch. Canapés were assembled and slid into the oven on large baking sheets, tables were set up, wine placed in decorative buckets full of ice to chill, glasses set out at the ready. Before I knew it, we were into what I thought of as the swirl—a state familiar to me from the old days when I was in college and worked banquets at fancy hotels. There was no time to stop, no time to escape the bustle, you just had to surrender to the swirling, clanking, well-choreographed but intense dance of preparation, service, clean up. At some point, a string quartet arrived and set up in one corner, tuned their instruments, and began playing a Bach prelude to warm up. I slipped into a guest bathroom and quickly changed into my service outfit of black pants, white shirt, black waiter jacket.

A few minutes after I finished dressing, Lucille's birthday party commenced with the arrival of the first guests. I soon learned that the proper terminology was hatch-day party. This seemed to be Carl's running joke for the evening, and I heard him repeating it to several different groups of guests as I passed through the various rooms with constantly replenished trays of hors-d'oeuvres. Through the blur of amiable conversation, well-dressed guests, baroque strings, lipsticked mouths gobbling canapés, champagne flutes drained and placed on my tray, I found time to glance at the art on the walls and my initial impression was reinforced. There was probably two million dollars or more worth of fine art hanging in the house. I liked Carl and Bill's taste. It was good stuff, well chosen. Their taste in furniture was nice too, simple but conservative. I didn't see a lot of the obvious stuff you'd see in every nouveau-riche tech worker's loft. I'd been to social events at more than a few houses, condos, and apartments where the host's idea of decorating was apparently walking into the fancy modern furniture store and ordering one of each.

Around nine p.m., the guests were all called into the living room/kitchen area and brought to order by Carl banging a fork on a wine glass. "Happy Hatchday" was sung to the accompaniment of the quartet with a series of shrieks and chatter from Lucille who was standing on her branch and bobbing to the music. Cake was cut and served. Lucille got some sort of bird treat that looked better to me than the sheet cake with too much icing the other guests were eating.

Not long after that, the party began to wind down. I ran into Fred, and he gave me the okay to leave. The workers who had arrived later would be staying to clean up and pack out. He handed me his clipboard so I could write in my hours next to my name. As I was filling in my hours, he turned to speak with Bill who had tracked him down to let him know that the downstairs bar was out of Chardonnay. I took the opportunity to glance at the top sheet on the clipboard. There it was, the code. I memorized it quickly and handed the clipboard back to Fred.

It seemed to be a date, easy to remember.

Outside the house, I passed a couple standing by the driver side door of a sleek black SUV, both obviously tipsy, fighting in low but strident voices over who was more sober. I recognized the woman. She was wearing a white wrap dress and shook her head of black, shoulder-length hair in a familiar gesture just as I was approaching. She held the car keys in a white-knuckle grip. She owned one of my sculptures. The man—I knew, though I had never met him—was a multimillionaire from the first tech boom, employee number three or four in one of the big ones. He was tall, wearing a sports coat, button-up, and jeans, with just the right amount of stubble covering his face. I ducked my head and gave them a wide berth. It was unlikely that they would recognize me, but I didn't want to take any chances.

As soon as I was well away, walking briskly down the hill, the cool night air of Marin on my face, I took out my phone, opened a new note, carefully entered the code, and saved it.

℮↷℮↷

Now, months later, I was back for my second visit to the bird house. The slope where I sat put me at the same height as the second floor of the house. Unfortunately, there were only two second floor windows at the front. During the party, I had wandered upstairs with a tray of hors-d'oeuvres as if I thought there might be hungry guests lurking in the master suite. While up there I had quickly checked the layout. I knew that one window belonged to a study, the other to a guest bathroom. The master suite was at the back. Still, I could see that all the lights were on downstairs.

I had a small, homemade device with me that I needed to place on the garage door. I dug through my pack until my fingers closed on the plastic box. I had painted it the same medium warm gray color used on the exterior of the house. I had also prepared it with a dual sided adhesive strip on the bottom. I peeled away the thin piece of plastic covering the adhesive and thumbed the switch to turn the device on. At the edge of the trees, I stood absolutely still for a moment, holding my breath. No sound of cars on the road. No neighbors out walking their dogs. I darted across the road, up the driveway, and adhered the box to the garage door near the ground. The color match was good. I was confident they wouldn't notice it.

Back in my hiding spot among the trees, I got a protein bar out of my pack and sat back to wait and observe. I knew Carl and Bill would be going out. When Fred from the caterers sent me the email asking me to work the party, he had lazily forwarded a general inquiry from Bill with details of the date, time, number of people needed, etc. This gave me Bill's personal email address. After the party, acting on a hunch, I tried logging in to Bill's account with variations of the bird's name as the password. It only took three tries:

Lucille!

A friend of mine once told me that even the most intelligent people usually have stupidly simple passwords—kid's names or birth dates, pet names, or one of the hundred or so most common passwords like 123456, password, etc. It was easy to find the lists online. My friend had a whole theory of human psychology built around this fact.

After that, I monitored Bill's email every few days. Nothing creepy, just looking for invitations and RSVPs. Tonight the couple would be attending a small dinner party at a friend's house in the city which meant they would be gone for at least three hours, probably longer.

After thirty-five minutes of sitting and waiting, I finally saw some movement through the small window above the front door. Indistinct figures moved past the window this way and that, engaged in last minute preparations before leaving: keys, jacket, phone. Soon, the garage door rolled up, I heard muffled sounds of car doors closing, and the Range Rover backed out. Carl was at the wheel, Bill in the passenger seat. I saw Carl reach up and press the button on the remote clipped to the visor. Nothing happened. He pressed it again, and the door began to close. The roll-jam device was working. It was getting dark now. Just before it disappeared around a curve, the bright headlamps of the Range Rover flicked on, turning the road and trees for an instant into a brilliant, artificial-looking tableau.

I sat back to meditate and wait for the last bit of daylight to drain out of the valley. Thirty minutes later, I stood and made my way down the slope to the edge of the road. The roll jam was simple but ingenious. It worked by capturing the code the remote broadcast and also jamming the signal so it didn't reach the receiver on the garage door opener. When the user tried again, it captured the second code, still jamming the signal, and then broadcast the first code it captured. This way, the door closed and the user thought it was a momentary glitch, but the device had the second code saved, which could then be used to open the door. I waited a moment, listening as I had before, then crossed the road, and pressed a button on the device. The garage door began to rise. I entered quickly and sent the door trundling back to its closed position.

Now was the moment of truth. Would the security code still work? If not, I would have decisions to make. If they were smart, the code would have been changed after the party. Or maybe their security system allowed for one-time codes. I pulled a small piece of paper from my left front pocket just to verify one last time the numbers running through my head. A date. Just then it struck me: the date was the date of the party. Almost certainly a single-use code. Hard to believe I hadn't noticed it before. But the year was wrong. Twelve years in the past. Twelve years struck a bell. I remembered a snatch of conversation from the party.

"How old is the bird?"

"Twelve, I think."

"Twelve! How long do these things live for?"

"Dear god, forever. Forty or fifty years."

"You might as well have a real child. At least you can kick them out when they're eighteen."

Twelve years. The date was Lucille's birthday. Or 'hatch day' I should say. Knowing this, I was certain the code would work. It had probably been chosen when the system was installed and had never been reset since.

I pulled my gloves on. The door connecting the garage to the house was locked, but the knob set was cheap. Interior doors seldom had good locks. I decided to try a bump key first. I pulled my lock pick set out of a cargo pocket and spread it open on the floor. I had several bump keys for different knob sets. I selected the right one, inserted it into the lock, and rapped on the end several times with a screwdriver handle. The lock disengaged and turned easily, but I kept the door closed, holding the knob while I put away my tools with my free hand.

With my tools stowed back in my pockets, I turned the handle, stepped through, and quickly entered the code on the security panel to disable the alarm system. The LEDs blinked green three times, and a robotic female voice reported that the system was disarmed. I took a moment, then, to close my eyes and go through my memory of the interior and the layout. My plan still seemed good. I pushed the button on the knob to lock it from the inside then fished a small tube of superglue from one of my cargo pockets and squirted some into the keyhole. If they did come home for some reason, they wouldn't be able to get through the door, and that would give me plenty of time to disappear out the back and off the balcony. I went to the front door next and repeated the super glue trick but left it ajar just a crack. That was my exit path. I could pull it closed if needed but would leave it open for the present.

On my previous visit, I had seen all the rooms, except for the master bedroom. I wanted to take a quick look before proceeding with my plan, so I carefully ascended the stairs in the dark. The bedroom was large and sparsely furnished. I walked the perimeter with a small flashlight, checking out the art. Nothing caught my eye until I shined the light on the wall above the headboard of the massive California king bed. Was that a Kline? Shit. I stepped up onto the bed and took a closer look. It did seem to be a Franz Kline mixed media work. Small but with those unmistakable, powerful lines. Mentally, I increased my estimation of the total value of the art in the house by perhaps a million. Still, the Kline didn't change my plan. I didn't want to try to move that kind of art.

Back downstairs, I started with the Rauschenbergs. I took each print off the wall. They were in very nicely constructed shadowbox frames. I popped the backs off the frames and carefully peeled the prints away from the backings where they had been stuck on with archival double-sided tape.

Next, I went to the dining room. The Lichtenstein's frame was screwed to the wall. I pulled a small, battery operated screwdriver from a cargo pocket and reversed the screws out of the wall. The frame came off cleanly, and I dismantled the back and removed the lithograph.

Next, I carried all three artworks to the coffee table in the seating area and stacked them neatly. Just as I was reaching around to pull the tube hanging against my back forward and slip the strap over my head, a deafening screech slashed through the dim room, and I jumped, spinning mid-air in the direction of the sound. Directly in front of me was a tall object covered by a sheet or blanket. Heart racing, I stepped forward and lifted a corner of the fabric. Thin metal bars. I lifted it farther. A cage. I lifted it farther still and saw Lucille's angry eye shining in the dark, glaring back at me. She clacked her beak a couple of times then seemed to deflate as her eye slowly closed and her breathing became deep and regular. I carefully lowered the fabric. I had forgotten about the bird.

Quickly, I rolled the art up and fitted it into the tube. I ran through an inventory of the things I had brought in with me, took one last look around, then left via the front door. Pausing in the shadows of the front porch, I held my breath and listened. The way was clear. I darted to the garage door and yanked the roll jam off then bolted across the road and into the woods. It took a moment in the dark, but I found my pack and hastily changed back to my anonymous hiker outfit then took a long drink of water from my bottle. I had a few of hours of night hiking ahead of me, but I would be back to the car, across the Golden Gate, and home before midnight. I hoped I'd be able to spot those mushrooms again in the dark. Some fresh pasta with wild chanterelles, garlic, olive oil, and parmesan sounded good.

CHAPTER 2

December 10:

There was a particular golden, Mediterranean quality of light we got in the Bay Area sometimes. It was one of those days, although I could already see wisps of condensing vapor swirling up over the edge of Twin Peaks. Late afternoon would bring cool air and fog spilling over the hills and rolling across the city toward the bay. The Chinese immigrants who came to California in the mid-1800s during the Gold Rush called San Francisco 舊金山. That translated to Old Gold Mountain. San Francisco was dirty, lawless, and remote back then. Now, though, with the fog held back by the hills and the warm sun shining down, the city looked pretty golden. I was sitting on a big rock on the summit of Bernal with the roofs of homes, churches, schools, and warehouses all spread out beneath me. Farther, past Bernal Heights and the Mission District, I could see the dense neighborhoods of SOMA and Hayes Valley, Potrero Hill, and the bay to my right, the downtown skyline in the distance straight ahead.

I pulled my phone from my pocket and checked the time. I had twenty-five minutes until my appointment. It was about five miles in city traffic through busy neighborhoods. Reluctantly, I stood, walked my bike to the road that spiraled up the hill, and hopped on.

Snaking down through the residential streets, I stood on the pedals and leaned on the brakes until I hit the flats at the bottom of the hill, crossed Cesar Chavez, and veered into the bike lane on Valencia. In the Mission, I passed hipster boys with Grizzly Adams beards and fixed-gear racing bikes. That trend seemed to be waning. It was hard to tell what would replace it. The Mission was my old neighborhood. Everything was different now, though. The new Mission involved a lot of Uber and Lyft drivers double parking in the bike lane and European tourists wandering around with guidebooks, looking for the artisanal coffee and food Valencia street was now becoming famous for. It was a far cry from the derelict storefronts, auto shops, and dive bars that had lined the street when I first moved to the neighborhood. Passing by Dog Eared, I was glad to see it still in business. It was one of the best book stores in the city and an old haunt of mine. Borderlands Books was still going strong too. They had opened a new café next door. Just past Fifteenth Street, I swerved out into traffic and back into the bike lane to get around an SUV dropping a group of shoppers off outside one of the street's fancy boutiques. Convincing people to call what was essentially an unregulated taxi service "ride sharing" was an impressive bit of legerdemain but it annoyed me.

Crossing under the 101 off ramp, I smelled piss, spray paint, and weed smoke, then Valencia ended, and I turned onto Market, lucked out on all the lights, stood, and pedaled hard to get across Van Ness just as yellow turned to red. The part of Market Street just east of Van Ness, I had recently learned, was now called Mid-Market or MIDMA. For years it had been a shambling, drunk, marginal, and squalid extension of the Tenderloin. Walk-

ing around that part of town used to make me feel like I
had stepped through a secret door onto the set of *Blade
Runner,* but the area had undergone a rapid transfor-
mation since they gave all the tech companies tax breaks
to move in. They were starting to get fancy coffee shops
over here too. That always seemed to be the first wave.
   I dodged between a taxi and a MUNI train, turned off
Market onto Kearney, and geared down for the hill. Just a
few more blocks, left on Columbus, and I was passing by
Chinatown and heading into North Beach. North Beach
was where my fence, Domenico, kept his office. I
reached back and patted my backpack reflexively, feeling
the PVC tube inside.
   Officially, Domenico ran an import/export business.
I didn't know how he made it look legitimate. That was
not something we discussed. I was on my way to his office to trade the bird house haul for a wad of cash. I
would put the cash in my backpack and Domenico would
put the art in his safe. It wouldn't stay there long, though.
It would be twenty-four hours max before the art would
be in the hands of an intermediary and on the way to an
art dealer who wouldn't ask questions. One of my rules,
and I knew Domenico felt the same way, was to never
keep any stolen goods in my possession longer than necessary.
   I'd met Domenico half way through my second year
in art school. I had started out as a painting major and
then switched to sculpture in my third year. We were
having a little reception for a show of student work, and a
big guy with a bristly crew cut and a nice suit was wandering around by himself. He stuck out in the crowd of
students and instructors, but he didn't seem to notice. He
was looking at each painting intently, getting really close
and wrinkling up his eyes. I guess he picked me because
my style was highly realistic. I was a Vermeer groupie

back then and would spend countless hours on drawing, underpainting, and layers. I was even grinding my own pigments. Domenico materialized at my side, smelling like baby powder. The event was winding down, and the gallery was almost empty. He wiped the back of his neck with a handkerchief and said he had a business proposition.

I met him at a bar a couple of doors down from the gallery. I ordered a whiskey, and he ordered soda water. It turned out he wanted me to paint a copy of another painting, working from high-res photos. It took eight months, but I did a good job, painting it up in layers and thin glazes just like the old masters, then drying time, then varnishing. There was no way it would pass for the real thing under careful observation, but I guess it was good enough to fool the owner for a while until the real painting was long gone, out of the country probably, and in somebody else's private collection. Or maybe the owner was half-blind, and my painting was still hanging in some grand old Pacific Heights mansion, nobody the wiser. I had a pretty good idea, even then, why Domenico wanted the copy, but I was a student, and he paid me a lot more than I was getting for my legitimate paintings—which was either nothing at all or another student's artwork in trade. I thought the painting was by a semi-famous artist, but I resisted doing any research. That was before online image search tools made it simple to find information for just about any artwork. I was very careful not to leave any fingerprints in the varnish.

Thinking back on it now, I guess maybe he saw something in me other than just a painter who could do the job. It was hard to explain, but it was as if there was something broken, or something wired differently in people like me and Domenico. It came through. We recognized each other. Other people saw it too, but they didn't know what it was. It made them nervous, so they talked. I thought it was like throwing stones into a well. That dark, gaping hole in the ground was weird, and people wanted to find a way to sound it out, comprehend its depth. I had often met people for the first time and had them nervously tell me their whole life story. This trait had been useful to me in a number of ways. I was not saying everybody who was wired like me became a thief. It could manifest in different forms. Anyway, that was how we met. I didn't see him for a while after that, but, eventually, I looked him up again when I needed his services.

ↄ‿ↄↄ

I had this episode just about every time I finished a job, usually the next day but definitely within a few days, always when I was at home and by myself. It started with a tightening in my stomach—a heaviness like my guts were twisted around something cold and hard. I could hear muffled sounds from outside—trucks passing, wind, the constant, low white noise of the bay—but those outside noises only seemed to make the silence inside more stifling and soon they were drowned out by the thumping roar of my own heartbeat pulsing in my ears, and the prickly, itchy feeling of nervous sweat breaking out on my forehead, lower back, palms. I usually walked carefully over to my favorite chair—a rehabilitated Eames lounge reproduction I rescued years ago from a pile of discarded furniture on the sidewalk—lowered myself into its familiar leather embrace, and just sat there, gripping the armrests until it was over. I looked it up. According to Google, those were the symptoms of a panic attack. Seemed reasonable. I'd never thought too hard about it. I'd always assumed it was a sort of release of the tight control and stress that built up when I was planning and

executing a job. I did know that I had come to dread it,
though. Maybe that was part of why I was glad to see Valerie. It was one of those days.

I lived near Pier 70 in a neighborhood called Mission
Bay or maybe the Dogpatch depending on what one's
personal idea of the boundaries was. When I moved here,
it was all old warehouses, stretches of blighted industrial
land surrounded by cyclone fences, brake shops, and—
here and there—dark bars exhaling stale beer and cigarette odors which catered to blue-collar, after-work drink-
ers. The city was growing, though, filling out—now for
every block of warehouses and garages, there was a brand
new condo development. Few of them were worth looking at twice. Most were just gray or tan boxes with bay
windows and useless, decorative balconies grafted on.
The Silicon Valley tech workers in jeans, hoodies, and
start-up T-shirts poured out of them in the mornings, got
on the company buses, returned, and flowed back into
them at night. Other businesses were starting to appear
too, just like the early days of gentrification in the Mission. Artisanal sandwich shops. Food trucks. High end
bars with cocktail menus. People had fixed up the old
Victorians west of Third Street. Families were moving in.
I saw them walking their dogs. The only dogs I used to
see here were lean, vicious Rottweilers chained to the
trailer hitches of RVs parked on the side streets.
Dogpatch was one of the only parts of town where you
could get away with living out of a vehicle. Those RVs
and their inhabitants reminded me of the people and
trucks in old dust bowl era photos. They were long gone.
I didn't know if there was any part of the city where you
could park an RV now.

Farther north toward downtown, they'd thrown up a
bunch of glass and concrete boxes to house the first wave
tech startups and biomedical research institutes, and they

were working on more. A lot of that land used to be covered with weeds, broken concrete, and interesting pieces of scrap metal. Along with my other, more lucrative occupation, I was a sculptor—mostly welded pieces. I missed jumping those chain link fences and wandering through the weeds looking for materials, but I guess it was progress. When the last vacant lot was turned into million dollar lofts, I could always move to Detroit. I'd rather stay, though. The weather was better here.

My building was a two-story cinderblock cube. It was the very definition of non-descript, and I liked to keep it that way. From the front, you couldn't tell anything. There was just a gray door a little darker than the gray wall, a small sign in traditional Chinese characters, and a mail slot. It was a rental when I first moved into the unfinished upstairs unit. It was supposed to be a studio space. Not a live/work. I rented it with my girlfriend at the time. We broke up, she kept the rent-controlled apartment in the Mission, and I moved into the studio. A couple of years later, the landlord decided to sell. I was sitting on a decent amount of money at the time from a lucrative evening's work, so I joined the ownership class. On the ground floor was a sweatshop run by Mr. L.C. Lee. It wasn't really a sweatshop, but I liked to call it that to get him worked up. He'd been renting the lower half of the building for something like forty years. I inherited him when I bought the place. I lived on the top floor. They turned off the industrial sewing machines and steam irons at five o'clock sharp, and a stream of middle-aged ladies flowed out the door and across the street to the bus stop. They stood there, drinking hot water out of Dollar Store thermoses and chattering in Cantonese until the bus came and took them away. Sometimes I wondered where they lived. What part of the Bay Area was still affordable enough for them? I had considered getting on the bus and riding until they get off so I could find out where that was. The machines started up again at eight a.m. the next morning. It was a cycle I'd come to depend on.

The sun was still out, but it was cold, and the wind was blowing dust in my eyes all the way down Third Street. I saw Valerie's car from a block away, parked across the street from my building. She drove an expensive-looking car. A long, low, shiny thing with one of those paint jobs that changed color from charcoal to puce to deep burgundy depending on the light and your perspective. It was hard to miss in this neighborhood, but in a year or two, it would probably fit right in.

I'd known Valerie for years. I wasn't sure I could explain our relationship in any conventional way. She owned a popular art gallery downtown on Geary. It was one of those places with high ceilings, exposed beams, big abstract canvasses on the pure white walls. There was always minimalist orchestral music playing in the background by some obscure Icelandic or Estonian composer I was not cool or connected enough to know about. We met when she wanted to include a few of my pieces in a group show she was arranging. Sometimes we slept together—when one or the other of us was feeling maudlin, which was most of the time. Mostly she tried to use me as an escort for various lectures, gallery openings, museum soirees. I generally resisted because I didn't want my face to be too well known in the tiny SF art world. Valerie was the only person, other than Domenico, who knew that I was a thief. She figured it out on her own. It didn't bother her, though—she was a profoundly amoral person. She cared about art, expensive clothes, and mid-century furniture. Like me, she had her own system of ethics. I guessed I maybe used my relationship with her as a way to avoid having a serious relationship with anybody else. Sometimes I thought that if she was doing the same thing,

if we were both working hard and seriously to avoid anything serious, maybe we should just give in and let it
happen. Or not happen. It was complicated.

Valerie was just starting her car when I pulled up. I
heard the purr of the engine stop. She stepped out of the
car and looked me up and down with a peeved expression, hand shading her eyes. "For god's sake, Justin, why
don't you answer your phone? I was just leaving."

I fished my phone out of a jacket pocket and looked
at the screen. Two missed calls. "Sorry, didn't hear it
ring," I answered, shrugging.

"Asshole," she said and stepped up for a hug but
wrinkled her nose and pushed me away almost as quickly. "You're sweaty, and this dress just came back from
the cleaners. You need to shower and put on something
presentable. We're going to the Heidrich opening reception at SFMOMA tonight," she said, looking at her
watch. "You have seven minutes."

"Heidrich? Really?"

She looked at me defiantly. "He's my best artist. I
told you about this two weeks ago. You know I represent
him. I'm premiering a new work by him this weekend.
You are also on the hook for that opening."

"Well, okay. Come on up. I guess I probably remember that conversation," I said over my shoulder,
rummaging in my backpack for my keys.

The main door was unlocked and, near the back of
the shop, I saw Mr. Lee in his little glassed-in office, beyond the ghostly shapes of cutting tables and dress forms.
The filthy blinds covering the back windows were closed.
It was after six o'clock, and the workers were all gone for
the day. Mr. Lee looked up from a pile of papers as we
came in and waved then bent his head back to his work.

"Hi, Mr. Lee, I found him," Valerie called out.

Mr. Lee waved dismissively, not bothering to look up a second time.

I shouldered my bike and climbed the steep stairway up to my second-floor unit. After hanging the bike on the hooks above the landing, I unlocked my door and pushed it open, allowing Valerie to enter first. She swept in and immediately strolled back toward my workshop while I turned on the lights. My place took up the entire top floor of the building, and it was all open, except for the bathroom and a loft where I slept, both of which I framed and finished myself shortly after purchasing the place. I wanted to at least protect my bed, clothes, and towels from the gritty black dust that blanketed everything when I welded. Through the many-paned windows at the back of the building, I could see the Oakland hills across the bay looking brown and desiccated, Val's tall form silhouetted against them. She flicked on my studio lamps and began to appraise my latest piece—a kind of large, welded basin built on a platform. It was an experiment for me.

When finished, the piece would be wired up with a microphone that would capture the sound of water dripping down into the basin from a large chunk of melting ice suspended above. The sound would be amplified and run through some audio filters then played throughout the exhibit space. I was constructing it from scrap metal and some nicely weathered pieces of two-by-four I found on the sidewalk. She walked around it slowly, tilting her head to the side so that her long bangs fell into her eyes. She swept her hair back with a quick gesture and folded her arms across her chest, lips pursing.

"Are you sure about this," she said, pointing. The tone of her voice made it obvious that she, at least, wasn't sure.

"Oh come on, Val, I just started that piece."

This was a long-standing argument. She was about to

let me know what she didn't like, but just then her attention was caught by a large painting in progress hanging on the far wall.

"What's this?" she called. "A painting? Have you gone back to painting? I hate it."

"It's not mine," I answered. "A friend's working here during the day. He got kicked out of his studio. You know the story—developer bought the building, everybody evicted, protestors are protesting, but it will be condos before you know it. I knew you wouldn't like it. It's not your taste, but you have to admit it's not terrible."

She nodded, now standing in front of the piece. "I have some customers who would buy this kind of crap."

"There's some wine in the fridge. I'll go hop in the shower."

"Don't forget to shave," she called as I closed the door.

In the bathroom, I got my razor out of the medicine cabinet, absent-mindedly taking it apart, putting in a new blade—all the time thinking about the wad of cash in my backpack, pinpricks of sweat on my forehead.

CHAPTER 3

December 11:

Have you heard the one about inbred aristocracy? It's not really a joke. They mostly knew it wasn't a great idea, but they really wanted to keep the money and the land in as few hands as possible. They wanted to literally keep it in the family. Almost all the pharaohs during the Ptolemaic Dynasty of ancient Egypt married full or half siblings. In Europe from the late Medieval period up almost to the present, aristocratic inbreeding was common. Jean V of Armagnac married his sister Isabelle. Ferdinand I of Portugal married his half-sister. Francis II of the house of Hapsburg-Lorraine married his double cousin Maria Theresa. Charles II of Spain's mother Mariana of Austria was his father Philip IV's niece. I guess that means his mother was his cousin. Many others married first cousins, uncles, aunts, etc. There were plenty of deformities, adverse hereditary conditions, and mental deficiencies stemming from this practice. The "Hapsburg Jaw" is one of the most well-known. Hemophilia and hydrocephaly were not uncommon.

The international art market was kind of like that: Inbred. Artworks passed from collector to thief to dealer to auction house to collector and so on. It was like a game of hot potato and, just like potatoes, the hot art works cooled as time passed, became more respectable, were imbued with a provenance. Everybody involved knew that a good proportion of the art that was bought and sold in the auction houses was probably stolen from somebody at some point in its history, just like the earl of wherever knew that his betrothed was his cousin, but it had become so normalized and accepted that nobody spent any time worrying about it. Most works of any value passed through the auction houses at some point, got stored at the Geneva Freeport, went back to an auction house, entered the black market, resurfaced at another auction. By some estimations, the international black market for art was the fourth largest in the world. Nobody asked questions when there was money to be made. It was one of the most corrupt industries there was.

This was why you invariably saw the same faces, made small talk with the same acquaintances, and caught up with the same old friends when you attended an event like the one Valerie and I were on our way to. As soon as Valerie pulled up to the curb outside the museum and we stepped out of the car, I began to recognize people. There was the bald head of the dean of the fine arts school I attended bobbing through the crowd and disappearing through the entrance. A well-known CEO of a tech firm shouldered past me with a beautiful woman on his arm. Valerie exchanged her keys for a claim ticket without so much as glancing at the valet's face and turned to wave to an older couple who had recognized her but were being inexorably pushed toward the entry by the flow of other attendees. One of the reasons I was able to case fancy homes the way I did was that, to rich people at parties, the workers in uniform were pretty much invisible, just interchangeable cogs who could park the car, fetch a drink, clean up a spill. As if to prove my point, I found myself shoulder to shoulder with none other than Carl and Bill as we began to make our way toward the door.

"Carl. Bill," Valerie sang out, "Wonderful to see you. This is Justin, a friend and a very talented sculptor. You've probably seen his work at the gallery."

I turned, shook hands, and exchanged nice-to-meet-yous with the couple, looking first Carl, then Bill in the eye. There was not the slightest flicker of recognition. As we passed into the vast museum lobby, Valerie launched into a conversation with the two about Heidrich's recent work, leaving me free to study the crowd. I liked to size people up at these events based on their place in the black-market cycle. Most of them, of course, were buyers and collectors—wealthy people who legitimately loved art or who liked the cultural capital they got from art, or some combination of the two. You could move those two sliders to describe a different ratio for each person who bought art, but they were all suckers, compared to the dealers and auction houses. The even bigger suckers, of course, were the artists who provided the raw material for the market but, except in rare cases, reaped almost none of the financial benefit. The artists and the collectors were sort of like the workers and patrons of a casino. The workers got paid minimum wage, and the patrons occasionally hit it big, but the house—the dealers and the auctioneers—always won. Before long, I thought I saw my friend Roberto—who fell solidly in the sucker category—about fifty feet away across the black-and-gray-striped expanse of marble floor. I excused myself and wove through the elegant crowd to intercept him. He was an old friend from school and was the artist whose half-finished painting, currently hanging in my house/studio, Valerie had disliked. He had stuck with painting when I bailed and was now managing to make a living from his art, just barely. He was sleeping on another friend's couch and was planning on moving to Oakland where he would join the mass exodus of artists leaving or being pushed out of the city by rising costs. I was surprised to see him at the opening. He had always been very critical of Heidrich's work.

He saw me coming and waved enthusiastically. He seemed to be trapped in an awkward conversation with an eccentrically dressed woman. Turning to me as I approached, he greeted me with obvious relief. "My old friend Justin is here. Justin, this is Mrs. Stella Robards, a collector known for her distinctive eye."

Mrs. Robards' hand felt like a small bird's nest. It made me awkwardly aware of my own calloused and battered appendage. The type of sculpture work I did was not kind to the hands.

"Such a nice compliment, Roberto," she trilled without letting go of my hand or my eyes. There was something predatory in her gaze, an unflinching reconnaissance of my essence, and she maintained her grip on my hand with an unexpected strength. "Are you an artist too, Justin?"

"Yes, he is," Roberto broke in, throwing his arm around my shoulder and pulling me back away from her. "A sculptor. Justin and I have a date to view the exhibit together. It was such a pleasure running into you, Mrs. Robards."

"Please, call me Stella. You're so formal, Roberto. And do get in touch to let me know when you will be available."

Roberto was pulling me along the whole time she was speaking, and we were already several paces away.

"Pleased to meet you, Mrs. Robards," I called as we were swallowed in the crowd moving toward the gallery where the Heidrich show was on display.

"Glad I ran into you," Roberto said then sighed, letting go of me. "Second time she's cornered me. Wants me to come to her house and 'consult on the proper hanging' of one of my paintings." He made air quotes with his fingers.

"Well," I replied, "you know you can't sell art if you don't Sell Your Art."

Roberto laughed. It was an in joke, a line from a course called Marketing for Artists we were required to take before graduating.

"Dear god, can you imagine? Even if I liked women..." Roberto threw his hands in the air.

"What are you doing here anyway," I asked. "You hate Heidrich."

"You know, I've changed my mind about him. I've been studying his work pretty intensively. Looking at his brush technique, his layering of color. There are minute details I never noticed before. I even did a few studies, copying sections from some of his paintings..." Roberto's voice trailed off. "That's boring, though. Let's look at the art."

We walked through the exhibit, stopping at each painting and taking our time. Half way through, we ran into Valerie who was schmoozing with yet another client—a tall man in an antique three-piece suit with an impeccable beard and the jowly, red nosed, loose bellied look of an alcoholic on the downward slope of a long decline. She wrapped her long fingers around my upper arm in a don't-go-anywhere grip while she finished her conversation.

"Ten more minutes," she whispered in my ear, and she kept her word. We left Roberto deep in conversation with another acquaintance and made a quick exit. Outside, while we waited for the car, the wind picked up, and damp, chilly waves of fog were rolling by. As usual, Val had not thought to bring a sweater or coat. She lived in the present and always dressed for whatever the weather was like at the moment she happened to step outside her condo. Years of living with the capricious weather of San Francisco had not altered her behavior.

"Let's go to my place," Val said, shivering, arms wrapped around me under my jacket, "I have a bottle of wine a client gave me. A reserve vintage from his winery."

I didn't need more convincing than that.

❧❧❧

The next morning, Val offered me a ride, but I refused. I felt like a walk in the fresh air might help clear out the wine-soaked cotton balls that seemed to have replaced my brain while I was asleep. As I walked down the Embarcadero, the bay on my left slopping against the sea wall and smelling like cold miso soup, I found myself ruminating again on a line of thought that had been preoccupying me recently: Why did I steal art?

It was actually an easy question to answer. If you were going to be a burglar, you should be a professional, and you should specialize. Art and jewelry were the most logical specialties. They were both easy to sell and had high value-to-risk ratios. Most burglaries were not committed by professionals. Amateurs broke into random cars and houses and took whatever they could find. Only about seventeen percent of those crimes were solved by police. Seventeen percent was low, but I wouldn't bet my personal freedom on those odds. Professionals were almost never caught because they planned carefully, executed with precision, and covered their tracks. So, jewelry or art? Precious metals and gems had never appealed to me. I didn't know anything about them and didn't have much desire to learn. Art, on the other hand, I knew a lot about and cared a lot about. It was an easy choice, if you could really call it a choice. Which led me to: Why did I steal?

That was a much more difficult question and one that I couldn't answer. I liked being able to answer questions, especially ones about things central to my life. Maybe that was why I had been coming back to this question, off and on, lately.

In the beginning, it was just because I needed money. It started when I was fresh out of school and broke, barely making enough money to pay my rent and eat. The occasion was a party in a "live-work" loft. Live-work was a scam that started in the late eighties when San Francisco passed an ordinance that was supposed to result in affordable housing for artists in areas previously zoned for industrial use. Developers took advantage of the law and built giant loft apartments with expensive furnishings that were neither affordable, nor designed for artists to work in. Eventually, after about fifteen years and thousands of units built, the city council was shocked, *shocked* to find that developers had not been building artist housing, and an indefinite moratorium was imposed. The loft where the party was held was a typical example—beautiful wood floors, granite counters, balcony with a view of downtown, expensive appliances, located in a completely renovated warehouse. The only piece of the original warehouse left seemed to be the heavy fire doors. It was a housewarming party, and the new owner was still in the process of moving in. Boxes full of his possessions were pushed up against the walls, brand new furniture and carpets were being trampled by the guests, who were mostly already drunk or rolling on MDMA when I arrived. House music loud enough to induce seizures was blasting from a shiny new audiophile-quality stereo system. It wasn't my type of scene.

Near the front door, there was a table with a stack of prints still packed in cellophane envelopes from the galleries where they had been purchased. There were also several large paintings leaned against the wall and one smaller one. I recognized the artist of the smaller painting. He was a "rising star" LA painter who did graffiti-inspired work. His stuff was selling for good money: maybe twenty-five thousand for a small piece like I was looking at. Clearly, the owner, or maybe a hired decorator with a generous budget, had gone shopping and hadn't had time to frame and hang the art before the party. The friend I came with was having fun, but I decided to leave after about half an hour. There was a wide, short, dark hallway that led from the main room of the loft to the door. On my way out, I was alone in that hallway and, acting on impulse, I picked up the smaller painting and walked out with it tucked under my arm. I can't remember my exact thinking or mental state. I was probably acting on more of an anarchistic, punk-rock impulse than a rational decision to take the thing and sell it.

The painting sat in the back of my closet for a couple of months but then, short on cash for rent, I got in touch with Domenico and found out how easy it is to move stolen art into the black market. Standard payment was about ten percent of the auction value. It was enough to cover my rent for a couple of months. After that, I became a little obsessed. I read every book I could find about famous burglars: Daniel Blanchard, Bill Mason, Vincenzo Pipino, Charles Peace. Those books convinced me that stealing from famous people or stealing famous things was stupid. I also read a lot about the industry, how stolen art moved through the marketplace, how the people who didn't get caught did what they did. That reading convinced me that staying under the radar and making a good living would be pretty easy.

Was it wrong to steal? I don't think that question has an easy answer. Nobody wanted to have their stuff stolen, but nobody wanted to be poor either. I had always, if I spent any time thinking about it, rationalized my avocation by the logic that rich people stole, too, but they did it via power. Money equaled power. Power allowed people to shape society and political systems to fit their own needs and desires. That power normally led to rich people gathering more and more wealth at the expense of poor people. So, using skill and intelligence to take some of that wealth away from them hadn't ever seemed like a moral failing to me. Now, though, I felt my philosophy shifting gradually, adapting. Maybe there was something to be said for the passion people put into the collection of their troves of art—

I looked up, breaking out of my thought bubble, and realized I was almost home. The street was deserted. I walked the last half-block, digging my keys out of my pocket. There was an old blanket and some greasy, flattened cardboard boxes in the doorway. I kicked them out of the way and let myself in.

It was a rare cold day in the city, the beginning of a cold front that would stay around for a few days, according to my weather app. I spent the morning and afternoon inside working on the sculpture. I cut two-by-fours, drilled long holes through them for the narrow-gauge steel rod that would hold them in place, and laid them down to form a sort of floor below the basin. By late afternoon, I was working with my battered old Makita grinder, smoothing down the welds along the corners of the central basin. I was grinding away with my respirator on to keep the steel dust out of my lungs, feeling like Darth Vader and making similar breathing noises, when I felt my phone vibrate in my pocket. It was a text from Valerie:

>*Heidrich reception tonight. Meet gallery 7 p.m.*

Shit. Another social event. I was an introvert. Not the kind who couldn't handle being out in public and dealing with people but definitely the kind who liked to keep social interactions with large groups to a minimum. I had promised Valerie, though, so I knocked off work around five-thirty, got cleaned up, ate some leftovers from the fridge, grabbed my backpack, and headed out by bike, aiming to arrive early in case they needed help setting up.

It was a cold ride. My fingers and ears were aching, and I was fog damp by the time I arrived at the gallery. I brought my bike to the alley around back and buzzed. Val's assistant Emilio let me in. He was in a panic.

"Justin! So glad you're here. Valerie ran late, and I need to get the tables set up and the wine..." His voice trailed off as he pinched the bridge of his nose between his thumb and forefinger and winced, squeezing his eyes closed.

"Headache?" I asked. He nodded, eyes still closed. "Don't worry, we'll get it set up. Go take six hundred milligrams of ibuprofen, STAT. I'll get the tables out."

He gave me a pained smile. "You're my hero, Justin."

I found Valerie in the main gallery space, checking over details.

She stood back and squinted at my clothes, looking me up and down. "Acceptable, barely."

"Always nice to be accepted," I replied and began setting up tables for wine and snacks.

Valerie had recently completed an expansion of the gallery into a space that had become vacant next door. "Become Vacant" was a nice euphemism for the old tenant having been priced out by a huge rent increase when their lease was up. This was a trend in neighborhoods around the city. There had been a few outraged articles in small, left-leaning community newspapers, but Valerie's clients were wealthy people who didn't much care if a non-profit immigrant-rights organization had to relocate. Valerie cared, but she also wasn't one to let an opportunity to expand slip away. Her reasoning was that her neighbor was going to have to move out one way or another. If she didn't seize the opportunity, somebody else would. At any rate, the gallery looked nice with its newly added space.

Günther Heidrich arrived by taxi at exactly seven p.m. He was a short man in his late-sixties with thin gray hair, a barrel chest, and the compact muscular build and ruddy complexion of a mountain climber. He was wearing gray jeans, a black button up tucked in, and purple suede Pumas. What was it, I wondered for the fiftieth time, about European jeans that made them immediately distinguishable from American jeans? Heidrich's jeans were obviously European, but I'd never been able to put my finger on what it was that was so obviously different. The fit? The wash?

Valerie introduced me, and he shook my hand with a firm grip. I noticed bushy hair sprouting from his ears and nostrils and equally bushy eyebrows. Heidrich had been painting for almost fifty years in near obscurity before suddenly being "discovered" by the international art world. His current work was highly abstract and, to my eye, nothing special. Sometimes it just took one or two reviews from respected writers, a retrospective, a fancy gallery deciding to represent your work, and the art world hive mind kicked in. Before you knew it, paintings from thirty years ago were selling for millions at auction. To his credit, he seemed unfazed by the buzz. Also to his credit, he hadn't forsaken Valerie, who had been championing his work for years. An artist of Heidrich's fame did not normally place new work in a San Francisco gallery. Famous artists premiered work at Zwirner, Gagossian, or one of the other five or so galleries in that league. Heidrich was giving Valerie the chance to show a new piece, though, and it was a big deal for her.

"Justin is an artist too, Günther," Valerie said as we were shaking hands. "I also show his work."

"A sculptor, I am guessing. Because of the hands," Heidrich replied.

"Yes," I said. "Sculpture. Pleased to meet you. Look, people are arriving. You two had better go greet the guests."

I skulked around the back rooms of the gallery for most of the reception, on the pretense of helping out with logistics. I even ran out to the market down the block for more wine, at one point. I did come out for the unveiling of Heidrich's new piece, though. It was more or less what I expected, but I found that I liked it. It was about six feet by four, vertical. The ground was dark and mottled, almost black in some places, deep grayish brown in others. Broad slashes of vermilion and phthalo blue stood out from the dark ground. These was a small patch of alizarin crimson near the top left, and a larger patch of mustard yellow a bit below the midpoint on the right. It was an abstract work, but it reminded me strongly of walking through the redwoods at night. I was pretty taken with it, actually. I stood and stared for some time, reliving that night walk, the cool air, the spider webs on my face, rotten bits of leaf and bark finding their way into my shoes, occasional glimpses of the moon through the trees. After a while, I felt an elbow poke me in the side. I looked over. Heidrich was standing next to me, nodding his head, smiling.

"A good one," he said.

I nodded, too. "Yes," I replied, looking back at the painting.

"I save this one for Valerie," he continued. "She understands my work."

We stood silently side by side for a while. Both taking in the painting and thinking our own thoughts.

After the reception was done and the last guests had finally stumbled out, Valerie sent her helpers home and locked up. She had an excellent alarm system and very good locks, which I had helped her pick out. Heidrich had declined Val's invitation for a late dinner in favor of room service and sleep. We drove through crowds of revelers, club goers, and peep-show connoisseurs in North Beach to Val's condo, parked in the underground lot, and rode the elevator up. The place was dark when we walked in. Through the big, north-facing windows I could see the Golden Gate Bridge shrouded in fog. The french doors that let onto the balcony were open a crack, and a cool breeze was fluttering the drawn curtains. Val took my hand and led me toward the bedroom. We stood at the foot of the bed, both tired, pressed together in a languid embrace. I ran my hands slowly up and down her back, down to her hips, while she nuzzled into my neck. I was looking at but not really seeing the wall above Val's bed. Something was nagging at me, though. Something was different. I focused and made a conscious effort to see what had changed.

"What happened to that painting you used to have above the bed?" I asked.

"Above the bed? I didn't—" Val turned, stopped speaking, breath caught.

A moment later, she whirled, flipped on the light switch, jumped onto the bed, and placed her hands on the wall above the headboard. In the light, I noticed there was a picture hanger still nailed into the wall and a square of slightly brighter paint where the painting had hung. She ran her hands over the bare wall then turned to look at me. Her eyes were manic, her body tense. "Tell me this is some kind of joke, Justin."

"No joke," I replied. "Was it there when you left for the gallery?"

"Yes, I think so." She stepped down off the bed and started frantically pacing the room, looking everywhere. "I'm sure it was."

"Did you have cleaners scheduled today?"

"No. They come on Wednesdays."

"Did you leave your balcony door open?"

She looked at me, suddenly focusing. "No. I never leave it open."

"It was open when we came in. Was it locked?"

"Maybe not. I don't know. I was in a hurry."

"Let's see if anything else is missing," I said, turning toward the door.

Valerie grabbed my arm, pulling me around to face her. "I don't care if anything else is missing." She was on the brink of tears, a tight, almost hysterical, edge to her voice. She raised her hands, placed them over her ears, shaking her head back and forth. "I don't care. That painting is the only thing I own that I care about, Justin."

I was standing close to her now, gripping her shoulders. "Why? What's special about that painting? I never liked it very much."

"It's a Heidrich, you fool. He gave it to me ten years ago almost, when I first started showing his work. We had a good show. Sold everything but one painting. That one. He was happy. Didn't want to ship it back to Germany with him. He told me to keep it for him." Her eyes were glassy now, turned inward, remembering. "I hung it above the bed. It's been there ever since."

"Shit. That painting is probably worth two million.

He gave it to you? Or he asked you to keep it for him?"

She was still shaking her head. "Gave. Loaned. I don't know. It's been years. Surely he would have asked for it back—"

"Is it insured?"

"Of course, it's insured! Of course. And recently appraised too. I used it as collateral for the loan to expand the gallery. Insurance won't get it back for me, though. I don't care about the money, Justin. I love that painting. It's one of the only things I've ever had that was just mine. Not for public consumption, not carefully chosen to fit an image. I can't tell him it's gone. How could I tell him? He's my most important artist."

I stood staring at her face. Her lower lip was quivering, mouth pinched tight at the corners. I had never seen her this upset before. Maybe I had never seen her betray real emotion in this way. I couldn't think of a time when she had. As this realization hit me, I also understood, suddenly, how facile our relationship had always been. I felt like I was looking into the eyes of a stranger. The shock of the missing artwork had opened her up, and I needed to respond.

"Okay," I said, "I understand. This is important. Let me go take a look around the apartment. I'm going to get you a glass of brandy. Sit here." I pushed gently on her shoulders, and she sat on the edge of her bed, eyes blank, retreating. Just then something caught my eye. I got down on hands and knees. Something was under the bed—just a corner showing. I reached under and pulled it out. It was a picture frame, empty. I looked at Valerie, and she nodded. It was the frame from the Heidrich painting.

I brought her the brandy then took my time examining the scene. Nothing else in the condo had been disturbed as far as I could tell. The lock on the french doors did not seem to have been forced. I turned on the balcony

light and went out. Everything seemed normal. The balcony was recessed with the concrete structure of the
building, and the balcony above formed the walls to right
and left and the roof. Along the open side, there were
metal safety bars with a stomach height railing about two
inches square. I walked the perimeter, carefully examining the railing. At the center, equidistant between right
and left walls, I thought I could make something out, but
the light was too dim. I went inside and found a flashlight. In the bright glare of the flashlight beam, I could
definitely see a partial shoe print on the railing, as if
someone had walked through dust, then stepped on the
railing. It looked like a sneaker sole. I leaned out and
looked up. Valerie's condo was one floor down from the
top. *Simple to rappel down*, I thought. *But risky if the
condo above was occupied.* I told Val I was going to the
roof. She looked up for a moment then bent her head
back down, eyes closed, and took a tiny sip of brandy.

I knew the way to the roof. We had gone up there
one time to watch the fireworks over the bay on the
fourth of July. I clanged up the metal stairs, each step
echoing down through the floors below. At the top, there
was a little landing and a door leading out. Shining the
flashlight on the floor there, I saw fine gray dust covering
the concrete and several footprints, some pointing toward
the door, some toward the stairs. The pattern seemed the
same as the one I had seen on the railing, but I would
have to compare to be sure. I took out my phone and got
a picture of the best print.

Outside, I walked across to the point I guessed to be
above Valerie's condo. There was a waist high wall
around the edge, two feet thick and capped with aluminum that wrapped down around the edges of the wall to
form a bezel. I shined the flashlight on the corners of the
bezel and walked back and forth a couple of times. About

four feet to the left of the point where I started, I saw marks where the aluminum was cleaner, as if something had forcefully rubbed off many years' worth of accumulated car exhaust and other particulate matter to reveal the metal below. Maybe something like a rope holding the weight of a man? I leaned out and looked down. There was Val's balcony, two floors down and directly below.

I went back downstairs and found Val still sitting where I left her. I sat down next to her on the bed. "The news isn't great," I said. "This looks like a pro job. Somebody came after that painting in particular. They knew it was here and knew you would be out. Probably also knew your neighbors upstairs would be out."

She turned to face me. "They're always out. Call the Police?" she asked.

I shrugged. "I don't think so. Not tonight anyway." I sighed, standing up and pacing. "You know as well as I do that the police are no good at this. They don't know anything about art. They don't even know where to start with an investigation like this. You'll want to call them tomorrow, so you can file a claim. Let me do a little digging. I have some connections. I can ask around. I need to ask you some questions first, though."

Val nodded, focusing. "What?"

"How many people knew about this painting, and who are they?"

"Not many. You know I don't normally let people into my bedroom."

I remembered Val telling me one time about how horrified she was when the hosts at a party she attended piled guests' coats on their own bed. "The bedroom is sacred space," she had said, "get a coat rack, put it by the door."

"I have parties sometimes," she went on. "A few people may have wandered in here over the years. It would be dark, though. The cleaners, of course, but I don't think they would recognize it for what it was. The signature is on the back, not visible in the frame." She glanced at the remains of the frame near her feet.

"I thought Heidrich didn't sign his paintings," I said, confused.

In fact, Heidrich was famous for not signing his work. I had read an interview with him one time in which he spoke forcefully about not sullying the picture plane with an autograph. He carried this prohibition even to the back of the work, saying that he was just a channel for the creative force of the universe, and it would be an unacceptable sign of ego to put his name on something that came to him that way.

"It's an early painting. He didn't develop those ideas until later. At the time, he still signed a few. Not many. I think he really just forgot to sign them. He's absent minded. He probably came up with that bullshit philosophy on the spot when somebody asked him to sign a piece they bought."

"When was the last party?"

She closed her eyes, thinking back. "A couple of months ago. A dinner party. All gallery people. Two couples, one or two singles. You were in LA for that opening."

I nodded. "I'll need a list of the people who were there."

Val nodded.

"Also, who did the appraisal?"

"Chatham's. Their twentieth-century-painting specialist. His name was Meyer, I think. Or Mather." Valerie took a ragged breath. "Christoph Mather. That was his name."

"That's good," I said, "It could be meaningless, but we need to think of everybody who knew about this painting. We need a full list of people who were here for dinner and also anyone else you can think of who might have known about it."

We spent the next hour talking it over, making lists. By the end of the hour, Valerie was exhausted, her voice edged with fatigue and emotional turmoil. We both collapsed into bed. As I was drifting off, her fingers closed around my wrist.

"I know it's unlikely, Justin, but if you can try for me, try to find it..." Her whisper trailed off, then, still whispering but slightly louder. "I can't tell Heidrich it's gone. I can't. I don't know what he would say. I don't even know that the painting is mine. I have to drive him to the airport tomorrow."

The next morning, I woke early. There was a sliver of red-tinged light falling across the bed. I propped myself up on my elbows and looked out the window. I could see the sky brightening over Angel Island. Valerie was tangled in the blankets, her hair a wild mass piled above her head. I pulled on my clothes and crept out, leaving a note on the bedside table:

Going to check with some contacts. Will let you know how it's going. I'll find out what I can, but it's a long shot.

CHAPTER 4

December 12:

I walked out the front doors of Valerie's building and stopped, standing stupidly on the sidewalk and squinting in the bright sunlight. Why had I told her I would try to track down the painting? It was a massive long shot and would probably just lead to more heartbreak. I, of all people, was well aware of how the system worked. Stolen art was almost never recovered because it was so easy to just drop it into the black market—like a leaf into a stream, out of sight in moments, and impossible to trace. Still, something bothered me about this job. It seemed like a major coincidence for the painting to be stolen while Heidrich was in town for only a couple of days, the very night of Valerie's opening. It was almost as if somebody wanted him to know about it.

My eyes were adjusted to the light now, and I let my gaze rest on the building across the street. It was a grand old art deco, eight stories high, with rounded corners and stepped toward the top to create large patios for the upper level units. Easy climbing, I thought, probably some good old art in those fancy condos. The doorman had his eye on me. I waved to him, chose a direction at random, and began walking. My jacket was zipped as high as it would

go, hands buried in my pockets, my shoulders hunched. It
was chilly out, despite the sun. Probably below fifty degrees. Not for the first time, I thought about the freezing
temperatures in the rest of the country, the snow and ice I
used to think was no big deal when I was a kid growing
up in the country. Living in coastal California tended to
turn people into wimps who couldn't handle cold weather. I was no exception.

The first order of business would be food and coffee.
I got my bearings at the next corner and turned west on
Lombard, heading for my favorite breakfast spot. It was a
small place and didn't look like much, but they had the
best omelets in the city. The secret ingredient was fresh
eggs from the proprietor's chicken coop out behind the
restaurant. She had taken me back to see it one time. The
building was an old Victorian with the diner on the
ground floor and the family's living space above. In the
back yard, the hens had a ten-by-twenty-foot patch of
sad-looking grass and dirt to run around on. There was an
old stove rusting by the back fence. Those chickens must
have found a lot of good bugs and worms to eat, though,
because the eggs were amazing. I had wandered into the
diner at random years before. In small letters at the bottom of the menu, it said: *special egg + $2.* Intrigued, I
asked for special eggs, and that was how I made the dis-
covery. I didn't think many other patrons bothered.

Mrs. Park greeted me when I came in and gestured
toward an empty seat at the counter. The diner was
crowded and warm, and the windows were fogged. A tel-
evision high up in the corner was showing a soccer match
with the sound off. The text on the screen was Korean.

"The usual?" she asked.

I nodded and sat down, and soon a steaming cup of
strong black coffee appeared on the worn, sun-wasted
linoleum in front of me. I let my thoughts drift back to

Val's painting. The weird thing, the thing that was nagging at me was that Heidrich's work was red hot. Selling a recently stolen Heidrich at auction would be tough, even if it was shipped to Europe or Asia. The assumption would be that the piece had been reported missing, and the theft would have made enough of a splash that somebody might see it and recognize it. This was precisely why I, and other smart thieves like me, preferred to steal less well-known work or pieces like the Rauschenberg and Lichtenstein prints.

Prints were perfect because there was normally at least a small run, so other very similar prints were out there on the market. This tended to muddy the waters for anybody trying to trace the origin. My best guess was that the theft had been commissioned, meaning that somebody wanted that specific piece and hired a thief to get it. If that was the case, my chances of recovering it were slightly better. Still pretty dismal though, all things considered.

I took out my phone and pulled up the Proton mail app. I had been using Proton for several months for all sensitive communication on the advice of my friend Ashna. She told me it was the only service the NSA couldn't access.

All their servers were in Switzerland and encryption was end to end. Not that I thought the NSA was interested in reading my email, but it never hurt to be safe. After entering two passwords—Ashna had explained why I needed two passwords: "one for your account and one to decrypt your data," but I still wasn't totally clear on how the tech worked—I started a new email and addressed it to an acquaintance:

Need to ask you something. If you are free today, send me time/place, and I will be there.

I hit send and started another email, this one to Domenico:

Need to speak with you briefly. Time today? If so, please let me know when/where to meet you.

I put down my phone just in time to see Mrs. Park's thirteen-year-old son, who was the weekend waiter/cashier and styled himself like a character from *Dragonball Z*, bringing a plate to my spot at the counter. He nodded to me and moved on, his prodigious wave of swept up anime hair barely moving. The omelet looked delicious as ever and smelled even better.

An hour later, after watching the Jeonnam Dragons defeat FC Seoul 1-0, I carried my check to the register, paid cash, and stepped back out into the brisk air and bright sun, bells ringing behind me as the door swung closed.

My bike was still in the back room at the gallery where I had left it the previous evening. I decided to walk over and get it.

The gallery wouldn't open until eleven but the walk would take a while, and I could get more coffee somewhere nearby and wait if I had to. Emilio usually arrived thirty minutes early to get the place ready for customers.

I walked over to Columbus and turned south, passing Washington Square Park and the cathedral poking its spires up into the clear air on my left. I always thought about Brautigan when walking that particular block. Then, after Brautigan, I thought about Dante and the first line of the Paradiso which wass carved across the facade of the Cathedral:

*La gloria di colui che tutto muove per l'universo
penetra e risplende.*

(The glory of him who moves everything, penetrates, and illuminates the universe.)

It would be nice to believe that. The tourist trap restaurants of little Italy were just starting to fill up with early brunch crowds. I decided to turn up Stockton and head straight through Chinatown and down past Union Square to Geary.

A dense mass of humanity was already out in Chinatown. I wove my way through the crowd, passing ladies in quilted jackets with rolling market carts full of vegetables, small children darting in and out of shops, old men on bikes, everybody emitting little puffs of condensed breath into the still air. The pungent aroma of dried herbs drifted out of open markets and blended with the ubiquitous incense and sewer gas. A couple of blocks and the throng became less dense. Soon, I was walking freely uphill, passing by the neoclassical port cochere of the Ritz when I felt my phone vibrate. I took it out and saw that I had a new email—a response to one of the emails I had sent earlier. It said simply: *Ferry Building. Red Rocket. 12:45 p.m.*

Red Rocket. Good coffee but it made me jittery. I was normally happy with crap coffee. I would even drink instant if it meant not waiting. I did appreciate fine, handmade, artisanal things but there was a line beyond which artisanal became fussy. You thought you were just getting coffee at an ordinary coffee shop but, all of a sudden, you found yourself caught up in someone else's fiendish obsession while you waited ten minutes for the intricate ritual dance of coffee preparation to culminate so you could finally get your caffeine fix. Still, Antoine had agreed to meet me on short notice so I couldn't complain about the location.

I passed by Union Square, where the ice skaters were

out and the giant tree was twinkling. There was a different kind of crowd here. Holiday shoppers. They seemed happy and red cheeked now, but they would be in foul moods by the afternoon—tired and hungry and aggravated by the amount of money they had spent. I gave silent thanks for the fact that I didn't have to buy Christmas presents for anybody as I slipped through the tumult and turned up Geary.

Emilio was already at the gallery. I saw him inside through the front windows, sweeping. The steel security grill was still closed. I reached through the bars, knocked on the glass, and waved. He looked up, smiled, and mouthed, "It's open," pointing toward the back, so I went around and let myself in. He came into the back room, broom in hand.

"Good opening last night. Thanks again for your help."

"No problem. It seemed like a good crowd," I said.

"Yeah. We had some out of town people who flew in just to see the new piece." Emilio was smiling, proud.

"Cool. I'm just grabbing my bike."

"Okay. I'm going to finish cleaning up. See you later."

"Have a good one," I called as he turned back toward the gallery.

I wheeled my bike out into the alley and hopped on. I had a couple of hours to kill but didn't want to go home then back out. I decided to just ride over to the Ferry Building and spend some time reading. Maybe get a second breakfast. It was all downhill or flat from the gallery to the Embarcadero, and auto traffic was at a standstill, so I coasted slowly, weaving in and out of the cars, rolling through the stop lights.

At the Ferry Building, I locked my bike up outside and waded through another crowd, straight through to the back, where I waited in line briefly at a chain coffee shop without pretensions of artisanal anything. The woman at the counter was cheerful and gave me a giant smile that showed off defiantly crooked teeth.

"What can I get for you?"

"Small coffee please, and a scone," I replied, smiling back.

Her cheerfulness was infectious.

A few minutes later, coffee and scone in hand, I headed out the back doors where I found an empty bench and a view of the ferry terminal, the Bay Bridge, and Treasure Island. Seagulls were screeching and turning slow circles high up above, and a massive cargo ship was passing by on its way to the Port of Oakland. I pulled out my phone and saw that I had a reply from Domenico. His response said:

>*After 2. Before 4:15. My office.*

Domenico always worked on Sundays and took Mondays off, so I wasn't surprised. I closed the email and pulled up my reading app. I kept only one book at a time on my phone. Usually something I would not otherwise choose to read. That way, when I was away from home and found myself with time on my hands, I would be forced to either read something difficult or do nothing. I picked up where I had left off in the *Iliad*: The Trojans advanced in a dense body, with Hector at their head pressing right on as a rock that came thundering down the side of some mountain from whose brow the winter torrents had torn it...

The light, the sound of the bay lapping against the piles, the Homeric prose, all blended together in some mysterious way to eradicate time. I looked up an hour and a half later, the armor of fallen warriors still ringing

in my ears, and realized it was nearly time for my rendezvous with Antoine.

I'd met Antoine a couple years after I began my
business relationship with Domenico. It was Domenico
who introduced us. There was a job some associates of
his wanted done. We met, went over the details, and then
both decided independently that we were not interested. It
was a smash and grab. Not my style and not Antoine's
either. I didn't know much about Antoine's work, and he
didn't know much about mine. I didn't even know his last
name. We were both in the same business, though. I
knew that much. And we ran into each other occasionally, at parties, openings, and other types of art world
events.

I saw him sitting at the counter as I approached. A
small, dark, wiry guy. He was dressed all in black. Black
501s, converse, jacket, T-shirt, and a baseball cap. I had
never seen him in anything else. There was a market bag
on the stool next to his. He saw me coming and moved
the bag. I pulled out the stool and sat down.

"Thanks for meeting me on short notice," I said.

He nodded, sipped his coffee. He was drinking es-
presso from a tiny cup the color of cinnamon. "No problem. I come here this time most days to do my shopping."
He gestured toward his bag on the floor at his feet. His
accent was French-African. Maybe Cameroon, or Congo.
Another thing among many I would probably never know
about him.

"I don't want to keep you, so I'll get right to business," I said, speaking softly and keeping my gaze on the
line of people waiting to order. "A friend had a piece of
art stolen. A piece very important to her. An early
Heidrich." Antoine drew breath sharply and nodded
twice. I went on, "It's almost certainly gone by now, but I
told her I would see what I could do. It seems like it was

a commissioned theft. A professional job. The thief definitely knew it was there and went in to get it. Nothing else was touched." Antoine was nodding, listening. "I know this is unusual, but I just wanted to ask you to keep your ear to the ground and let me know if you hear anything that could give me a clue where to start. Of course, I'm not asking you to betray any confidences or—"

Antoine waved his hand in a dismissive gesture. "That is understood. You wouldn't ask me if this was not important. What method of entry? Any other details?"

I gave him a rundown of the break in and theft.

He sat for a while, thinking. Finally, he nodded and glanced over at me. "I will let you know if I hear anything," he said, raising an eyebrow.

"Thanks."

We sat for a few moments in silence. It was an easy silence of kinship. We were not friends, just acquaintances. We didn't know much of anything about each other, but we did know that we both belonged to a sort of club with a small membership. Even if we did not talk about what we did, it was nice to sit with a comrade.

Rising, I clapped him on the shoulder lightly. "I can't thank you enough. Please let me know if there's ever something I can do in return."

Antoine nodded again and looked me in the eye. "I will."

It was one o'clock. I wanted to go home, take a shower, and have a nap, but I decided once again to stay downtown until my business was done. Domenico had said to come by after two. Outside, I unlocked my bike, stood for a moment, thinking, then hopped on, and started pedaling. My destination was a Krav Maga class I often dropped in on. It was an open class that combined conditioning and advanced Krav training. I had been studying Krav Maga for several years. Besides biking, it was the

only regular exercise I did. Sometimes, if I was doing a
job that required a specific type of conditioning, I would
do specialized training for a couple of months. Not all my
jobs were as simple as the one at Carl and Bill's house.
Sometimes, they involved climbing and ropes. In general,
though, Krav and biking kept me in good all-around
shape. I always kept gym clothes in my backpack, so I
was set. I had time to drop into the one-thirty class, get a
workout in, and be at Domenico's office by two-forty-
five.

☙❧☙

    After class, feeling beat but also energized, I stripped
my sweaty clothes off and stepped into the locker room
shower. Nobody else was waiting, so I spent several
minutes letting the warm water pummel my back. We had
practiced wrist manipulations in class, and my forearms
were particularly sore. Standing under the water, I
thought about Val, the painting, Antoine. Would he be
able to find out anything useful? *Wait and see*, I thought.
Back at my locker, I toweled off, dressed, and headed out
for North Beach.
    The entrance to Domenico's building was off a nar-
row, cobblestone alley. There was a front entrance, of
course, but he preferred visitors to come in by the less
obvious door. The building was a two-story brick box
built in the early- 1910s with a warehouse on the ground
floor and offices above. The alley was dark, graffiti covered, and foul smelling. I rattled over the cobblestones on
my bike and hopped off when I got to the door. It was a
plain, unmarked metal door with many layers of washed,
scraped, and painted over graffiti forming an interesting
palimpsest of tone-on-tone grays. A small callbox was
mounted in the brick next to the door and a security cam-

era five feet above the lintel. I pushed the single button on the box and waited a few seconds. Soon it crackled to life, and a woman's voice spoke, tired and raspy. It was Sylvia, Domenico's secretary and receptionist.

"Who's there?"

"It's Justin," I answered, looking up toward the security camera. "Domenico said I could stop by."

A loud buzzing was quickly followed by the slinky clack of the lock disengaging. I pulled the door open, shouldered my bike, and stepped through.

I left my bike in the entry and climbed the stairs, running my fingers along the rough brick and the old, age-darkened mortar between them. There was a landing, a switchback, another flight, then the stairs opened up into a long narrow reception area with Sylvia seated at the far end behind a big old oak desk. Two black-leather-covered couches were placed against the walls, and a large Persian carpet with a gold and red mandala-like pattern lay across the floorboards. A row of windows on the left wall faced another warehouse across the alley and let in a dull, grayish light. Sylvia looked up from her computer but kept her fingers on the keyboard in touch-typing position. She was probably in her mid-fifties, plump but stylish with black hair and a sharp crow-like face. I stopped, standing in the center of the rug.

"He's on a phone call. Sit. Coffee?" she asked.

"No thanks," I answered, sitting down on the couch facing the windows.

I had tried to hold a conversation with Sylvia my first few times in the reception room, but she had discouraged it by answering in monosyllables. I didn't try anymore. Most likely, she had a good idea of the kind of business her boss conducted and didn't want to get to know the people who visited him. She tapped away on her keyboard while I waited, staring out the window. I

could see a small patch of sky above the roof of the
warehouse next door. Occasionally, a pigeon or two
would fly past, dark gray spots on the washed-out blue
sky.

A few minutes later, Sylvia cleared her throat. Domenico's office door was open, and she gestured with her
head toward it. I thanked her and walked back, skirting
her desk.

Domenico was seated when I entered but stood and
grasped my hand. He had one of those bone-crushing
handshakes, but I thought he went easy on me because he
knew my hands were important in my various lines of
work. He had aged very little since I first met him. The
lines on his forehead were a bit deeper, and he had a bit
more silver in his hair.

"More merchandise for me so soon?" he asked, sitting and leaning back in his big executive office chair,
fingers lacing behind his head.

He was making a show of relaxation, but he was on
guard. It was unusual for me to make an appointment
with him so soon after the last one. Unusual was not good
in Domenico's world.

"No," I replied. "I know this is a bit out of the ordinary, but I just came by to ask for your help with something." He nodded, sitting forward and placing his elbows
on the desk, so I continued and told him about the theft,
giving him the same rundown as I had given Antoine.
"Obviously, it's understood that you might not be able to
tell me anything, even if you have knowledge of this. I
respect your discretion completely," I finished.

Domenico leaned back again and turned his chair
slightly to the side. He kept his gaze on me, obviously
pondering his response. I looked around the office. Dark
wood paneling covered the walls up to about waist
height. From there, the plaster wall rose to a coved ceil-

ing with a decorative egg-and-dart plaster motif running around the periphery, just below where the inward curve of the wall began. He had one of those old console stereo systems all built into a massive wooden cabinet. On top of it was a tray with small glasses and a crystal decanter half full with some light brownish liquid. It had been half full since my first visit to the office years before but it was never dusty.

Domenico rose, walked to the cabinet, and lifted the hinged top of the center portion to reveal a turntable. He then bent down and opened one of the cabinet doors behind which was a collection of records. He took his time, his broad back to me, selecting a record. When he eventually made his choice, he extracted the album and slid the record out of its sleeve, placing it on the turntable and pushing the button that set the machine in motion. He crossed back to his desk and sat. The music had begun to play, softly. It was cello music, choppy, emotional.

"You know this music?"

I shook my head no.

"It's Elgar's Cello Concerto. London Philharmonic. Beatrice Harrison. I'll make you a tape." Domenico had given me several cassette tapes dubbed from his old records. I had a feeling he gave them to everybody. Either he had no idea that people no longer owned tape decks, or it was some kind of private joke. We listened in silence for a moment, then he turned to me, all business.

"Do you know about Darwin's finches?"

"A little," I answered.

"He found fifteen different species of finch in the Galapagos. They all were evolved to eat different kinds of foods. Different beak shapes." Domenico made a beak with the thumb and fingers of his left hand, opening and closing it. "It was a big part of the evidence for his theory. This business—" He made a gesture that encompassed both of us. "—that we are a part of, is like that. There are different species who make their living in different ways. Maybe I can help you. Maybe I can't. It depends on how the deal started, who lined it up, what connections I might have. Are we the same species? Closely related? Or distant cousins? You see what I mean?"

I nodded again. "I appreciate any help you can give me but, like I said, I totally understand that you might not be able to tell me anything."

"Good. Our working relationship is productive, Justin. And, I like you. We think alike. I'll help you if I can." He leaned back again, resuming his relaxed posture. "Please ask Sylvia to hold my calls on your way out."

I stood, and we shook hands again. "Thanks, Domenico. Let me know if I can do anything for you."

His face crinkled into a pained expression, and he waved off my offer. "If you hear from me, it will be today or tomorrow. Longer than that, and I haven't found any information."

୧ଽୣୠ

Later that evening, I was standing on the roof of my building, looking out over the bay and finishing a glass of Pinot Grigio. There were lights of big ships anchored or moving slowly, cars flowing across the bridge, and a three-quarter moon hanging low over it all. I had made salmon for dinner with sweet potatoes and brown rice—a meal I could eat every night. My roof had two big planter boxes where I grew vegetables and berries. I also had a small lemon tree. I had just finished watering, and the rich, earthy aroma of wet dirt smelled good. At the back edge of the roof, my solar panels were reflecting the moon. Were they generating any power from the moonlight? I wondered. My phone buzzed in my pocket. I took it out, glanced at the screen. It was an address in China-town. Waverly Place, just off Clay. There was an apart-ment number. The message was from an anonymous Guerrilla Mail address, sent to my Proton account. I tapped the address to open it in maps and shifted to street view. The building was five stories, characterless, with a brick facade and a chiropractor's office on the ground floor. It was the clue I was waiting for. I owed either Domenico or Antoine a favor. Eventually, I would have to find out which of them had sent it.

CHAPTER 5

I debated for a minute, wanting to go to bed and follow the lead in the morning, but decided I needed to act immediately. Downstairs, I changed into some anonymous clothes, pulled on a jacket, threw a few things I thought might be helpful in my backpack, and was out the door. As I shouldered my bike and started down the stairs, I checked the time on my phone. Seven-forty-two.

Outside and on my bike, I was wishing I hadn't had two glasses of wine, but I knew it would wear off with a few minutes of vigorous activity so I turned off Third Street onto the relatively deserted Terry Francois Boulevard and started pedaling hard. Soon, I was just south of the ballpark, curving around and joining back up with Third Street. My head felt clearer, and the fuzzy aura around the streetlights was lessening. Crossing China Basin, I smelled the creosote on the pilings and saw a pelican swoop by. I kept going straight up Third, passing South Park, the freeway, Yerba Buena, and the SFMOMA. It was hard to believe that it had only been forty-eight hours since I attended the opening with Valerie.

At Market, I had a green light so I bunny hopped the streetcar tracks, swerved around a taxi creeping out into the intersection, and continued up Kearny. A few more blocks of uphill, and I was nearing my destination, so I pulled over, found a well-lit portion of sidewalk, and locked up my bike. I had a good U-lock and a heavy chain to go through the wheels. Nonetheless, whenever I left my bike outside, I always assumed it wouldn't be there when I returned. The Miata was my seventh or eighth bike since moving to the city when I was seventeen years old.

On Clay Street, approaching Waverly, I pulled my hood up and walked slowly, checking out the neighborhood. This wasn't a part of the city I knew well. I was very close to, if not in, the heart of Chinatown. I'd never been sure exactly where the geographic center of Chinatown was. There was, undoubtedly, strong disagreement on the subject. The buildings were all four or five stories with restaurants, nail salons, markets, herb shops, and other similar businesses on the ground floors. Chinatown had been completely decimated by the 1906 earthquake and resulting fires, so the buildings were mostly from the 1910s and 1920s. The foot traffic was sparse, but cars and trucks were packed onto Clay, honking and moving slowly.

I turned left on Waverly and strolled casually. It was more an alley than a street. Parking was on one side only, and the roadway was barely wide enough for two cars to pass in opposite directions. The building was halfway down the block on the left. I crossed to the right side and gave it a good, sidelong look as I passed by. The top four floors seemed to be apartments, and there was a main entrance with a no-nonsense gate and call box. I doubled back, crossed the street, and approached the entrance. The street was fairly dark, and nobody else was around, so I spent some time inspecting the callbox. There were no names, just the apartment numbers next to the buttons printed out on one of those old-style label makers that actually embossed the numbers into a rigid plastic strip. Grime was embedded around the edges of the labels and the green plastic was faded from many years of sun exposure. The apartment number from the email was 403. Fourth floor. Avoiding that one, I chose a number at random and pushed the button. I waited a minute, but no answer came so I chose another. This time, after about twenty seconds, a voice crackled through the speaker.

"Wei?" It sounded like an old woman.

"UPS," I said, trying to sound urgent and tired at the same time. After a few seconds which seemed to draw out into an eternity, I heard a loud buzzing and immediately pulled the gate open, then pushed through the inner door.

The lobby was tiny with just enough room for a small table where the residents apparently left flyers and misdelivered mail. Above the table was a two-by-three grid of those stick-on mirror tiles with gold veins. Classy. I kept my hood up and peeked around the edge at the walls and ceiling. No cameras. The dark gray carpet was newish but looked like probably the lowest cost per square foot available at the discount carpet center. There was no elevator, just a narrow staircase going up to a landing, turning ninety degrees, going up again. There were several Amazon boxes under the lobby table. I found one addressed to a fourth-floor apartment, tucked it under my arm as a prop, in case anybody questioned me, and started up the stairs. At the fourth floor, I pulled open the fire door and stepped into the corridor. It looked like there were six apartments per floor. I went to a window at the end of the hallway to orient myself then strode down, passing each door. Four-oh-three was on my left, which meant it faced the street. At the opposite end of the corridor, there was another fire door and a back staircase leading down. I left the package at the door of the apartment it was addressed to and then took the back stairs down. The stairs ended up in a narrow breezeway beside the building which led past cobweb-and-grime-covered electrical meters to a door that opened back out into the street.

I went ahead through the door but stood in the recessed doorway for a moment, checking out the buildings on the opposite side of Waverly. Directly across was another, similar building with an insurance office on the ground floor. To the left was a dingy-looking, five-story hotel. To the right a two-story box with an auto body shop at ground level. The roof of the auto body shop building would do, but the hotel would be better so I headed there first.

There was a button outside the locked door. I pushed it and heard a buzzing sound from somewhere inside. A moment later, the lock clicked open, and I stepped in. The hotel lobby was scarcely larger than the lobby of the apartment building I had just left. At the back was a small reception desk where a balding, middle-aged man in a blue button up shirt sat. He had a computer terminal with an ancient tan plastic CRT monitor.

"Hello," I said, walking up to the desk. "I need a room. Fourth floor if possible. Facing the street. The man nodded and two finger typed a search on his terminal. After a moment, he turned, took a key from the board behind the desk, and slapped it down on the brown Formica counter.

"Four-eleven. How many nights?"

"One night. What's the rate?"

"One sixty-five. All tax included."

I didn't have time to haggle, so I took out my wallet and counted out the price in cash. He handed me a registration card and a pen. I filled it out minimally with a fake name, address in Cleveland, Ohio, and random digit telephone number. He didn't even look at it.

"Elevator there," he said, pointing to a contraption that appeared to be as old as the building. I thanked him, took the key, and stepped into the elevator. The interior was paneled in fake wood. There was a heavy door, and rattly bars that closed automatically then rattled open again when it reached the fourth floor. The hallway was dark, but I found room 411 and managed to open the door after fiddling with the lock for a while.

Once inside, I flipped on the light. The room was small but tidy and didn't smell nearly as bad as I expected—just a faint aroma of mildew and industrial strength cleaning products. I turned the light back off and opened the curtains. I was on the corner nearest to the apartment building and had a good view across the way. Four-oh-three was the middle apartment and had two large windows facing the street. There were no curtains in the windows. There appeared to be blinds that were currently rolled up. I could see the blue light of a TV reflecting on a wall and some dark shapes of furniture. I sat on the bed, old springs groaning, and got binoculars out of my backpack. With the binoculars, I could make out the end of a couch and a pair of feet in white socks. This could take a while, I thought as I settled back.

I spent almost two hours sitting on the bed, watching the window of apartment 402, getting up only once for a glass of water. The feet moved occasionally. While I was sitting there, watching, I thought about what the hell I was doing. I felt as if I had been somehow drawn into a choreographed dance, pulled in by an invisible partner. It was totally out of character for me to be doing something like this, but it felt right at the same time. I knew the steps of this dance. In fact, I felt like a sixteenth-century aristocrat might have when the band started up a stately pavane, and everybody filed out onto the ballroom floor.

My body was moving automatically, and I couldn't think of a reason to stop.

Finally, just as I was about to give up and lay back on the bed for a nap, the feet swung off the couch and disappeared from view. A moment later, a man walked up to the window and opened it. He lit a cigarette and stood, smoking thoughtfully. He was small, maybe five feet six inches, with a slight build but lean and capable looking in a tight black T-shirt and jeans. His face was expressionless and highlighted in red and green by the neon sign of the body shop across the street. He reminded me of a protagonist in a Wong Kar Wai movie. He had that kind of sangfroid swagger. After a couple of minutes, he threw his cigarette butt out the window, lit another, then made a small jerk and pulled a phone from his back pocket.

He answered the call, spoke a few words, nodded his head several times, hung up. Two more drags and the second butt followed the first, exploding in a shower of orange sparks as it hit the pavement below. He moved away from the window, the light from the TV drained away suddenly, and he reappeared wearing a dark hoodie. The window slammed closed. It was go time for me.

I grabbed my stuff and hurried out. Luckily, the desk clerk was not there when I bolted through the lobby. I opened the front door carefully and looked out. The man was half a block away, walking toward Clay Street. I followed, matching his pace and trying to be quiet. He was carrying a tube, like architects use for blueprints. A shock ran through me, and I felt my fingertips prickle. I had a pretty good idea what was in that tube. For a moment, I considered chasing him down and wrestling it away. I quickly quelled the impulse.

The last thing I wanted was a fight in an alley with a guy who might kick my ass. Also, I knew he was probably just hired help for the job. I wanted to know where he was going, who he was meeting.

He turned up Clay, and I continued to follow. He didn't seem to be checking for followers. I didn't know why he would. He had no reason to suspect anybody would know what he was carrying. He turned right on Stockton and continued several more blocks until he came to the big six-way intersection at Columbus. He was lost to view for a moment as a bus passed between us, but then I saw him again heading north on the east side of Columbus. I stayed on the west side and kept him on my right, staying a few paces behind. Half a block later, he stopped, looked up at the sign above a small trattoria, nodded, and stepped through the door. On my side of the street, there was a wine bar one door down with outdoor seating. Two tables were empty so I sat, keeping my eyes on the restaurant across the street. The interior was dim, but the entire front of the place was windows. It didn't look very popular. I could see two tables occupied by couples, all of whom were looking at their phones. There were several more empty tables and a couple of shadowy booths at the back upholstered in red. A moment later, a waiter led the man to one of the booths. He sat but did not pick up the menu.

The waiter seemed to ask him a question. He shook his head and gestured toward a water glass on the table. Just then I felt I tap on my shoulder. A waitress was standing next to my table.

"You're supposed to check in with the hostess before sitting down…" Her voice trailed off meekly as if she was not interested in confrontation with a customer.

"Sorry," I said, glancing back across the street. He was still seated, alone. "If I can keep this table, I'll make it worth your while. I'm waiting for somebody. Need to be able to see the people going by."

She nodded, frowning. "Fine. Here's the wine menu. Food's on the back."

"Just bring me a glass of your favorite wine. I trust your judgement."

She brightened up a little. "Okay. Be right back."

I continued watching the booth. The man had his phone out now and was reading something but looking up at the door every now and then.

A few minutes later, the waitress stopped back by and placed a large glass of red on my table. "It's a Nero D'Avola, Sicilian."

She was waiting so I took a sip. "Delicious. Thanks."

She wandered off to another table, and I turned my attention back. A tall, bearded man in a suit was coming up the sidewalk. He looked familiar. I watched him approach the trattoria, slow his already ponderous pace, and enter. My neurons were firing, trying to recall where I had seen him before, then it hit me. He was the guy from the Heidrich opening at the SFMOMA, who Valerie had been talking with just before we left. She hadn't told me his name. I had a terrible memory for names, anyway, but I never forgot a face. I watched him walk back and take a seat at the booth. The waiter approached, and he waved him away with a come-back-in-a-minute gesture. The two seemed to be conversing. A very short conversation followed by the tall man slipping something out of the inside pocket of his suit jacket and handing it across the table. The smaller man pocketed it and stood. They shook hands, and the nameless resident of apartment 403 walked out. I watched him for a moment as he disappeared back down Columbus.

He did not have the tube. When I looked back, the tall man was smiling, waving the waiter away again. He took out his wallet, placed some cash on the table, and stood, slinging the tube over his shoulder. I quickly took two twenties out of my wallet and weighted them down with my still full wine glass.

I was standing when he emerged from the restaurant and turned down Columbus, heading back in the direction he had come from. This guy would be no contest. Given the chance, I would definitely take the painting from him. It didn't look like I was going to get the chance, though. Half a block down Columbus, he took a key fob out of his pocket, pushed a button, and the lights of the big, gray Mercedes sedan he was standing next to flashed. Shit. I was still standing at the corner, waiting for a chance to dart across the street through the heavy traffic when he opened the door, tossed the tube into the passenger seat, and got in. The car started up, and he pulled away from the curb.

I saw my opening and bolted across, dodging past a delivery van and seeing for a moment the surprised face of the driver illuminated by oncoming headlights. Across the street, I saw the Mercedes stopped at a traffic light halfway up the block. I ran, reaching back and fumbling with the zipper on my backpack as I went. I dug down and found what I was looking for. One of the items I had tossed into my backpack before leaving was a small GPS tracking device, magnetic on one side. I pushed down the button to turn it on and made it to the corner with three seconds left on the flashing walk signal across the street.

The device was in my left hand, my phone in my right. I flipped my hood up and hurried out into the crosswalk. As I passed in front of the Mercedes, keeping my face turned away, I let my phone slip out of my hand, trying to make it look like an accident. I immediately dropped to one knee, recovered the phone, and slapped the tracker onto the back side of the license plate holder. Standing, I continued across the street at a jog and stepped onto the opposite curb just as the light turned red.

When I looked back the Mercedes was already a block away, tail lights flashing as it slowed then turned right onto Filbert Street.

I stepped into an apartment building doorway and stood for a moment, catching my breath. Adrenaline was still flowing, and my heart was racing. I allowed myself to calm down for thirty seconds then lifted my phone and pushed the button to wake it. The screen was fine, no damage from the fall. It was in a good, sturdy case so I hadn't been worried. I opened my SMS app and found Val's name.

>*Who was the guy at the Heidrich opening you were talking to before we left? Tall. Suit. Beard. Red nose.*

I tapped the send button then scrolled through my apps until I found the one for the GPS tracker. I hadn't ever used the thing, but I had gone through the steps to set it up, so I was hoping it actually worked. I tapped the app icon and waited an excruciating few seconds while it flashed a "connecting" message. Finally, the message faded out, and a map appeared. On the map was a blinking dot, moving slowly up Broadway toward Pacific Heights. I watched it for a few seconds, moving, stopping, moving, stopping, then a reply from Val popped up. She always responded to text messages with alarming speed.

>*Jenkins Booth. He's an asshole. What's going on? Do you have a lead?*

I thought for a moment, then typed back:

>*Nothing solid. Don't do anything rash. I'm working on it. Let me do my thing and I'll get back to you soon. Where does Booth live?*

I sent the message then flipped back to the tracker app. Booth was turning off Broadway now and heading south toward Lafayette Park. He was in one of the fanciest areas of the city. Val's reply came back:

>*Pac Heights*

>*Alone? Wife? Kids? Insane woman in the attic?* I asked.

>*Alone I think. Scion of an old SF family. Inherited the house. Runs an antique shop.*

I flipped back to the tracker again. He had stopped. I watched for another twenty seconds, but the dot stayed where it was. He was home. What was my next move? The chance that he would move the painting anywhere else tonight seemed small. I needed more info, though. Did he pay Mr. 403 to seal the painting? Or was he a middleman? Would he keep the painting in his house? Take it to a safe deposit box? Planning on selling it? He had to be rich if he lived in the area of Pac Heights where the little blue dot had stopped. Sometimes, though, people seemed wealthy but were actually on the edge of insolvency.

There were many possibilities. I needed to get into the house and look around. Maybe I could even get the painting while he slept. He looked like the kind of guy who would drink himself to sleep. I was going to need some help, though. I scrolled through my contact list and found my friend Ashna's name.

>*Are you free for a drink?*

After sending the text, I started walking back down

Columbus toward where I had left my bike. As I passed the wine bar, the waitress from earlier was taking an order at one of the outdoor tables. She looked up and stared at me with an astonished expression as I passed by. Maybe she had seen me dash across the street. I smiled and kept walking. Soon I felt my phone buzz, and Ashna's reply was there on the screen:

>*At Syn Bar. Come over.*

Syn Bar. I hadn't been there in years. I was surprised it still existed. My last, hazy memory of a night out at Syn Bar involved experimental electronic music played by two guys hunched over laptops. They had live, psychedelic video accompaniment by another guy with a laptop and some sort of homemade grid of unmarked buttons that applied freakish effects to the video clips when pressed. I remember it going on for hours.

I found my bike miraculously still where I left it and in one piece. Syn Bar was in the Tenderloin. Definitely not a good place to leave a bike outside. They had indoor bike parking if I remembered correctly, though.

It was not a long ride. Fifteen minutes later, I passed through a crowd of smokers out front, walked through the front door, and found a spot for my bike on the jam packed rack just inside. It was a cavernous space with a bar, seating on the ground level, and more seating in a loft upstairs. The stage area was at the front, to the left of the door, and was currently inhabited by a young woman with two tables full of arcane equipment all wired together in a tangle of cables and running into a big mixing console. She was moving back and forth, turning knobs, pushing buttons, flipping switches. The sound coming out of the speakers was a kind of low droning with little explosions of static and occasional blips and bloops.

I looked around. The place was crowded with people who looked like they probably spent a lot of time in front of screens, writing code. I waited for a few minutes at the bar for a beer then did a circuit of the downstairs. No Ashna downstairs, so I headed up to the loft. As I reached the top of the stairs, I saw her. She was seated at a corner table. Two guys with sculpted, tattoo-covered arms were just getting up from the table and passed me as they headed down the stairs. I walked over.

Ashna jumped up and gave me a hug. "Justin! Nice to see you."

"You, too. It's been a while. Who are those guys? I don't want to intrude."

She wrinkled her nose. "Don't worry about them. The taller one is my boyfriend. The other one is his friend."

"Boyfriend?" I asked, raising an eyebrow.

Ashna and I went way back. I was used to her calling people her lovers but rarely boyfriend.

"Yeah. He wants me to call him that. I'm trying it out."

"Where did you meet? Work?"

Ashna was a hotshot programmer for one of the big tech companies. We met at art school on orientation day and had been friends since. Freshman year, she took a digital art elective. Pretty soon, she was making installation pieces that involved servo motors, circuits, and microcontrollers running generative algorithms. As part of her work, she started going deep into code— programming stuff in low-level languages and making conceptual pieces based on the flow of data over networks. By the time she graduated, she had no trouble getting a job at a start-up company and hopped from there to her current employer.

"No. Friend of a friend. He's a paleo blogger."

"A what?"

"You know, paleo-diet, paleo-lifestyle. You can't tell me you haven't heard about this, Justin. It's huge in the Bay Area."

"I might have heard something about it. I didn't know people could make a living blogging about it. though."

"Don't be an asshole to him. He takes it seriously. He was just giving me shit for eating this." She gestured to a sandwich on the table.

"Is that from here?" I asked.

All the biking and chasing people had made me hungry, despite my earlier dinner.

"No. Hipster sandwich place down the street. Say what you want about hipsters, they make good sandwiches. You can have half if you want. I'm not that hungry." She pushed the sandwich across the table. "The bacon is kind of wimpy, though. Not crispy enough."

"Thanks," I said, and took a bite. "You're right about the bacon."

She nodded thoughtfully. "Yeah," she said. "Somebody sent that little piggy to college where the soft Marxist ivory tower elite taught him it wasn't his job to be crispy for the man."

I burst out laughing. Couldn't help myself. Statements like that were one of the reasons I loved Ashna. "Listen," I said, "I need your help with something."

Her eyes sparkled. "Like last time? Some kind of cloak and dagger shit? You still never explained that to me."

"I know. Sorry. I promise to tell you someday." I sat back, looked around, then leaned forward again. "I need to get into a house. I want to make sure there isn't a security system. Maybe shut it off if there is. I can tell you this: there's something in the house that was stolen from

a friend. It's not a good guy's house. You would be helping me defeat the bad guys."

Ashna looked me in the eyes. "When."

"Right now."

"Let's go," she said, standing and lifting the strap of
a messenger bag over her head.

CHAPTER 6

December 12 ~ 13:

We left Syn Bar via a back door which let out into an alley damp with billowing fog. I stepped carefully over a pile of rotting vegetables and coffee grounds, used syringes, a garbage bag ripped open and spilling out brightly colored children's clothes. Ashna turned right when we reached the street. I followed half a block to where her car was parked. She thumbed the button on her key, and the doors unlocked with a beep.

"Okay," she said, sliding into the driver's seat, "where to?"

"Pac Heights," I answered, "near Lafayette park."

She hit the ignition, plugged her phone into an aux cable, and started some music playing. Bone shaking sub bass notes began to emanate from the speakers as we rolled away from the curb. Ashna drove like the car was a cyborg extension of her body. Anybody else pulling the moves she made would have had me stomping the floor boards, trying to find the non-existent passenger side brake pedal. I was relaxed with her, though. I knew she was more than capable.

Soon, we were out of the Tenderloin, across Van

Ness, and headed into Pacific Heights. Modest Victorians and apartment buildings gave way to gated mansions with elegant landscaping. Ashna turned up Octavia. A couple of blocks later we were approaching the south end of the park. She gave me a look, slowing the car.

"Left," I shouted over the music, reaching to turn down the volume. "Then around to the other side of the park. I need to turn this down. Wake people up in this neighborhood, and the police will be here in seconds."

She nodded. We made our way around the west side of the park.

I had my phone out, checking the map. "Pull over. It's the house right there."

It was a two-story, red-brick Edwardian, smaller than its neighbors but still good sized. It had a fence with an automatic gate at the driveway and an attached garage that was newer than the rest of the building. Booth's Mercedes was parked in the driveway. Altogether, though, it had a look of neglect. The landscaping was beginning to go to weeds. There was moss on the roof. A couple of newspapers still in bags were just outside the gate. Ashna was gazing across the street, nodding her head. Around the edges of one ground-floor window with heavy red drapes pulled closed, I could see some dim hint of light. The rest of the street-facing windows were dark.

"Hand me my bag," Ashna said, reaching her arm out but not taking her eyes away from the house.

I got her bag out of the back seat where she had thrown it when we got into the car. She tore open the Velcro and pulled a laptop out. It was a sleek, ultra-thin, gunmetal-colored thing with no logos I could see. The machine came alive almost instantly when she opened it. There were several command line terminal windows open, all tiled to fit the screen real estate exactly. She began typing commands into one of the windows.

"Need to find the right network," she muttered and jumped out of the car. I watched her stand and rotate ninety degrees in each direction while watching the screen of the laptop. She moved ten feet and did it again, then ducked back into the car. "Okay," she said, "there's one called boothnet that seems to be strongest in the direction of the house. Pretty weak signal but good enough."

"Definitely the right one," I answered. "His name's Booth."

"Good. It might take a while, but I can probably get in." She typed a command into one of the windows which returned a dense block of output in green text. "WEP! How old is this guy's router? That makes things easy."

She began typing commands so quickly I literally could not follow what was happening on the screen.

"What's WEP? What are you doing?" I asked.

"Wired Equivalent Privacy. Security protocol. Running an injection test now," she murmured. "Be quiet so I can concentrate."

I shut my mouth and sat back, looking back and forth between the screen, her fingers typing, and her face bathed in the green light. She worked for another couple of minutes then, "Cracked it." She looked up and gave me a devious smile. "I'm going to connect now. I can use this key." She pointed at something on the screen. "Okay. Now I'm on the network. Let's see what I can find." She began typing again. I leaned my head back and closed my eyes for a minute while she worked. "Found the security server," she said, "let's see if this thing has a web interface."

"Thanks for helping me with this," I said.

She gave a sharp head nod. "No problem. You know I love this shit. I will bet you one million dollars that the default password will work on this thing."

"I wouldn't take that bet. How do you know the default password?"

"Just downloaded the manual. This security system is as old as the router. I'm in. People never change default passwords. This thing is remotely accessible. He's got a static IP address. Looks like there used to be a company doing remote monitoring but the service contract wasn't renewed. Big warning message here. Admin account probably isn't accessible from outside the LAN but I can change the password on this other account with full permissions. Must have been the account the security company used..." Her voice trailed off, and then she suddenly slammed her laptop closed, leaned over the console, wrapped her arms around me, and began to kiss me with a surprising fervor. I tried to pull away, but she held on tighter.

"What the—"

"Just play along for a minute."

I heard the sound of a car approaching slowly. A light moved over us. The car continued past, and I saw it was a police cruiser. It turned the corner, and Ashna let go of me, smiling.

"Saw it in the rear-view mirror," she said. "Nice kiss, Justin. I thought you were enjoying it there for a second."

"You started it. Did you learn that counter surveillance technique from an old detective movie?"

"Seemed like the best course of action at the moment."

We were both laughing now.

"I'm not complaining."

"Get serious for a second. We've got what we need. I can disable this security system whenever I want. Although it doesn't look like anybody's listening anyway."

"Good," I answered, thinking. "I don't really want to break into an occupied house. It's against my principles. I need to keep an eye on this place, though. I need to know if he leaves or has visitors." I was looking around. "Stay here for just a minute."

I climbed out of the car, closed the door softly, and walked a few paces into the park along a concrete pathway. There was a small building just ahead. It looked like a shed. Maybe for storing grounds-keeping equipment. The door had a cheap padlock on it. There were no windows, but there was a louvered vent high up on the wall facing the street. I went back to the car.

"I found a good spot to keep a lookout from."

"That shed?"

"Yeah. I can get in pretty easily."

"Stakeout! You're into some weird shit, Justin, but it's fun. I'll bring you some coffee and snacks later. You'll know it's me if you hear three sharp knocks, a pause, two knocks, another pause, then a sound like an owl hooting in the distance."

"You're a natural at this."

"Text me if you want me to turn off the security system."

"Okay," I said, reaching into the back seat for my backpack. "Thanks again. I owe you a nice dinner and two explanations."

"The pleasure's all mine."

It took me less than a minute to pick the padlock. I hurried in and closed the door behind me. The shed was damp and chilly and smelled like gasoline. I shifted a lawn mower and a couple of rakes out of the way then kicked a couple of bags of fertilizer over to stand on. The two screws holding the vent in place came out easily with the screwdriver on my multitool. I now had a nice, nine-inch-by-four-inch window and a perfect view of Booth's house. There was no way I could stand there all night staring out at the house, though. What I needed was some

sort of motion-activated alarm. I ran a quick search on
my phone and found an app that might work, so I downloaded and installed it. It used the phone's camera and
said it could send text messages, emails, take pictures,
and also flash a warning on the screen whenever it de-
tected movement. There was an outlet in the shed, and I
had a charger with me, so I plugged my phone in and
managed to set it up facing the house by propping it up
between the claws of a gardening tool I found hanging on
the wall. With my improvised surveillance set up complete, I was able to arrange a couple more bags of fertilizer into a semi-comfortable seat. Sure enough, the phone
gave a quiet beep, and the screen was briefly overlaid
with a red exclamation point the next time a car drove by.
The system was working.

Seated there, I found myself musing on the fact that I
had constructed for myself a sort of real-life version of
Plato's cave. I was sitting in the dark, staring at a digital
shadow of a puppet show involving myself, Booth, and
the Heidrich painting. What was the reality? I hoped I
could find the clue that would lead me out of the cave. I
think I dozed off for a minute, woke when my phone
beeped and flashed to alert me about another passing car,
dozed again, then woke with a start to a beep and the image of Booth on my phone as he walked out the footpath
gate at the front of his property, to the right of the automatic driveway gate. I jumped up and looked through the
opening. He was wearing the same suit as earlier and did
not appear to have anything else with him, certainly not
the painting.

As he closed the gate, I saw him weave, almost lose
his balance, right himself. He turned left and strolled
down the sidewalk, out of my sight.

The house was empty. I had no idea how long Booth
would be gone but now was my chance. It couldn't take

long to find the painting. I got my phone down and texted Ashna.

>*It's time. Disable everything please.*

Twenty seconds later I received her reply:

>*Done. I was just about to bring you some coffee.*

I typed quickly:

>*Thx. Hold off on that. I'll get in touch soon.*

I left things as they were in the shed, locked it back up, and loped across the park to the street. There was no traffic I could see, so I continued across and vaulted over Booth's fence. My feet sank into the damp grass on the other side. I headed straight for the front door and tried it. Locked. Both the knob set and a bolt lock. I glanced back at the road. No activity there so I headed around toward the back of the house, appraising as I went. The windows were old and would be easy to break or force open. I continued, bending low to duck under some overgrown fruit trees, then turned the corner into the back yard which was small and dark with tall trees planted around the perimeter. Near where I stood there was a veranda with french doors.

I hopped over the low balustrade onto the mossy stone floor of the veranda and bent down to inspect the door handle. It was too dark to see anything. I took my backpack off and dug through it until I found a small keychain LED flashlight I always kept with me. I turned the beam on the lock. It was old—probably not as old as the house but weathered and showing spots of rust. I generally didn't bother trying to pick old locks since I didn't have any practice with them. I didn't have time, anyway, so I took my jacket off, wrapped it around my hand, and punched out the pane nearest to the knob. The glass was old and brittle and offered almost no resistance. Pieces fell to the floor inside with a pleasant tinkling sound. I reached in, turned the lock, then pushed in against resistance from heavy draperies which were pulled across the doors.

I entered Booth's house slowly, sweeping the broken glass back with my foot so that it would be hidden by the drapes. My guess was that the broken window pane would not be discovered any time soon. It didn't look like Booth opened his curtains very often. I lifted my flash-light and shined it around the room I had entered. It was about twenty by fifteen feet and seemed to be a library. Wooden shelves covered all the walls. I could see the spines of old books, stacks of magazines, and loose pa-pers weighted down with various objects as the beam of my light passed over the shelves. There was a large rug covering most of the floor, a desk piled with papers, books, plates, and teacups at the far end of the room, and, near where I had entered, an antique sofa. The air in the house had a stale, pungent odor—the aroma of unwashed clothes, dirty dishes, garbage not emptied, floors not vac-uumed, windows kept closed. Behind the desk was a wide doorway leading into another room which was dim-ly lit by some unseen light source.

It must be the room I could see from the street, I thought, the only one with any light on. A good place to start looking for the painting.

I walked slowly to the doorway, crouched low, and leaned my head around the frame. I was looking into a large living room. I guessed they would have called it a drawing room when the house was built. There were two seating areas in the room. Near where I was crouched was a grouping of ornate Louis XV sofas and chairs up-holstered in gold and cream striped fabric. Near the far end of the room, facing a fireplace where a half-burnt log was smoldering, were two leather club chairs with a table between them holding a lamp with what looked like a Tiffany shade. The lamp was the source of the light I had seen. Also on the table were a folded newspaper, an empty crystal goblet, and a wine bottle. I heard a sudden, loud crack and jumped but quickly realized it had come from the log in the fireplace.

There were several large windows which faced the street, but all were covered with the red curtains I had seen from outside. Beyond the club chairs was another doorway which led into an entry hall with a marble-tiled floor.

The seat by the fireplace seemed to be where Booth had been sitting before going out, so I made my way over and looked around. The wine bottle was empty which ex-plained his unsteady walk. I checked the label—a cheap Bordeaux. The price tag was still on the bottom. I scanned the area around the chairs, but there was no sign of the painting. On either side of the hearth were pot-bellied, marble topped Louis XV chests with two drawers each. I went to the one on the left and opened the top drawer.

It was full of pornographic magazines. Booth's tastes were not what I would have expected. The lower drawer held an antique revolver and the pieces of a broken ce-ramic figurine. I checked my watch. About fifteen minutes had passed since I had watched Booth walk through the gate. Where had he gone at this time of night?

I moved to the next chest and opened the top drawer. Age-darkened lace doilies and linens. The bottom drawer held a cigar box with three cigars in it, one of those things you use to cut the end off a cigar, a couple of Zippo lighters, and a bottle of lighter fluid. I was just sliding the drawer closed when I heard the sound of a key sliding into a lock, echoing through the entry hall as the sound waves bounced off the hard marble floor. Shit. Booth was back.

For a moment, I crouched there, indecisive. My instinct was to leave at once, back through the library, out the french doors, over the fence. If I left, though, if he noticed the broken window, I would never get the painting back. He would know somebody was snooping around, and he would hide it well, maybe take it somewhere else more secure. I made a decision, stood, ran to the dark end of the room, and lowered myself to the floor behind one of the sofas. I would wait and see what happened. My guess was that he would continue drinking and eventually pass out in the chair by the fire. Once he was out, I could continue my search.

The front door opened with a whine of old hinges then thumped closed. I heard his footsteps on the marble, diminishing. There was a dull clattering from another room then I heard him coming back across the hall. He clomped into the room and put something down on the table with a clunk. The sofa behind which I hid was raised about ten inches off the floor, resting on eight carved legs. The floor beneath was thick with dust which had formed delicate drifts around several ancient insect carcasses. Peering under the sofa, though, I could see Booth's feet.

He crouched down and prodded the log in the fireplace with a poker, rolling it onto its side. Flames jumped up. He plucked a smaller log out of a basket on the hearth and threw it on. Once he had the fire going again, he stood, and I heard the distinctive sound of a wine bottle being opened with a waiter's corkscrew followed by the rush of liquid pouring into his glass. He had gone out for more wine, it seemed. I remembered, then, biking up Gough Street a few days before. I had passed by a little market just a block away. I had remarked on it because it looked a lot nicer than the usual cigarettes, beer, and junk food mini marts you saw all over the city. Booth settled into his chair with a grunt and picked up his newspaper.

I lay there behind the sofa for about ten or fifteen minutes, listening to the fire, the rustle of newspaper, the clink of the glass as he picked it up, drank, and set it down. He refilled the glass, and the cycle recommenced. After another ten minutes, I was starting to feel a bit crazy. Laying still and silent on a cold wooden floor in a stranger's house was not something I was cut out for. I liked action, movement.

It was one of the reasons I never went into occupied houses. I didn't like creeping or hiding. Finally, something different happened. Booth's phone rang. I heard him shift in his chair, dig into a pocket, and pull it out. There was a beep, and he answered.

"Jenkins Booth speaking." His voice was deep and phlegmy, his speech a little slurred. He was silent for several seconds then spoke again. "Yes...yes...it is...I'll be waiting."

There was another beep as he hung up. He cleared his throat and took another long drink of wine. He sat still in his chair for another minute then stood and walked to the closest window. I heard him pull back the drapes and stand still for some time, looking out. A mini-eternity passed. My left arm was beginning to cramp painfully.

Finally, I heard a car pull up out front and sit idling. Booth walked unsteadily back into the entry hall and must have pushed a button to activate the gate because I heard it sliding open. The car pulled into the driveway, and the gate clattered slowly shut. The engine shut off, a door opened and closed. I heard Booth open the front door, indistinct voices, then the front door closing and two sets of feet reentered the room.

"Have a seat here by the fire. Glass of wine?"

I could hear in his voice the attempt to speak slowly, without slurring. The voice that answered was male, nasal, and accented. The man sounded French, but it was not a classic French accent. There was something a bit more enunciated and sharp about it. Maybe Swiss? His shoes were expensive—shiny brown leather with hard leather soles.

"Just half a glass, please. I have to get on a plane soon." Booth wandered off, probably to fetch another glass. When he returned, the other man took up the conversation again.

"Drinking wine before a long flight always leaves me with a headache, Mr. Booth."

"Me as well. You are flying back tonight."

"Yes. SFO direct to Milan Malpensa. Leaving at two a.m. I get in late so stay over then driving from there next morning."

"I see. Why not fly in to some place closer?"

"My employer prefers Milan. He has connections there. No issues with customs if you see what I mean."

"Yes, of course. Very prudent." Booth paused, taking a sip of his own wine. "Shall we go ahead and get down to business Mr. Legere?"

"Naturally. I have here the sum we discussed. I assume you have the item close by?"

"Yes. Just upstairs. I'll be right back."

Booth stood, and I heard his footsteps recede again across the marble entry. He was gone for a couple of minutes, during which the other man sat very still. Finally, Booth was back.

"Very good. The condition is as expected?"

"I haven't removed it from the tube. You are all set to meet the appraiser at the airport?"

"Yes, of course."

"You may contact me if there are any problems."

"I will do that, Mr. Booth. Please open the briefcase and verify the payment."

I heard the clack of briefcase fasteners opening. There was a pause.

"Everything looks fine."

"Very good. Now, I thank you for the wine. It has been a pleasure."

They both stood and walked into the entry hall. The painting was leaving the house. There was no reason for me to stay. As soon as I saw their feet go around the corner, I stood quietly, crouching, and crept back through the doorway into the dark library. As silently as possible, I squeezed back between the curtains and the french doors, narrowly avoided stepping directly in the pile of broken glass, and slipped out, closing the doors behind me.

Once outside, I hurried around to the front of the house, batting away a damp spider web that wrapped around my face as I passed by the fruit trees again. At the corner of the house, I stopped and peered around the edge.

Mr. Legere was just closing the rear hatchback door of a sleek, dark burgundy SUV. He was of medium size but well built, wearing a dark suit, a chocolate brown trench coat, and a black Ascot cap. Altogether, a well-dressed guy.

I couldn't see much of his face in the dark, but I could tell his jaw was strong. If I had to guess, I'd say he was in his late-thirties or early-forties.

He circled around, opened the driver's side door, and got into the car, moving with a brisk athleticism like a martial artist or ballet dancer. The car started with a purr, the gate rolled open, and he backed out. I watched the tail lights recede, wondering what I should do.

I had most of the information I needed to make some good guesses. It looked like Mr. Legere was acting as an agent for a buyer in Europe, somewhere within reasonably close driving distance of Milan. He had commissioned Booth to acquire the painting. Booth had hired the thief from Chinatown who I had trailed, possibly through yet another intermediary, to steal the painting. As I had suspected, it was not a random theft. The European buyer had wanted this piece in particular, or, perhaps, had just put out a request for any early Heidrich work. I needed to book a ticket on Mr. Legere's flight.

There was a possibility I could steal the painting back from him before he left. If not, though, I needed to follow him to Milan and determine where he was spending the night before setting off by car the next day. The absurdity of what I was doing suddenly struck me again as I crouched there at the corner of a stranger's house on a cold night when I could have been home with my own glass of wine.

Booth had stolen something from somebody I cared about, though. Yes—he was just a middleman who had probably fallen on hard times and needed some cash. It had to be hard to keep a house in Pac Heights on the income from an antique shop. He had probably spent his inheritance on wine and property taxes and had turned to this as a way to pay his bills. I was in no position to judge somebody for stealing a painting. I was going to get it back, though. I had invested serious time and energy in getting it back already.

I knew about the sunk-cost fallacy. I was aware that continuing to put time and resources into a fruitless endeavor simply because you did not want to waste the time and resources you had already put in was a classic failing of human nature. I was still pretty sure I could get the painting back, though. Also, I had to admit I was having fun. I found that the "cloak and dagger shit" as Ashna had called it suited me. Everything except the creeping and hiding, anyway.

Thinking about creeping, I crept self-consciously around the front of the house, ducking under the windows, to where Booth's Mercedes was parked in the driveway and retrieved my GPS tracker. Across the street, I found a secluded bench in the park and got my phone out. There was only one airline with a two a.m. direct flight to Milan from SFO. It had to be the right one. There were two seats left in first class. Nothing else. The last-minute price was astronomical, but I went ahead and bought the ticket. I needed to get home, pick up my passport, and get to the airport quickly, so I stood, shouldering my backpack, and headed for Gough Street where I would be likely to find a taxi.

It took less than a minute to find one. The first cab that passed by pulled to the curb when I raised my arm. I hopped in, exchanged greetings with the driver, and gave him my address. He was a Sikh. My favorite taxi drivers were always Sikhs.

I sent several text messages while the cab meandered through downtown and SOMA on the way to my place. First, I thanked Ashna and let her know I would get back in touch soon. Next, I texted Roberto to tell him I would probably be out of town for a few days. Since he already had keys, I asked him to water my rooftop garden and told him he could stay at my place if he wanted. Finally, I sent a text to Val. I took a while composing it because I didn't want her to be worried or suspect the crazy lengths I was going to, to recover the painting. In the end, I just told her I had to go out of town for a couple of days, but I had a good lead and was continuing to pursue it.

At my place, I asked the driver to wait while I ran upstairs. My dirty dishes were still in the sink, but I left them there. I didn't like leaving a mess when going out of town, but I didn't have any choice. Roberto would probably wash them. I grabbed a change of clothes, toiletries, my passport, my laptop, and took all of the things out of my backpack that would give me trouble in the security line, except for a couple of items that I would just have to take a chance on. I almost left the pile of gadgets and tools on the bed where I had dumped them but remembered at the last second that Roberto might sleep there while I was gone. Quickly, I tossed them all into a box which I put on the top shelf of my closet.

Once I was back in the cab, I slouched in my seat and gave myself a few moments to relax and breathe deeply while the driver headed down Third Street and turned onto Cesar Chavez, taking us toward 101. From there, it was only fifteen minutes to the airport. It felt good to sit for a moment in the warm car and empty my head. The headlights of cars streaming into the city in the opposing lanes blurred in my half-closed eyes, and I drifted off for a few minutes. Before I knew it, though, we were rolling up to the curb at the SFO international terminal. I roused, rubbed my eyes, paid the driver, and stepped out onto the cold, blustery loading zone sidewalk. It was just after one a.m.

CHAPTER 7

December 14:

Inside the airport, I found the correct ticket counter and stepped into the empty first-class lane. An agent waved me over, and I slid my passport and credit card across the spotless linoleum. I waited for a minute, staring blankly at the display above the counter that showed arrivals and departures, while she typed something into her computer, smiled, and handed me my freshly printed boarding pass.

The small crowd of people waiting in the coach line gave me hostile glances as I picked up my backpack and headed toward the security checkpoint.

I loved airports—especially international terminals. Some people hated them—mostly people who traveled for business. For me, they were waystations I got to pass through on my way to someplace new and interesting. When I was a kid, I loved the Narnia books, especially *The Magician's Nephew*. They were the only fantasy books I was allowed to have. C. S. Lewis was a Christian theologian, so his writing was acceptable. Airports were like the Wood Between the Worlds. Jump into a pool and see where you end up. Even now, with the weird circumstances and last minute, middle-of-the-night flight, I was happy to be swallowed up in the glass, steel, and concrete embrace of SFO.

Getting through security was no problem. The line was short, and I only had my backpack. I did have a couple of interesting things in my pack, so I was a little worried about being pulled aside for extra screening, especially since I had booked my ticket at the last minute. Nobody seemed to care, though. I stepped into the backscatter machine, held my arms up, and stepped out the other side where my bag was just emerging from the X-ray scanner. TSA screening was futile, but I tried to take it seriously, anyway. Undercover agents routinely smuggled mock weapons and explosives through checkpoints and then published reports that got filed away with no action taken.

Still, it was a good show that maybe made people feel safer. I just assumed that the chance of the terrorists choosing the plane I was on was negligible and put my faith in statistics. I stopped at a bench and laced up my shoes then headed out into the terminal.

My guess was that I would find Legere in the first-class lounge, so I headed straight there, following the clearly posted signs. At this time of night, the terminal was sparsely populated, and most of the shops and restaurants were closed. I hurried through the vast emptiness because the flight would be boarding soon, and I wanted to at least have a chance of stealing the painting back before it was on the plane. At the lounge, there was a small entry area where I showed my boarding pass to the attendant and was admitted with a smile. People smiled at you a lot when you flew first class, I was discovering.

The room was all tan and gold with tasteful, patinaed lamps and squishy, comfortable-looking chairs and sofas upholstered in shades of brown. It looked like the lobby of a nice hotel. A few people were scattered around the room, sitting in the cozy chairs, sipping complimentary beverages and staring at laptops or smart phones. A counter staffed by two airline representatives in crisp uniforms took up half of one side of the room. Large windows on the opposite wall overlooked the tarmac and the dark waters of the bay beyond. There was a hushed atmosphere and some tinkly piano music playing softly. I walked a slow circuit, pretending to look for a place to sit. In the corner farthest from the entry, I saw him.

His appointment with the appraiser must have been quick. I imagined a rendezvous in the airport parking garage. The hatch open and the painting unrolled in the back of the SUV. I recognized his shoes first. He was still wearing his ascot cap, but I could see his face now. He had a pointy nose, high cheekbones, and was wearing gold-rimmed reading glasses through which he stared intently at his phone.

I took a seat in a grouping of chairs halfway across the room where I had a good view of him. On the floor next to his chair was a small leather overnight bag. Next to that was the tube containing the painting. I had no doubt that he would carry it with him everywhere he went. My only chance would be if he went into a bathroom stall. I could grab it and have perhaps twenty seconds to get as far away as possible while he got himself together enough to follow and/or raise an alarm. I sat there, thinking about it, and the more I pondered it, the more it seemed impossible. Even if I got the painting away from him, I would be in a secure, well-lit terminal with no place to hide.

I would have to somehow get back through the security checkpoint and out, into a cab. I resigned myself to following him onto the airplane and trying to steal the painting from his hotel room in Milan.

Just as I decided this, a disembodied female voice

announced that the flight was beginning to board. They seemed to have sprung for better speakers in the lounge than in the terminal because I could actually understand what the woman was saying. Legere looked up, listened to the announcement, put his phone in his pocket, and stood, gathering his bag and the painting. I watched him walk to the exit.

He was shorter than I had thought before and powerfully built. After he passed through the doorway, I counted to twenty then stood and followed.

There was a crowd of tired-looking travelers at the gate. I recognized a few faces from the check in line. They glared at me some more as I breezed through the first-class lane, handed my boarding pass to a woman wearing a jaunty gold scarf, and entered the jet way. On board, I found my seat, tossed my backpack into the overhead bin, and gave Legere a sidelong glance. He was already seated, one row behind mine and on the opposite side of the center row of seats. He was looking at his phone, frowning. I sat down and checked out some of the first-class amenities.

I had flown first class before but not recently. The seat reclined fully into a bed and had its own monitor with a variety of movie, shows, and games available. I suddenly felt very tired. *Sleep on the plane*, I thought, *then back to work in Milan.*

I closed my eyes and leaned back, relaxing while the rest of the passengers boarded and the flight crew gave the emergency briefing.

Just before take-off, I checked my phone messages. Roberto had responded, letting me know that my garden would be safe and well nurtured. Valerie had also responded. Her message simply said:

>*Be safe. It's just a painting.*

Yes, just a painting, I thought, closing my eyes again, *but I am going to get to the bottom of this and get it back.*

⌘⌘⌘

When I woke up, we were in the air, still two hours away from our destination. The cabin was hushed and dark with just the lights lining the aisles lit. I looked over and saw Legere reclined in his seat, asleep, the toes of his fancy shoes poking out of the end of his blanket. *Not the kind of guy who takes his shoes off in public.* I looked out the window and saw nothing but dense clouds and blackness beyond, so I got my phone out and dropped back in on Hector leading the Trojan force into battle. A couple hours of the *Iliad* would doubtless put me in the right frame of mind for action once we were on the ground.

⌘⌘⌘

The landing was bumpy, jolting me out of an *Iliad* delirium. The captain informed us that the local time was eleven-oh-three p.m., the weather was clear, and the temperature five degrees Celsius. I did a quick calculation: approximately forty degrees Fahrenheit. I looked over at Legere again. He was awake, sitting up in his seat with the painting in its tube across his knees. His face was impassive, staring straight ahead. I needed to follow him closely and, hopefully, keep him in sight through the passport control area and somehow find out what hotel he was staying at.

The plane rolled up to the terminal after several minutes of taxiing, and my fellow passengers began to stand, stretch, and pull bags down from overhead bins. There were only two rows of seats between me and the exit door. Soon the flight crew had the door open, and we began to file toward it. If I followed the regular flow, I would exit before Legere. I went ahead but walked slowly in the jet way, pretending to read something urgent on my phone. Legere passed me, and I sped up, staying behind him.

At the passport control area, I had to split off to go through the non-EU lane. Luckily, since I had flown first class, there was only one person ahead of me—a woman who appeared to be traveling for business, based on her no-nonsense rolling suitcase and business-casual attire. Legere made it through ahead of me and was almost to the exit into the main terminal before the agent, a young woman who looked like a sleepy Isabella Rossellini from *Wild at Heart*, handed me back my passport.

I headed off as fast as I could without looking suspicious and caught sight of him moving through the crowd. He took an escalator downward, and I followed. We passed through a broad hallway with elegant, barrel vaulted skylights, which suddenly opened out into a massive lobby. There were groupings of red and purple chairs and couches; recessed alcoves splashed with orange and yellow light; dark wood; a shiny, highly reflective black floor; and curvilinear white forms rising up from the periphery to weave together into a kind of abstracted basket that formed the ceiling some twenty feet above my head. I stood there for a minute in a daze before I realized we were in a hotel lobby. I looked around and eventually saw a sign. Apparently, there was a hotel and conference center with direct access to the terminal, and I was standing in the lobby.

Legere was at the reception desk, so I took a seat in one of the red chairs close by, partially concealed by a potted palm, and pretended to look at my phone again while he checked in. I peered through a gap between two giant fronds as he signed the paper and the desk clerk handed him his key card. Luckily, Legere didn't seem to speak Italian well, and the two had landed on English as their lingua franca. A vacuum cleaner was running somewhere in the lobby, and I couldn't make out much of what they said. Finally though, the vacuum turned off, and I heard the clerk say, in response to a question from Legere, "Yes—in the Campo Rosso bar until two a.m."

I assumed he had asked about food. So, with any luck, he would be going to the bar for a late dinner which would give me an opportunity to get into his room. I waited for Legere to cross the lobby and get into an elevator then hurried over and watched the panel above the doors that showed what floor the car was on. It passed one and stopped at two for perhaps ten seconds, then dropped back down to one.

Knowing which floor he was on was good, but I needed to know his room number too. I wandered back over to the reception desk. There were two desk clerks available. The clerk who had checked in Legere was farther away down a long expanse of dark wood desk, but I headed that way, avoiding eye contact with the closer one.

When I stepped up to the counter, the young man looked up and gave me a nod. He had hair of impressive thickness carefully sculpted with large quantities of gel.

"*Mi dispiace, non parlo italiano,*" I said, hoping that my semester of Italian in high school had at least taught me how to properly communicate the fact that I couldn't speak Italian.

"English?" the clerk replied.

"Yes, if it's okay. I need a room for tonight. There was a mix up, and my assistant did not make a reservation. I would like something on the second floor if possible. I believe my colleague, Mr. Legere, is on the second

floor. We will be working together while we are here so
something close by would be good."

The clerk nodded and turned to his computer terminal, typing quickly. "Ah, Signore Legere. Yes, he just
checked in a moment ago." He did some searching on his
computer. "I have a room across the hall. Junior suite.
King bed. Two hundred thirty-five euro per night."

"Perfect." I handed him my credit card and passport.

He turned his attention to his terminal. While he has
busy typing, I leaned over the counter as inconspicuously
as possible and looked at the stack of check-in slips next
to his computer. Legere's was on top, the room number
plainly visible. The clerk printed out a similar check-in
receipt for me, and, once I had signed it, deposited it on
top of Legere's. He then programmed two key cards, put
them in a cardboard holder, and handed them to me. I
took one out, flipped it over quickly, and noted the logo
of the company that supplied the hotel door locks. I was
in luck.

Some people would call it luck anyway. I guess you
could also look at it as a statistical probability. That company made the majority of key card locks installed in hotels—especially large chain hotels. You could also look
at it as being prepared. With the advent of personal blogs
and amateur online video, it had become very easy to stay
current on how to bypass many different kinds of locks
and security systems. There were always people posting
new video tutorials and discovering new exploits. I made
a habit of watching those videos and reading the blogs on
a semi-regular basis.

There was a chance Legere had gone straight from
his room to the bar. A sign in the elevator announced that
the Campo Rosso lounge was on the first floor, so I got
off there and wandered around, trying to find it. Walking
the halls, it was difficult to escape the feeling of being in

a vast, alien space ship. Something about the lighting and the architecture made the atmosphere of the hotel both surreal and cinematic. The place seemed to be not proportioned for humans, beginning with its raw square footage. It was almost as large as the airport it was connected to and was made up of five or six massive interconnected volumes that looked like a flattened burrito in a snow-white tortilla, chopped into unequal, separated segments.

When I found the lounge at last, I paused for a moment at the entrance. The bar itself featured a glowing red panel stretching it's full length of some forty feet and a panoramic bank of windows through which I could see the night sky and glowing lights of indistinct airport facilities. The customer side of the bar projected out about a foot and was made of clear, two-inch thick Lucite. The back side where the bartender worked was blond wood. The decor only served to enhance the alienness of the architecture.

Legere was seated there at the bar, alone except for a businessman twenty stools away. He had a full glass of wine in front of him which glowed ruby red in the light from the panel below. The painting was propped against the bar at his feet. A full glass of wine and presumably food on the way meant I had to act now. If I could get into his room, I could hopefully find some useful information, although I would not be able to get the painting. I turned and headed back toward the elevators, walking quickly.

I found my room on the second floor and took a moment to inspect the door handle and key card device, feeling along the bottom with my fingers. The port I was expecting to find was there, and it hadn't been blocked. The exploit I was planning on using was well known and some hotels had blocked physical access to the port. Inside my room, I tossed my backpack onto the bed and got out the things I would need. I had brought with me a device I built myself by following tutorials online. It was a whiteboard marker with the insides removed and replaced with some circuitry. The tip of the marker was a plug that would interface with the lock via the port on the bottom. If the TSA had found it and opened it up, I might have had to answer some questions. To their scanner, though, it would have just looked like a standard marker. I also had two small, plastic handled screwdrivers and a tension wrench and pick, all of which I had hidden inside the hollow handle of my razor. I didn't anticipate needing anything else.

Legere's room was across the hall and several doors down. I walked briskly to the door, took the cap off the marker, and plugged it into the port on the bottom of the lock. Almost immediately, the green LED flashed, and I was able to open the door. Inside, I started the stopwatch on my phone then flipped on the light and looked around. It was not a suite like mine, just a regular room with a single, king-sized bed. Legere's bag was on top of the bed, and his coat was hanging in the closet. I quickly searched the coat pockets but came up with only an old cough drop and a parking garage receipt. I took the receipt and left the cough drop. Next, I looked through his bag.

There was some clothing, most of which was in a laundry bag, a pair of sneakers, a dopp kit with the usual things, and nothing else. I went back to the closet and pushed his coat aside. There was a standard hotel room safe at the back of the closet, built in to a low shelf for shoes. The scrolling red letters on the safe's LCD panel said *bloccato*. He had put something in the safe before going to the bar.

Most people didn't realize that the safes in hotel rooms had an easily accessible lock that overrode the electronic code panel. It was there so that security and maintenance staff could open safes when people either forgot their codes or forgot to empty their safe before checking out. On the front of the safe was a diamond-shaped logo plate held on by two small screws. I reversed the screws and removed it, exposing the lock behind. I didn't practice as much as I should, so I was not great at picking locks, but this one was fairly simple. It took me about a minute and a half of work to get it open. I pulled open the door of the safe and surveyed the contents.

There was an eleven-inch Macbook air, on top of which was a light brown calf skin passport case and a wad of several hundred Euros. I took out the passport case. It felt expensive and definitely went with what I had seen so far of Legere's style. I opened it and flipped to the front page of the passport inside. Legere was looking back at me, a little younger, with an impassive expression.

He was a citizen of the République Française. Full name, Benoit Olivier Légère. I got my phone out and took a picture of the page. Tucked into the inside pocket of the case were several identical business cards. They were his own cards and said that he was an attorney with an office in Nice. I took a photo of his business card as well, put everything back, then hesitated for a moment, indecisively considering the laptop. No, not enough time to search his digital world, I decided. I closed the safe back up and replaced the logo plate. According to the timer on my phone, I had been in the room for only seven minutes. I was satisfied that I wouldn't find anything else useful, though, so I slipped out into the empty hallway.

Back in my luxurious junior suite, I consulted the menu then called room service and ordered a Caesar salad with grilled salmon and a beer. I hadn't eaten on the plane and was starting to feel light-headed. Sitting back on the bed, I took some time to study my pictures of the passport and business card. Legere's birthplace was listed as Osani, Département Corse-du-Sud. I had never heard of it but it seemed to be on the island of Corsica. He was forty-two years old, one-point-seven meters tall, and had blue eyes.

There was not much else I could glean from the passport so I turned to the business card. It was a plain white card with a small icon representing the scales of justice. His full name was listed. Under that it simply said *Avocat*. At the bottom of the card, there was an address and a phone number. I got out my laptop, connected to the hotel WiFi, and mapped the address. It was in downtown Nice only a couple of blocks from the harbor. I switched to street view.

The building was several stories tall with pinkish stucco walls, wrought iron balconies, and ornamental dentils along the roof line. There was a typical looking French brasserie and a women's shoe store with windows displaying a variety of chic-looking high heels on the ground floor. The upper floors all appeared to be offices. Legere's office seemed to be on the second floor, based on the suite number.

The narrow street below was restricted to pedestrian traffic, although it intersected with a larger street just one building down. Across the way, there was another cafe with sidewalk seating. A family with two small children, all their faces blurred, were seated outside enjoying a nice-looking lunch. My stomach grumbled while I marveled at the technological miracle that allowed me to peek into this moment in the life of an anonymous family, frozen in time. I didn't need to wait long, though—just then there was a knock at my door. Room service had arrived.

I settled back on the bed with the tray and my laptop

in front of me, eating while I searched for more information. I typed Legere's full name into the search bar and got a few hits. One of them led me to an article on the 1996 French Olympic freestyle wrestling team in which Legere's name was mentioned. I ran an image search and found an old, grainy photo that looked like it had been scanned from a magazine. They were posed in a stadium, on a red wrestling mat.

They all looked tough. A much younger Legere was in the front row, kneeling. They didn't win any medals that year. The medal count was dominated by North and South Korea, Russia, the US, and several Eastern European countries. I continued searching but couldn't find anything more about Legere. He didn't seem to exist after 1996 as far as the world wide web was concerned. So, Olympic wrestler goes to law school and opens private practice. I decided he must represent private clients, such as the one who was no doubt eagerly awaiting the Heidrich painting and had sent Legere to San Francisco to pick it up.

It wasn't exactly drafting a will or arguing a court case, but I guessed it probably paid well. I looked up Osani, too, while I was at it. It was a small commune or civil township on the west coast of Corsica. Several stone towers built by the Republic of Genoa in the fifteen-hundreds were located near Osani and were now designated as historical monuments. Aside from that, there was almost no information about the place online.

It looked like I was going to have to take a trip to Nice and search Legere's office. I would need to studiously avoid running into him there, though, if I wanted to emerge in one piece—one of my many roommates while in college had been a former Olympic wrestler who had taken up ballet and was working on a BFA in dance. Many years of training and fighting had given him some amazing cauliflower ears and had also replaced his normal human pain reaction with blunt dismissal. I had once mentioned this with curiosity to another friend who was a dancer, and she had immediately seen the connection. "Wrestling and ballet are two highly demanding physical occupations," she had told me, "both require participants to develop an exceptional tolerance for pain."

I was sure that if Legere got his hands on me, I would regret it.

I finished my meal while browsing rental car sites and comparing rates. I settled on one and booked it for a week beginning the next day. My destiny was well defined, at least for the next twenty-four hours. Could any mortal ask for more than that? Hector, Achilles, and the rest of the heroes of the *Iliad* would have been fine with it.

I took a shower, donned a complimentary robe, and collapsed into bed with my alarm set for eight a.m. Despite the time difference and the sleep I had gotten on the plane, I drifted off pretty quickly. I had the ability to sleep anywhere, at any time, under just about any circumstances. It was my only known super power.

CHAPTER 8

December 15:

Some mornings waking up was like a slow, pleasant climb, rung by rung out of a dark well. Other mornings, it was like struggling out of a black, viscous pool that dragged and pulled me backward. That morning, though, it was more like riding a rocket that accelerated suddenly into a bright sky and exploded, jolting me into consciousness.

I bolted up in bed, panting and squinting my eyes against the bright light from the window. I smacked the alarm to turn it off and, my heart racing, sat for a minute going through everything, figuring out where I was and why: Milan, airport, hotel, Legere, Heidrich, painting, Valerie.

Once I had the pieces stacked and sorted to form a more or less reasonable timeline, I got out of bed and picked up the phone. A woman answered, and I stumbled through ordering eggs, bacon, fruit, and coffee in my rudimentary Italian.

I was just out of the shower and getting dressed when a cheerful server arrived with my food. She rolled the cart into my room and waited while I signed the check. The coffee and bacon smelled good so I sat down on the edge of the bed and started eating while I planned my day.

The drive to Nice would take about four hours. I wouldn't be able to attempt a break-in at Legere's office until late at night, so there was no rush. I wished there was a way for me to track or follow him, but it didn't seem feasible. I would just have to take my chances on finding something that could lead me to the painting once I was in Nice. I decided to spend the morning in Milan shopping for some items I would need. First on the list: warmer clothes. I hadn't counted on it being so cold.

The train into the city from the airport was modern and efficient, arriving at Cadorna station in central Milan in less than half an hour. I came out of the station and saw the Castello Sforzesco looming up, gray and imposing down the Via Marco Minghetti. Turning away, I headed east along a tree-lined street. The sky was dull gray, a shade lighter than the walls of the castle. The windshields of parked cars were frosted over, and I was shivering in my T-shirt and hoodie. When I reached the Via Dante, a broad pedestrian throughway lined with shops and restaurants, I turned onto it and headed southeast toward the Duomo and the Galleria. I had been to Milan many years before and knew I could find a coat at the Galleria if not along the Via Dante. The shops were just beginning to open, and waiters were out trying to entice tourists into their eateries.

I politely declined several invitations to sit down and have breakfast. After a little more walking, I saw a clothing store that looked like it would do and went in to browse. Inside, there was loud pop music playing and lots of bold color choices, but I managed to find a few acceptable items. Fifteen minutes later, I emerged wearing a gray merino sweater under a black, hooded parka with a few more items in a shopping bag. I imagined the fashion-conscious Milanese would cast fewer sidelong glances my way now.

Next, I stopped at a cell phone shop and spent a few minutes discussing SIM cards with the elderly proprietor. He wanted to sell me one that I was pretty sure wouldn't work outside of Italy. I chose a different one. There was a lot of hand waving and attitude, but I managed to purchase it at last. It was a pre-paid card with data. Seated at a cafe next door with an authentic cappuccino in front of me, I popped the card out of my phone and replaced it with the new one. When the phone booted back up, it immediately found a strong cell signal and everything seemed to be working fine. I tested it by searching for hardware stores and found several *Ferramentas* nearby. These seemed to be small, specialized shops but might have what I needed, so I finished my cappuccino and left to check out the closest one.

After a short walk, I found the shop on a narrow side street with streetcar tracks down the middle and lots of scooters and motorcycles parked along the sidewalk. A yellow antique tram similar to the imported streetcars in San Francisco rumbled by just as I turned onto the street. I waited for it to pass, the cobblestones shaking under my feet. The shop was just across the way—a storefront with a narrow door and two small display windows on either side. I crossed and entered.

Inside, it was dim and packed to the roof with shelves of tools, miscellaneous hardware, and plumbing, building, and electrical supplies. The owner was at the front counter chatting with a guy who looked like he knew his way around a sewer pipe, so I wandered, browsing. I had no trouble finding the things I needed. It was a small shop but well curated.

I waited for a few minutes while the owner finished delivering a long diatribe to the other customer. I didn't understand a word. Finally, he turned and gestured for me to bring my purchases up to the counter, and, a few minutes later, I was on my way, heading back toward the train station. Milan was a beautiful city, and, under other circumstances, I would have done some sightseeing, but I was on a mission. I needed to get back to the hotel, check out, and get my rental car.

ↄ⁄ↄↄ⁄ↄ

The first car the rental company tried to give me was a lemon-yellow Citroen with a bizarre panel along both sides that looked like a giant Hershey's chocolate bar. I walked slowly around the car twice, shaking my head in disbelief, before deciding it was far too ugly and far too recognizable. I went back to the rental counter and waited in line again while using my phone to look up a translation for the phrase "I want a boring car please, preferably gray."

"*Voglio una macchina noioso prega, preferibilmente grigia,*" I said, as politely as possible, placing the keys to the Citroen on the counter.

The rental clerk gave me a look like I was crazy, whispered something into the ear of the other clerk, then spent some time passive-aggressively looking through the keys hanging on the big pegboard behind the counter. Finally, he selected a set of keys and slapped them on the counter.

"Grigia," he said and turned to his terminal to process the swap in his computer system.

I signed again, thanked the clerk, and walked back to the lot. The car was a putty-gray Fiat 500x. I walked around it, decided it would do, and hopped in.

It didn't take long to get away from the airport, and I headed south on SP52 toward Genoa. It was a pleasant highway, two lanes in each direction, with trees and grassy-green embankments rising up along both sides. Following my phone's instructions, I turned onto E64 and was soon passing through bucolic farmland and rolling hills. I saw old stone houses crumbling into the ground, ancient walls and fences, farm houses billowing smoke from chimneys.

I turned onto a highway labeled A26 which somehow became E25 a few miles later. After that, I gave up on trying to figure out the Italian highway and freeway numbering system and just let my phone navigate for me. There were lots of trucks on the road, probably carrying cargo from the port of Genoa north to Milan and beyond. As I neared the sea, the landscape became hilly with deciduous trees and exposed rock faces, long tunnels, and more small villages. I reached the coast around midday and turned onto a highway called E80. It was busier, with three lanes in each direction.

The highway ran a little bit inland, but I saw occasional vistas of the blue Mediterranean opening out when the road temporarily meandered closer to the coast. I decided to stop at a small town called Varazze for lunch and swung off the highway, down a local access road, and onto the main street that ran directly along the seaside. I saw a parking spot almost immediately, paralleled into it, and stepped out into a blustery, sunny day. The Mediterranean was choppy. Small white capped waves were rolling in and pedestrians were walking along a broad sidewalk bordering the sea wall, holding their hats to keep them from being tossed away on the wind. I had parked one door down from a Ristorante Pizzeria that was open and looked nice, so I stepped in and was soon greeted and led to a table.

Over a pizza topped with taggiasca olives, onions, sea salt, and sardines—and a glass of the house white that the waitress talked me into—I researched hotels in Nice. I decided on a modest place about ten minutes walking from Legere's office and booked online for three nights. When the waitress returned, I politely refused another glass of wine, paid in Euros I had withdrawn from a machine in the airport before leaving Milan, and headed back to my car.

The remainder of the drive to Nice was uneventful, and soon I was entering the industrial outskirts of the city. I turned off the A8 and took Boulevard Gorbella straight into the heart of the town, where I skirted the Gare De Nice, made a few more turns, and ended up on the Boulevard Victor Hugo where my hotel was located. It was early afternoon, and there were crowds of pedestrians out on the sidewalks. Daredevils on scooters shot by me in a lane marked for bikes. Six and seven story buildings with white or off-white facades and french doors leading out onto balconies with carved stone balustrades rose up along either side of the tree lined boulevard. I passed a small park with palm trees, an ancient stone church, and saw red-tiled mansard roofs beyond. Finally, I saw the sign for my hotel and turned off into their tiny roundabout, shut off the engine, and stepped out of the car, stretching my back and shoulders which were stiff from the long drive.

There was a fishy, salty breeze blowing in from the harbor. A doorman stepped out, took my keys, and gave me a claim check. With my backpack over my shoulder and my shopping bag holding the items I had purchased earlier, I headed for the registration desk.

On the way up to my room, I thought about my first trip to Europe as a college student. I had traveled with only a backpack then, too. Unlike now, though, I had stayed in hostels and subsisted on a diet of baguettes and cheese. My obsession back then had been seeing as many old master paintings as possible. Now my obsession was recovering a new master painting. Life was a trajectory, but sometimes that trajectory looped and cycled, bringing us back again to places and experiences we'd been through before, giving us a chance to relive things through the filter of our evolving knowledge and values.

I collapsed on the bed in my room, feeling the jet lag. It was just after three p.m. I decided to nap for a few hours then get up and see what I could find out by perusing the outside of the building where Legere kept his office. First though, I sent a text message to Valerie, mindful of the fact that it would be coming from an unfamiliar, European number at six a.m. in the morning her time.

>*This is Justin. Sorry for the early text. Do you have any art world friends in Nice?*

It was worth a try. Valerie knew people just about everywhere. Her father had been a diplomat assigned to Western Europe, so she had attended fancy boarding schools in England and France then had gone on to one of the ivy league colleges on the east coast. She had a vast web of friends and acquaintances all over the world. Her reply, as usual, came quickly:

>*What the hell are you doing in Nice? Yes. Gabrielle Cartini. Friend from school. Gallery owner. Very wealthy. Father some sort of gangster. Will send contact info by email. Need to look it up.*

>*Why in Nice? Too hard to explain by text. Please let her know I'll be in touch. Thanks. Xoxo*

I tapped the send button, shut off my phone, rolled over, and fell asleep.

℃ↄ℃ↄ

It was seven o'clock when I woke up. I stood, stretched, and pulled back the curtains of my room's only window. Night had fallen while I was sleeping. There was a park across the way, the street below alive with pedestrians, cars, and scooters, and more stately buildings like the one I was standing in marching away into the distance. The street lamps cast a greenish light, giving the scene below an underwater feeling. I turned away from the window, pulled on my new jacket, gathered some things in my backpack, and left the room.

Downstairs and on the street, I joined the fishbowl scene. I found a small brasserie a couple of blocks from the hotel and ordered steak frites. I didn't normally eat steak or french fries when I was home, but the meal was so quintessentially French, I couldn't resist. After my meal, I strolled down toward the harbor, heading toward the address from Legere's business card. It was after eight p.m., so I assumed he would not be there. The air became colder and damper as I approached, walking down Rue de Congrès.

I turned, walked another block, turned again, and saw the building, looking just as it had in street view. There were pylons to keep auto traffic off the pedestrian street, but the scooter drivers were not deterred. Lots of people were out, walking, filling the tables at the restaurants, eating, smoking, laughing, and talking.

I put on a black knit hat I had purchased along with my new parka and pulled it low, then took stock of the building as I passed. On one side, it was up against a building of similar height. On the far side, it bordered a single-story restaurant. I kept walking and turned left just past the restaurant down another narrow pedestrian alley. There was a side door that looked like it led to the restaurant's kitchen. It would be a fairly easy climb onto the roof of the restaurant and from there trivial to reach several of the balconies of Legere's building. I still didn't know where his office was located in the building, though, so I circled back around to the front and stopped across the street, leaning in a doorway of the opposite building and pretending to look at my phone while checking out the entrance. I had seen no lights on in the building, so I was fairly sure it was only offices, not residential.

The recessed entryway had a brass call box on one wall and a heavy oak door with a solid looking lock. I could wait until late at night, but I had a feeling this street stayed pretty busy with foot traffic throughout the evening and into the early morning. It would take me a long time to get through that door, if I could do it at all. Even if no pedestrians happened by, there might be an alarm.

As I was standing there pondering, the door opened, and an elderly woman came out, pulling blue kidskin gloves onto her hands. She walked briskly away as the door swung slowly closed. I almost missed my chance, standing there dumbly staring after her, but, at the last moment, I darted across the street and placed my toe between the door and the jamb. The hydraulic mechanism that closed the door was industrial strength and squeezed my toe painfully, but I stood there for a few moments, pretending to study the directory on the call box. I fake pushed a button, pretended to speak into the microphone, waited another moment, then pulled the door open. I glanced around as I entered, but nobody seemed to have noticed me. Either that or my comical acting was convincing enough.

Inside, there was a small, marble-floored lobby with a dark wood, glass-doored letter board on the wall. The letter board showed names and suite numbers of the tenants in gold lettering on a black velvet backing. I made a note of Legere's suite number and turned toward the staircase that twisted up around the periphery of a central atrium like a corkscrew. In the center of the staircase, in what had once been open space, a small elevator in a glass walled shaft had been installed. I had seen other old buildings similarly retrofitted before. I eschewed the cramped-looking elevator and began climbing the stairs. The building smelled like oiled wood, old carpet, and dusty books.

Each floor had two wings, each with its own hallway leading toward the back of the building on either side of a central courtyard, which I could see through windows, along the back wall of the staircase. At the second floor, I stepped from the landing, turned randomly to the right, and started down a hall the center of which was covered in a thick, spongy, burgundy-colored carpet. The numbers were wrong, so I turned back and headed down the other hallway. Legere's office was two doors from the end on the inside, facing the courtyard.

The doors all had bolt locks and new knob sets produced by a company I was unfamiliar with. There wasn't much chance of me getting through the front door so I walked back to the stairs and climbed to the top. At the fifth floor, the stairs continued up to an unlocked door which led out onto the roof of the building. I stepped out into cold wind and fresh air, walked to the edge, and looked down into the courtyard. There were rose bushes, a patch of lawn, and a stone pathway with a bench. Each suite or office appeared to have a balcony with french doors.

I walked back from the edge and leaned against an AC unit, facing away from the wind and looking out toward the sea. I needed to think. I've never liked heights or having to climb, jump, or rappel to get into a house or building. It increases the possibility of random accidents, and that is anathema to a careful planner like me. Still, I had done it before. Getting down to Legere's balcony would require a simple series of jumps, one balcony to the next. Once I was there, I was confident it would be simple to get through the french doors.

I wasn't ready to give up. First, though, I needed to know how far down it was from the roof to a fifth-floor balcony. I sat, scooted up to the edge of the roof, and leaned over. It looked like about ten feet. If I hung from the edge of the roof and let go, it would be about a three-foot drop. I wanted to be sure, though. It could be difficult to judge heights from above, so I got a coil of nylon cord out of my backpack and unspooled it until the end was touching the floor of the balcony below. I then reeled it back in and counted how many feet it was by measuring repeatedly from the tip of my fingers up to a spot on my forearm I knew to be exactly one foot. It was just over ten feet.

I got up and walked all the way around the inside perimeter of the building. There were no lights on in any of the suites as far as I could tell. The courtyard was not visible from any other buildings nearby. On the far side, there was a blank, windowless wall of the building next door. The buildings abutted each other, but there appeared to be a passageway from the courtyard back out to the street. There was no reason to wait.

I walked over to the area above Legere's office and scooted up to the edge of the roof again. The wind was picking up, but it wasn't strong enough to worry about. I dropped my backpack first, and it landed with a dull thump to one side of the balcony below. Taking a deep breath, I turned and lowered myself to a hanging position, fingers curled around the edge of the roof, and let go. I had a brief sensation of ultimate freedom mixed with terror, flying through darkness, then my feet hit the balcony below, and I absorbed the shock by sinking to one knee. As I landed, my dinner did a flop in my stomach, and I briefly regretted the steak frites. My face was almost up against the nearest pane of glass. I knelt there for ten seconds, just staring at the ornate gold and green curtains which had been pulled across the doors inside. Eventually, my breathing and heart rate returned to normal. I stood and tossed my backpack down to the next balcony, climbed over the wrought iron railing and lowered myself hand over hand until I was again hanging. This jump would be a little more difficult since I needed to swing inward and let go in order to land on the next balcony down. I swung a few times, building up speed, then let go and flew down again. This time I landed off balance and had to stagger to the side and grasp the railing to steady myself. I was on the fourth floor now. Two jumps to go.

The next jump went better. I landed square and in a crouch as I had the first time. As my eyes focused on the door in front of me, though, I froze, heart racing. Two big, glowing eyes were staring directly into mine. It took a few seconds, but gradually I realized it was a cat. The eyes were surrounded by fluffy white fur. It was a long-haired Persian with a flattened face, and it was staring at me casually, as if seeing someone plummet down onto this balcony was a normal, everyday occurrence. I stood and looked in through the windowed doors. It was dark inside, but it seemed to be a design studio that took up at least two office suites with the walls between them removed. There were drafting tables, flat files, and steel cabinets. I shrugged my shoulders, waved goodbye to the office cat, threw my backpack down to the next balcony, and kept going.

When I finally reached Legere's balcony, I sat for a minute, catching my breath and calming down. I was sheltered from the wind now, down in the courtyard. The air was cool and damp and smelled of earth and grass. I heard the distant trills and chirps of a nightingale singing. Rested and ready, I dug through my backpack until I found a flathead screwdriver I had purchased earlier that day in Milan. French doors normally locked via pins on one of the doors that slid into holes at the top and bottom of the door frame. The second door usually had a knob set lock. If the pins weren't slid into place, the knob set lock was useless. If you could get a screwdriver or slim jim between the doors, it was fairly easy to slide the pins out of the holes and just pull the doors open.

The doors were old, probably original to the building. As a result, they were loose and rickety from many years of weathering temperature and humidity changes. I pried them apart with the screwdriver and slid the top pin down then repeated with the bottom pin. It took about ten seconds. With the pins retracted, I just pulled the doors open and stepped inside, closing the doors after me. There were curtains similar to the ones I had seen three floors up, held back by hooks. I closed them, got my flashlight out of my pack, and turned to the office.

I was in a room about fifteen feet by ten feet. Opposite the balcony was an open doorway leading out into a waiting room with a couch and small receptionist desk. The outer door to the hallway was located in the reception area. Both waiting room and inner office had dark, carved wainscoting, wood floors, and nice, antique looking carpets. Legere's desk was a big, flat plane of wood with ornate, carved legs. It had one small drawer which held a few pens, paper clips, stapler, tape. On the desk was a sleek, new iMac. Under the desk, on a small table, was an inkjet printer. The computer was sleeping, not shut down. I tapped the return key on the wireless keyboard, and the screen came to life. It showed Legere's name and a password entry field. Aside from the desk, computer, printer, an Aeron chair, desk lamp, empty wastebasket, and two regency-style button-tufted side chairs facing the desk, there was very little in the room. Legere seemed to be minimalist in his tastes. Either that, or he didn't really use this office much. There was a large safe mounted in the wall opposite the desk with a door as big as a two-drawer file cabinet. It had a number pad and a small LCD screen. Clearly, it required a code to open. Legere probably kept his files in the safe.

I sat down on the Aeron chair and flipped on the green glass shaded desk lamp. Seated there, I opened the drawer and went through the contents again, pulled the drawer all the way out, looked under the desk, put it back, looked under the printer, checked the wastebasket again. Nothing. I needed to get into either the safe or the computer.

I got my phone out and texted Ashna. It was about one p.m. in San Francisco, so, hopefully, she was at her desk, at work, with her phone handy.

>*It's Justin. Any way to get into a password protected iMac?*

I waited about forty-five seconds, staring at my phone, emptying my mind. When it buzzed and Ashna's reply popped up, it startled me. Her reply was just a URL. I tapped the URL, and a web page opened titled "How To Reset Mac OS X User Password In Recovery Mode." I followed the directions which required a forced shut down, reboot into recovery mode, a terminal command, and then choosing a new password. There were two accounts on the computer, Legere's and one just called Admin. I chose to reset the password for Admin, since resetting Legere's would tip him off immediately that somebody had been tampering with his computer. The machine booted back up, and I logged in as Admin. I soon figured out that I couldn't access Legere's user folder from the Admin account, though. I had forgotten that OS X did not allow even an administrator user to access another user's files. I sent another text to Ashna:

>*How to access another user account's files?*

>*you have to be root. This will only work if root hasn't already been enabled.*

Another text rolled in with a URL. I tapped it and was taken to a page with instructions on how to enable the root user in OS X and set a password. Ashna sent me another text with a URL for a page that explained how, with root access, to open a finder window under another user's account. I had to run some more terminal commands, but, at last, I could see Legere's files. I opened his Documents folder and sorted by date modified. The newest file was over a week old. Next, I tried his desktop. There was a folder on the desktop labeled "courant," so I opened it and sorted by date modified again. At the top of the list was an MS Word document that was last edited that day at three-seventeen p.m. It was called: *Antonetti_15_12*

I double clicked the document and waited a moment while Word started up. My ability to read French was limited, but I quickly gathered that the document was an invoice. It contained a chart with a column for date, one for description, and one for cost. Listed there were travel expenses such as plane tickets, hotel, and meals. The dates were all from the previous few days. At the bottom was an item simply labeled "Frais d'acquisition"— acquisition fee or maybe procurement fee, I thought. The amount was twenty-five thousand euros. So, here was Legere's invoice for collecting the painting from Booth. He had probably typed it up to bring with him when he delivered the Heidrich. The invoice was addressed to a monsieur Patrice Antonetti. There was an address, but it was a PO box.

I took a photo of the document with my phone and checked to make sure it was legible, then closed it, logged out, and shut down the computer. I booted it back up just to see what would happen. It came up with a login screen asking for a username and password. When I came in, Legere had been logged in, and the computer was locked. He would know that it had been rebooted, but he wouldn't know anything else unless he tried logging in to the Admin account.

My guess was that the Admin account was created by whoever set up the computer for him. He probably never used it. The iMac was plugged into a power strip under the desk with an extension cord running under the carpet to a wall outlet. Judging by the sparkling cleanliness of the office and the lack of any trash in the wastebasket, I guessed that there must be daily cleaning service provided by the building. I decided to shut the computer back down and then pulled the extension cord plug halfway out of the outlet, cutting current to the power strip. Hopefully, he would think a cleaner had accidentally knocked the cord loose.

It was time to get out of there. I put the curtains back where I had found them and checked around one last time to make sure I hadn't dropped anything or left any items out of place. Satisfied, I turned off the desk lamp and exited via the balcony doors. Outside, I used my screwdriver to slide the pins back into place. From Legere's balcony, it was about eleven feet down to the soft lawn below. I hung off and let go, dropping into the darkness.

CHAPTER 9

December 16 ~ 17:

Back at the hotel, I poured myself a glass of whiskey then dropped an ice cube from the machine down the hall into the glass and watched the melted water swirl and mix with the golden liquid. Twenty-five thousand Euros was a pretty good payday for flying to San Francisco, picking up a painting, and flying back. It had already been obvious to me, based on Legere's conversation with Booth, that he was yet another middle man. Now, hopefully, I had the name of the man at the other end of the deal. I pulled up the image of the invoice on my phone. Patrice Antonetti. Not a particularly French-sounding name. I switched to my email and found one from Valerie amidst the accumulation of spam. It contained a phone number, email address, and physical address for the gallery owned by Gabrielle Cartini. I typed a quick thank you to Val then composed an email to Ms. Cartini asking for a meeting the next day.

Sitting by the window, sipping my whiskey, I watched the people and automobiles flow by down below. I was well past the feeling of absurdity I had felt sitting in the cheap hotel room in San Francisco, staking out the apartment of the unnamed thief who had stolen the

Heidrich. I was acting without introspection. I had no
thought of giving up, going back to San Francisco and
my regular life. Momentum was carrying me forward. Or
maybe it was inertia. I'd never really grasped the difference.

✞✠✞✠

    I woke early the next morning, made coffee with the
coffee maker provided in the room, and sat at the desk,
searching for information about Patrice Antonetti. I found
a lot of mentions in articles about fancy society soirees
and also found several photos of him. In nearly all the
photos, he was wearing a tuxedo, holding a glass of
champagne, his free arm wrapped around the waists of
various beautiful women in filmy gowns. He was tall
with aquiline features, dark, leathery looking skin and
thick white hair swept back from his forehead. He was
listed as a contributor to several arts organizations such
as the Orchestre Philharmonique de Nice, the Ballet Nice
Méditerrannée, and the Nice Muséé d'Art Moderne et
d'Art Contemporain. Beyond that, there was not much
information about him available on the web.
    I gave up and decided to get some breakfast. Before I
closed my laptop, though, I checked my email and found
that Gabrielle Cartini had answered me already. She invited me to drop by the gallery any time between eleven
a.m. and three p.m. I answered, letting her know I would
come by at eleven, then shut down my laptop and headed
for the shower.
    Later, out on the street, I headed for the Vieille Ville,
the oldest part of the city where the streets were too narrow for auto traffic and the buildings dated back as far as
the Middle Ages. I walked amongst the ancient, Italianate
houses and shops for a while, admiring the faded greens,

burgundies, golds, pinks, and blues of the roughly plastered walls and wooden shutters, the ancient cobblestones, arches, spires, and glimpses of hidden gardens tucked away in courtyards. Eventually, I found a restaurant with a scattering of outdoor tables in a small cobbled square and had a leisurely breakfast and more coffee.

Even the most leisurely breakfast has to end eventually. I still had an hour to kill before I could go to meet Ms. Cartini, so I walked up the hill to the Fort du Mont Alban, a sixteenth century military fortification built by the Duke of Savoy. I had just enough time to climb up, enjoy the view overlooking the Bay of Angels for a few minutes, then head back down into the city. I walked, immersed in my own thoughts, until I arrived abruptly at the front door of the gallery.

Gallerie Cartini was in the heart of the city, not far from my hotel and the Gare de Nice. It's funny how high-end contemporary art galleries all looked more or less the same. It was similar to the way tourist streets all over the world look eerily similar with their racks of baseball caps, sunglasses, key chains, T-shirts, paintings of dolphins, ice cream, and chain restaurants. Instead of appealing universally to the average person, though, fancy galleries make their appeal to the wealthy. The high ceilings with exposed beams, white walls, and minimal furnishings are signifiers of a certain milieu. Ms. Cartini's gallery was no exception.

I entered from the busy street and immediately felt a calmness wash over me. The current exhibit consisted of large paintings by a Chinese artist who worked in a surreal, hazy style. The colors were muted, and vague forms of buildings and people could just be made out through green and yellow washes like mist or veils. The gallery attendant allowed me to view the art for several minutes before wandering over and asking if I liked the work. She was a young woman in all black with a severe hair style and chunky glasses. I made apologies for my terrible French, and she immediately switched to English.

"I like the paintings very much," I said. "They're very evocative. I'd like to spend some more time studying them, but I have an appointment to meet with Madame Cartini at eleven, and I don't want to keep her waiting."

"Of course, Monsieur. I will let her know you are here." She turned on her heel and disappeared through a door at the back of the gallery. I spent another minute looking at the painting in front of me. It seemed there was a promontory, a woman walking along a causeway, maybe a castle on a hill. I felt a tap on my arm and turned to see that the attendant was back. "Please follow me, monsieur."

I followed her through the rear door into an immaculate store room with racks of artwork wrapped in brown paper, and on up a wooden staircase. At the top of the stairs was a loft-like office as large as the gallery. The rear half of the office was taken up by flat files and racks like the ones below. We passed through the storage area and found Gabrielle Cartini seated at a Nelson swag leg work table. Behind her were floor to ceiling windows that looked out on the street below. She rose, strode out from behind the desk, and offered her hand.

"Madame Cartini, it's a pleasure to meet you. Your gallery is lovely," I said, taking her hand.

"Monsieur Vincent. Enchanté," she replied, holding my eyes with her own which were pale blue and striking. "Please, call me Gabrielle." She gestured to a pair of tubular steel chairs upholstered in soft white leather with an interesting, welded steel table that looked like a one off a kind custom piece between them. We both sat. She was a tall, strongly built woman with an olive complexion and dark, wavy hair. She was attractive and comported herself with a self-assurance that made me think of Frida Kahlo staring out at me from one of her self-portraits. She wore black jeans and a dark gray silk blouse. The chairs and table rested on a pure white rug with a felt-like texture. I hoped my shoes weren't too dirty from my morning walk. "So, you are a friend of Valerie?" She spoke English with a British accent.

"Yes," I replied, "she's a good friend. I asked her if she knew anyone in the art business here in Nice, and she mentioned your name. Do you know her well?"

"Very well. We were in boarding school together and were roommates our last year before university. I still see her often at Art Basel, the Venice Biennale, sometimes other events. Valerie wrote and asked me to meet with you. She tells me you are a sculptor?"

"Yes."

"Is it about your artwork that you are here? I'm afraid I don't show sculpture in the gallery."

"No. I'm here on a different type of business. It's a little unusual, but I hope you can help me with some information about a man named Patrice Antonetti."

Her nose wrinkled and she made a sour face, involuntarily it seemed, when I said the name, but she recovered quickly. "I know the man," she said. "I wouldn't be interested in any business involving him." I held up my hand placatingly.

"Please, I am not here to ask for your involvement in any way. I'm simply trying to collect any information I can find about him. I'm conducting a sort of investigation into a missing artwork, and he seems to be involved."

She raised an eyebrow, inviting me to explain, so I launched into the story of what I was doing in Nice. I decided not to hold back or cover up in any way, instead giving her all the details necessary to explain. I did not talk about breaking into Booth's house or Legere's office, but otherwise gave a full account.

When I was done speaking, she sat back, crossed her arms, and studied my face for a full ten seconds. "This is a very interesting story. A troubling problem for Valerie to have this painting missing. I think your relationship with Valerie must be more than just friendly?" I nodded. "Very well," she said. "Let me tell you about Patrice Antonetti. Do you know the history of Corsica?"

"Very little, aside from it being the birthplace of Napoleon Bonaparte."

"Yes. That is what most people know. It is also my birthplace. Officially, it is a region of France, but we have a long history and culture going back millennia before the island was annexed by France. There are very old, very powerful families in Corsica. Some people would call them clans. I belong to one of those families. Patrice Antonetti also belongs to one but that family no longer has power. Various events took their toll on his family, and he is one of the last survivors. He still has money, plenty of it, but he does not go back to Corsica. It would not be a safe place for him. Still, he is a man of means. He lives well in an old chateau outside of Nice, which belonged to his family, and keeps an apartment in the city as well but I believe he rarely says there. He goes to the soirees and attends the openings. I am well acquainted with him from meeting him often at these types of events. Nearly every time I see him, he invites me to a dinner or cocktail party. He would like to be in favor with my family. He appears devoted to art, but my opinion of him is not good. I think what he really likes is power. He is both a coward and a bully. He surrounds himself with people who have less, so that he can have power over them. He buys art. If you visited his house, you would see plenty, but there are rumors that he also collects on the black market, that he has a secret collection that he keeps to himself. These are just rumors I have heard. I can't say whether they are true." Gabrielle stopped speaking and appraised my reaction to her words, staring me down with those blue eyes.

"Thank you. This is just what I needed to know," I responded. I sat for a moment then, thinking, fitting this new information into the puzzle. Legere was from Corsica too. It made sense. "So," I said, "If Antonetti wanted an early Heidrich for this private collection of his, he might have arranged to get one, possibly without knowing, or wanting to know, the details of how it was procured?"

"I think he would not be ignorant of the details, although it's possible. Heidrich has a reputation for refusing to sell his work to certain collectors who he believes are involved in the black-market trade."

"Interesting. I wonder if Antonetti is one of those?"

"You would have to ask Monsieur Heidrich."

"Can you tell me where Antonetti's house is located?"

"Of course, I can tell you," she said, waving a hand, sounding exasperated all of a sudden. "But you can't really be planning to go there, to take back the painting if he has it. Who are you? My father employs many capable men, if you know my meaning. I can recognize men like this. You look like a capable man. You could even be Corsican by your looks. There is something ambiguous in your face and coloring. But you are an artist, a sculptor. You have to understand that Patrice Antonetti comes from a family that is dissolute, but this does not mean he isn't dangerous. He is from a tradition that does not shun violence."

"I understand that. Thank you for your concern. I do have a certain...expertise...in this area, though. I wouldn't consider this if I didn't have a fair belief that I can succeed. I would need to gather more information first, though. I need to see his house."

"And you are doing this for Valerie? Purely out of the goodness of your heart?"

"Yes. I'm doing it for Valerie. I wouldn't call my heart good, though. I've been thinking—I was thinking on the way here as a matter of fact. Walking around the Vieille Ville put me in a Medieval frame of mind. Do you know about the crusades and papal indulgences? How a lot of the crusaders officially went to reconquer the holy land as a form of penance? To absolve them of their sins? Of course, the real motive was often financial. I haven't always lived the most ethical life. I've been pretty thoughtless at times. Maybe I'm on a kind of crusade of my own to bring this painting back. Maybe I'm doing it for myself as much as for Valerie."

"Do you love Valerie?"

"Yes. I think so."

"Ah, romance. If you love her, you should be able to just say yes. No matter. You're going to need my help. There are two things I can do. First, I can take you out to the area near Antonetti's house so you can see it. Second, tomorrow night is the opening performance of a new ballet at the Opéra. I have tickets, and I'm sure Antonetti will be there if you would like to meet him. He attends all the openings. I have work to do this afternoon, but tomorrow I will call at your hotel in the morning, and we can drive out."

"That's not necessary. If you can just tell me."

"Nonsense. I'll take you. When asked for a favor by a friend, I don't go halfway. My presence might be useful. What hotel are you staying at?"

I could see by her look that she was not going to take no for an answer. We made plans to meet at ten a.m. the next morning, then I thanked her, and we said goodbye.

Out on the street, I walked for a while without any destination in mind. It took several blocks for me to process my meeting with Gabrielle Cartini. She had a powerful presence. I didn't feel like going back to my hotel and sitting around all afternoon. I did want to speak with Heidrich, though. I looked at my watch and did a quick calculation. It was nine p.m. in San Francisco. I stopped in a doorway and texted Valerie. She texted back soon after with Heidrich's phone number. She appeared to have given up asking me what I was doing or why I needed the information I asked for. I dug my earbuds out of my backpack and dialed the number, walking aimlessly while the call connected.

Heidrich answered on the second ring. "Ja?"

His voice was rough. I imagined I might have disturbed him in the middle of his work. He sounded like it might be the first word he had spoken all day.

"Herr Heidrich. This is Valerie's friend Justin. We met at your opening in San Francisco."

"Yes. I remember. The sculptor."

"Do you have a moment? I wanted to ask a question about a collector who may have wanted to purchase one of your paintings."

"Yes, go on."

"Patrice Antonetti is his name. Do you know him?"

"Yes. He contacted me through an agent. A year maybe? The agent would not say who he worked for, but I found out. Antonetti wanted an early piece for his collection. I know this man's reputation. I refused. Of course, he can buy from a gallery or private collector, and I can't stop him, but few people have my early paintings for sale. Has he approached Valerie?"

"No. His name came up in a different context. There are rumors about him."

"I believe the rumors to be true."

"Thank you. That's the information I needed."

"You are welcome. My advice, do not deal with the man."

"I'll take that advice. Thanks for your time."

"Again, you are welcome. Say hello to Valerie."

After hanging up, I continued to wander the streets of Nice and ended up back in the old quarter. I found myself in the square outside the Cathedral of Saint Reparata. My speech to Gabrielle about the crusaders had been off the cuff, but it felt true in some sense. I considered for a moment but held back from entering the church. I hadn't been inside a church since I left home at seventeen. Gazing up at the baroque facade of the cathedral, I thought about the crusaders who had probably taken their last communion there in the old church, before it was rebuilt. They were hard men, undoubtedly, leaving on a long journey, believing strongly in the righteousness of their task, although with the backward gaze of modernity we judged their undertakings differently. My personal crusade was nowhere near as difficult but might be just as dangerous, based on Gabrielle's warnings about Antonetti. Still, I had entered many homes in many places and come out every time with what I went in to get. Antonetti's chateau was just another one. With the right planning and proper caution, I would prevail.

ᘒᘒᘒ

The next morning, I was ready and waiting in the lobby when Gabrielle pulled up in a white BMW SUV. I slid into the passenger seat and was immediately assaulted by a wet tongue slurping my ear.

"*Leo! Arrete!*" Gabrielle said, reaching back and pushing a massive furry creature away from me.

I turned in my seat. Leo was a standard poodle with dark, almost black, fur. He was big, maybe seventy pounds, and hunkered down on the back seat, head resting on his paws, staring back at me with sad brown eyes. I held out my hand, received a lick, and patted him on the head.

"Nice to meet you Leo," I said and turned back to Gabrielle. "Thanks again for coming to pick me up and show me around the countryside."

"It's my pleasure," she replied. "We're going to drive out to a village called Le Broc. It's about twenty-eight kilometers up into the mountains. Antonetti's house is close to the village. I know a place where we can hike to an overlook and see the house and grounds."

She was wearing jeans, sturdy hiking shoes, and a cable-knit sweater. I had foreseen some walking in nature and had chosen similar clothes. The day was bright, cloudless, and cool—maybe fifty-five or sixty degrees.

"I'm glad I dressed for a walk," I replied. "Is hiking something you do a lot?"

"Yes. Nearly every weekend if the weather is good. Leo needs to get out and run."

Gabrielle piloted the SUV deftly among the pedestrians, scooters, and taxis in the city center and then onto the A8 and through the outskirts of Nice. The car was comfortable and quiet. I could never bring myself to purchase a luxury automobile—one of the few things that had stuck with me from my childhood was a distaste for conspicuous consumption—but I did appreciate the high-end experience of riding in one. As we drove, we talked about art and artists. She knew a lot about contemporary sculpture, much more than I did, as a matter of fact. After a while, we turned off the A8 onto a smaller highway that led inland and up into the southern foothills of the Alps. The farther we got from the city center, the fewer office parks and subdivisions we passed. Farms and forest took over, and I saw glimpses of the Var river, paralleling the highway. Ahead, rising above the horizon far in the distance were hazy blue, snowcapped mountains. After about twenty minutes of driving, we came to a bridge and crossed the river. Looking out over its green-brown expanse, I thought about T. S. Eliot's "strong brown god," "destroyer, reminder of what men choose to forget." Slow, broad, silty rivers like the Var always bring that poem to my mind. I mentioned it to Gabrielle, and she nodded.

"Yes. It's an unassuming river. The name Var comes from the Ligurian word for waterway. Sort of like naming your dog 'canine,' or your city 'inhabited place.'"

After the bridge, we turned onto a narrower road, barely wide enough for two cars. We passed through several small villages as we climbed into the hills, but mostly the road was bordered by forest close on either side. Occasionally, a low branch would scrape the roof of the car. We passed a few daredevil motorcyclists coming down the hill at breakneck speed. Also, a few cars and small trucks, requiring both us and the opposing drivers to swerve precariously onto the almost non-existent shoulder. After the first truck passed us within mere inches, Gabrielle pressed a button that caused the side mirrors to fold in.

"Lost a mirror on this road one time," she explained.

The road twisted and turned through the hills, switching back, and climbing steadily. We passed through a small town called Carros, then, about ten minutes later, we rounded a curve and looking out over the valley I caught a glimpse of a village on the far side, clinging to a rocky slope. The old stone buildings with their red tiled roofs were all crowded and jumbled together, and in the center, a clock tower or church steeple poked up, the tallest structure in the town. Thick forest climbed up the hills, right to the edge of the village, and the mountains rose up behind it. We continued around the curve and came to the outskirts of Le Broc. Stone walls and houses rose up along both sides of the highway. I saw an old woman on a balcony, shaking dust out of a rug. A cat darted across the road. Soon we were into the town proper, and the buildings were two and three stories high, the road even narrower.

We passed a tabac and a patisserie, then the road widened a bit, and Gabrielle swung into a parking spot between two tiny Peugeots.

"We're close to the center of town," she said. "We should walk to the main square and see the church, then we can get something to eat for our hike and head out."

Leo was hopping around excitedly in the back seat, shaking the entire vehicle.

"No, you stay here, Leo. We'll be back in a few minutes."

She rolled down the windows enough so the dog could get some fresh air then we both stepped out, and she locked the doors.

We strolled through the narrow, shady streets, stopping at various shops to buy cheese, bread, fruit, and saucisson sec. I loaded the foods into my backpack as we purchased them and we continued another block, via a street so narrow that it felt like a tunnel, to the main town square. A fountain was splashing in the center of the square and a Christmas village had been set up around the periphery. There were gift stands selling ceramics, hand crafted furniture and toys, and a variety of foods. We made a circuit of the square then headed back toward the car.

"I thought you should see the village," Gabrielle said. "This is very close to Antonetti's house. He comes here often to shop, to eat lunch, and the people know him."

"It's a nice place," I replied. "Quaint. Almost untouched."

Leo was happy to see us and was very interested in the smell of cured meat coming from my backpack. Gabrielle made a U-turn, and we headed back out of Le Broc and onto a forest road even narrower than the one we had taken to get to the village. We drove for a couple of miles amongst the trees until Gabrielle suddenly swung the car to the right and we pulled to a stop, on a patch of dirt, at a point where the shoulder briefly widened.

"This is the trailhead," she said, opening her door and climbing out.

She pulled open the rear driver's side door, and Leo bolted out, running furiously up the road, almost out of sight, then back toward us. I climbed out, too, and shouldered my backpack. Gabrielle whistled to Leo and headed straight into the underbrush between two trees, crunching through dry leaves. I followed and soon saw that there was, indeed, a path. It was rocky and overgrown and almost fully covered over in some places by grass and weeds but still walkable.

Gabrielle set a fast pace, while Leo bounded in and out of the trees ahead of us, chasing woodland creatures and barking at birds. The trees around us were a mixture of deciduous oaks and pines, which gave the forest an open, airy feel, although the path was narrow. A blanket of leaves and fallen branches covered the ground with occasional outcroppings of sedimentary rock poking up through the duff.

We walked for about half an hour, climbing steadily, before the trees began to thin and give way to bare hillsides dotted with thickets. Another few minutes of walking brought us to a shelf of rock overhanging a steep slope that receded into a forested valley. Gabrielle stopped and waited until I was standing next to her then turned and pointed down into the valley.

Perhaps half a mile away was a large clearing in the forest the size of several football fields. A gravel road ran down the center of the clearing, through what seemed to be well maintained landscaping of lawns, hedges, and topiary, to a circular drive and a large, stone house three stories high with a black-tiled mansard roof and turrets flanking the main entrance. There were several outbuildings as well including a small greenhouse, a carriage house squatting next to the main house, and, nearby, a stable with a fenced yard. The forest edged close up to the rear of the house. In the space between the house and trees was a terrace with a large, rectangular swimming pool and narrow stretch of lawn.

"Nice house," I said.

"Yes. I believe it has twelve bedrooms. There is a ballroom, library, sitting room, and dining room as well as the kitchen on the main floor. Family bedrooms mainly on the second floor. Servants' quarters probably on the top floor. Completely remodeled twenty years ago to add modern comforts. Antonetti has many parties—one every weekend almost. I have only been inside once for a dinner party several years ago, before I knew as much about him, although I have been invited often as I mentioned. His cars are in the carriage house there," she said, pointing. "He had a Rolls Royce, a Land Rover, and a Porsche when I visited. He insisted on showing them to me. Shall we have our picnic here?"

"Seems like a good spot," I replied and took my backpack off. We spread out a blanket Gabrielle had brought, sat, and unpacked the food. It was warm in the sun and pleasant to sit and gaze out over the valley. Leo wandered over and lay down on the blanket with us, begging for sausage. I spent some time looking over the house with binoculars. A sophisticated alarm system seemed unlikely for a house so far from anything else. It would take a private security company or police at least half an hour to respond to an alarm—hardly worth paying for. Strong physical security was more likely. I needed a closer look at the house, and I needed to know who the permanent occupants were, including servants.

"Who lives in the house besides Antonetti? Do you know?"

"I believe his mother lives with him. She would be very old. He is not married and has no children. I think he also has a woman who cleans and cooks and a man who maintains the property."

Just as she finished speaking, I saw a figure emerge from behind the main house and walk around toward the carriage house. I trained the binoculars on him. It was not Antonetti. He was a big, dark-haired guy wearing work boots, jeans, and a heavy green over shirt. It was probably Antonetti's maintenance man. He stopped in front of the carriage house, fiddled with something for a minute, then swung large double doors open and stepped into the dark interior. I kept the binoculars trained on the doorway. Soon, I saw a safari style SUV pull slowly out. The man hopped out of the car, closed the double doors, then lit a cigarette and stood leaning against the car smoking for a couple of minutes. Suddenly, he straightened up, as if at some noise, and dropped his cigarette, grinding it into the gravel with his heel. I swung the binoculars over and saw Antonetti himself approaching the car.

"Looks like Antonetti and his work man are heading out somewhere."

"Probably to the village for supplies," Gabrielle replied.

I watched them circle around the drive, head down the road, and disappear around a bend. We sat for a few minutes in silence, finishing our picnic. Leo was napping on the blanket in the sun, his legs twitching.

"Is there a path from here down to the woods near the house?" I asked.

"Yes. Continue around that outcropping. On the other side is an easy slope. The trail continues on across the valley and joins up with another in a couple of kilometers. To reach the house one would have to turn off the trail and walk through the forest perhaps two hundred meters to the edge of the property. Ready to go back now?"

I nodded and knelt, packing the remains of our picnic into my bag while Gabrielle folded and stowed the blanket.

"Leo! *Allons-y!*" Gabrielle called and took off running, the dog following and bounding ahead of her.

We headed back down the trail at a jog. I watched Gabrielle hop nimbly over fallen trees and rocks. She was light on her feet, a good trail runner. I kept up, copying her moves until we were back at the car. We packed our things in and headed back down the road, toward Nice.

◠◡◠

Several hours later I, set out from my hotel, on my way to meet Gabrielle. She had offered to pick me up again, but the Opéra de Nice was a short walk, so I had refused. I had spent the afternoon shopping and was wearing a new suit and stiff new shoes. In San Francisco, people went to formal events in every type of clothing imaginable, but I assumed it would be a dressier affair in France.

I spent a few minutes standing out front, leaning

against the monolithic facade of the theater and watching people walk by. There was a well-dressed crowd out front, chatting amiably, meeting and exchanging French double air kisses, and smoking their last cigarettes before entering.

With five minutes to spare before the performance was slated to start, I saw Gabrielle coming toward me through the crowd wearing a blue wrap dress and towering heels. I waved and strode over to meet her.

"That looks like a brand-new suit."

"Yes. I thought I should try to dress appropriately."

"You did well. Let's go in. Antonetti's box is across from mine. If he is here as I assume he will be, we can run into him at intermission."

She took my arm and we entered. The interior of the theater was all gilded plaster and marble and grand red carpeted stairways. We climbed up a couple of floors then turned down a corridor and stepped through a door into a luxurious loge upholstered in red. I wandered to the front and looked out over the crowd. We were two floors above the orchestra and there was yet another floor of loges before the first balcony.

"Nice seats," I commented.

"My father," she replied. "He keeps this box for all performances, but he almost never attends. He gives the tickets to whoever wants them. Nobody else likes ballet."

I nodded and we took our seats. The sounds of the orchestra tuning their instruments and the low murmur of the crowd blended nicely.

Gabrielle leaned toward me. "Look straight across and count five boxes this way from the stage. Antonetti is there."

I did as she instructed and saw Antonetti in an immaculate black suit and tie seated in the front row of his box with a young woman in a filmy green gown and a necklace with an enormous yellow jewel that flashed as she moved. Another couple was seated behind them. I watched Antonetti for a moment. He seemed to be telling a joke. The woman at his side laughed, raising a hand to her throat. The other couple chortled merrily. Just then the lights darkened and the conductor emerged from the shadows and mounted his rostrum.

The first half of the ballet passed slowly. I had trouble paying attention. I was thinking about Antonetti sitting across from us, his house, the painting. Just before the end of the first act, Gabrielle stood and gestured for me to follow.

"Let's hurry to the other side so we can be there when he comes out." I rose and followed after her. We rounded the corridor and stopped at a marble topped bar where I bought two glasses of champagne. I handed one to Gabrielle, just as the loge doors began to open and people started to emerge, blinking and stretching. She was facing toward the door to Antonetti's box. We pretended to converse but her eyes were searching. Suddenly, she smiled and waved.

"Ah! Monsieur Antonetti."

He had spotted her and approached, greeting her warmly. They began speaking in a language I thought at first was Italian but soon decided must be Corsican. Close up, I could see that he was at the far end of middle age— maybe sixty-five—with the deep, craggy wrinkles that came from a lifetime of sun exposure. He was lean though and fit looking for his age. After a moment, Gabrielle gestured toward me and switched to English.

"This is a friend from the US—"

I stepped forward, cutting her off and offering my hand. "Dustin Cruz. Pleased to meet you."

"Patrice Antonetti," he replied, shaking hands and looking down the length of his aquiline nose at me.

"Dustin is an artist," Gabrielle offered. Antonetti nodded, turned back to Gabrielle, and said something in Corsican, smiling in an obvious attempt to be charming. She turned to me. "Monsieur Antonetti invites us to come out to his house for cocktails tomorrow evening if you are free. He is having a small party."

"Yes, of course." I turned to Antonetti. "Thank you for the invitation."

They spoke for another minute, then Antonetti nodded politely to me and turned back to his friends. Gabrielle and I wandered back toward our seats.

"I told you he would invite us," she said. "He never fails. He seemed surprised that I accepted."

"It's great luck," I replied. "It will be very helpful to see the inside of his house."

We parted out in front of the theater after the ballet was done. I thanked Gabrielle for helping me, and we made a plan for the following evening. I would drive my rental and meet her at the place where we had pulled off the road for our hike. From there we would go in her car. I wanted to have the rental car handy in case an opportunity presented itself. The weather had turned colder, and a light mist was swirling in the air, silver halos of water droplets dancing around streetlamps as I made my way back to the hotel. I thought about Valerie. Gabrielle's wrap dress had reminded me of Val. It was the kind of dress she wore for almost every occasion. I decided to call her and check in. I wouldn't tell her yet what I was doing or what I had found out, though. I didn't want her to try to talk me out of it.

CHAPTER 10

December 18:

I woke early and made coffee in my room again, as I had the previous day, then spent the morning doing research online, eventually ordering room service as I dug deep on Antonetti. Unfortunately, I was not able to learn much more about him than Gabrielle had already told me. I did learn a good deal of Corsican history though—particularly regarding the Union Corse which was the group of Corsican clans that organized the heroin trade known as the French Connection between France and the US during the 1960s and early 1970s. It was a fascinating story stretching all the way back to WWII. The Union Corse had aided the Gaullist wing of the French resistance in Marseille during the German occupation.

After the war, they had continued their cozy relationship with the French Government by assisting in strike-breaking and anti-communist initiatives. This relationship gave the mafia families unofficial immunity from law enforcement which enabled members to start up and expand the heroin trade. They smuggled opium from France's colonial outposts in Indochina and Turkey to Marseille where it was processed into heroin and then smuggled further around the globe to end up on the streets of New York and other American cities. Eventually a combination of stricter enforcement and gang warfare brought down the French Connection. The families continued to run gambling, money laundering, prostitution, contract killing, and smaller drug trafficking operations. Then, in the mid-2000s, the two most powerful families on Corsica—the Brise-de-Mer and Colonna clans—became embroiled in a violent gang war which decimated their ranks. In the aftermath, other families rose to fill the power vacuum.

As I read the history, Gabrielle's story began to make sense. Antonetti must have come from one of the clans that lost power during the conflict, and Gabrielle's father must have come from one of the families that rose to power. If I had judged Antonetti's age correctly, he would have been born around 1950 which would mean he grew up and came of age at a time when the Union Corse was at the height of its power and influence. His wealth was undoubtedly made up of profits from the drug trade hidden away over the years in Swiss bank accounts and offshore financial structures. An exile from his homeland, he lived now in an old chateau probably also purchased with drug money. He whiled away his time by patronizing arts institutions and collecting priceless art via unscrupulous means using his underground network of criminal contacts. Legere, too, was Corsican. He was probably a low-ranking associate who had also fled the island in the wake of the conflict and now did odd jobs for Antonetti. Gabrielle had tried to warn me. These were not nice people. Knowing more about the history made me wary, but it did not soften my resolve.

I had nothing to do until the evening when we would attend the cocktail party, but I was restless and felt like an animal in a cage, pacing my hotel room. I decided to

drive out and survey the woods around Antonetti's chateau. Hopefully, I could get closer to the place and gather
useful information. I collected my car from the valet and
headed out, following the route we had taken the day before. The drive was uneventful, and I found the turn-out
where we had parked after overshooting it, turning
around, and then backtracking slowly. I hiked through
sun-dappled woods to the spot where we had picnicked
and spent some time surveying the house and checking
out the terrain. There was no activity as far as I could tell
from my vantage point. It seemed that everybody was
either away or staying inside. As Gabrielle had said, the
trail continued around a bluff, curved down, and lead on
through the valley. I estimated the distance to the point
where I would be even with Antonetti's house at perhaps
half a mile.

There was nothing to do but start walking so I set off
following the trail down into thicker woods. The day was
unseasonably warm, and I was sweating, my T-shirt
damp by the time my watch told me I had covered the
half mile. I had seen some fairly recent horse droppings
on the trail which made me suspect that there would be a
connecting trail leading toward the house. There was a
stable next to Antonetti's house that had seemed to be in
good repair. He and his guests probably went riding
around the surrounding countryside. I began keeping an
eye out for any sign of a junction, and it didn't take long
before I found it.

Two large, mossy stones were set on end at either
side of the connecting path, like a gate. The last thing I
wanted was to run into Antonetti, so I kept to the trees
about fifteen feet into the forest and paralleled the trail. It
was not too bad in the underbrush but definitely slower
than walking on the path. Soon, though, I came to the
edge of the woods and could see the house and outbuild-

ings ahead of me. I was even with the west side of the house. To my left the woods curved around, following the edge of the grounds.

I kept moving, staying hidden in the woods, and following the curve around until I was facing the rear of the building. Between my position and the house were the pool and terrace. Steam was rising from the pool and a few leaves floated on the surface of the water. My nose caught a faint whiff of chlorine on the light breeze that rustled the leaves around me. At the back of the house on the right was a loggia with Doric columns supporting the impost of each arch. The floor of the loggia and connecting terrace was gray flagstone. The pool seemed to be a recent addition but had been surrounded with matching flagstone. Dark wood and canvas patio furniture was scattered in groupings around the terrace.

I turned my attention to the house itself. The original windows had probably been made up of multiple square panes but had been replaced with modern, solid looking casement windows that opened outward. One window on the second floor was open a few inches, but green curtains blocked my view of the interior. The walls of the house were made up of fitted stone blocks with plenty of good looking finger holds, and there were ornamental ledges and cornices which together would make for an easy climb.

On the first floor to my left there was light coming from two windows, but I couldn't see inside from where I was standing. I bushwhacked my way a little farther and stood on top of a fallen tree. Just as I stepped up onto the tree a woman in a gray dress and black apron passed in front of one of the windows. I held still and watched her walk to a large stainless-steel stove and stir something simmering in a big pot. She lifted the wooden stirring spoon out of the pot and brought it up to her face, blowing to cool it. She had dark hair in a loose bun and appeared to be middle aged. She had to be Antonetti's housekeeper. After tasting whatever it was she was making in the pot, she moved away, out of my sight. I felt fairly certain now that getting into the house would not be much of a challenge. The challenge would come once I was inside. I would have to wait until the cocktail party to get a feel for the interior.

I began working my way back around through the trees but froze at the distant sound of a horse whinnying. I stood still for a few moments then carefully continued until I could see the front of the house, the stable, and fenced stable yard. Two horses were now out in the yard. They stood side by side, one large and dark brown, the other smaller and white. A large door was open to the interior of the stable, and I saw Antonetti's workman come out with a wheelbarrow full of straw and wood shavings.

I had seen enough now. I continued on deeper into the woods, paralleling the path, until I came back to the junction and turned, heading toward my car.

e⁄ɔe⁄ɔ

I was back in the city by one p.m. and spent the rest of the afternoon walking around and doing some shopping. At six-thirty, after a light dinner, I headed out again in my rental car, retracing my route from earlier. This time, despite the fact that the sun was already down, I didn't miss the turn-out. I parked and shut off the car and all the lights. It was very dark and very quiet on that road with the tree branches overhead, the moon not yet risen, and only the faint glimmer of a few stars. I got out of the car and stood, leaning on the warm hood, listening to the faint rustle of creatures, the whisper of the breeze through the leaves above. I felt very lonely and very distant from all human society at that moment. Both of my professions were lonely ones. Most of the time it didn't bother me.

About fifteen minutes later, I saw headlights approaching. The car slowed, and I recognized Gabrielle's BMW. She pulled over, and I got into the passenger seat. No wet tongue attack came from the rear seat this time.

"Did Leo stay home?"

Gabrielle turned to me and smiled. She was wearing an elegant burgundy dress and black jacket, her hair up. "Yes. He would have to wait in the car. Antonetti is afraid of dogs."

"That explains the lack of dogs at his estate. I expected a guard dog or two."

"Did you hike out there today? I thought you might. He was attacked when he was a boy. My father told me this. It's a kind of joke about his manhood, but I think it's terrible. Do you have a dog?"

"No. We had lots of dogs when I was growing up, but I'm away from home too often to have any pets now."

"I see," she said, getting the car turned around and heading back down the road, "What sort of dogs did you have?"

"Mutts. They were farm dogs."

"Your parents were farmers?"

"No. I mean, I don't know. I've never met my parents. I was raised by a foster family. They were farmers." Gabrielle nodded. "I like standard poodles though," I added, to ease the awkwardness. "That's a noble breed."

"Noble indeed. Before the revolution, poodles were a favorite of the French nobility. They were hunting dogs."

We continued, passing by Le Broc and heading back into the forest. We drove for another half mile before coming to a turnoff. There was a large, ornate steel gate standing open on hinges embedded in a Medieval-looking carved stone gate post. Gabrielle turned and passed through, putting us on the road I had seen from the bluff above during our picnic. The long driveway was lined with shrubberies trimmed into cones and lights on posts with little solar panels to charge their batteries during the day. We drove into the circle, gravel crunching under the tires, and parked.

Several guests had already arrived. I ran my fingers along the smooth, shiny flanks of their Jaguars and Mercedes as we strolled up to the main entrance. There was a small, raised portico around the front door. I took Gabrielle's hand as she stepped up. Antonetti was just inside the door, dressed in a shiny black shirt unbuttoned to show white chest hair, immaculate burgundy jacket, black slacks, and loafers. He greeted her effusively, offered a hand to me, and then almost immediately turned back to her. It was clear that he had invited me out of politeness. His attentions would be all for Gabrielle. I realized then what she was putting herself through for my sake and resolved to do something nice for her.

Stepping through the doorway, following Gabrielle, I took a look around. The entry hall was bright with a vaulted ceiling rising two stories up and walls of off-white marble. The floor was glossy white and gray-checkered stone. There were wreaths, mistletoe, festive candles burning, and other colorful and fragrant decorations in honor of the season. To the right was a staircase that curved around and led to a gallery and hallways which, I guessed, gave access to the upstairs bedrooms. There was also a door below the staircase that I knew from my earlier reconnaissance must lead back toward the kitchen and pantry and maybe other non-public areas of the house such as laundry, wine cellars, etc.

To my left, an arched doorway led into a huge room that looked like it must be the ballroom Gabrielle had told me about. Directly across from the main entry, another arched doorway led into a library or drawing room. The guests who had arrived before us seemed to be congregated there. Antonetti led us forward, through the arch.

The room was enormous. It had a polished floor of robust wooden planks, tasteful, modern furniture, and exposed stone walls. Fashionable people stood around the room in conversational groups, holding drinks, bathed in pools of honey colored light from recessed fixtures. Baroque music played softly from hidden speakers.

Antonetti and Gabrielle were speaking Corsican as he led us to the bar in the corner of the room. A young woman in a gray dress with a white collar offered an array of options in French. She seemed to be hired help based on the uniform. Gabrielle asked for a glass of Bordeaux, and I followed her lead.

As we turned back toward the room, Gabrielle leaned over and whispered in my ear. "Go explore. I will handle Antonetti."

"Okay. Thanks for helping with this," I whispered back then nodded to Antonetti and wandered off.

The dominant language in the room was French. My French was rudimentary at best, so I meandered, nodding and smiling.

More guests were arriving. I passed the doorway to the entry hall where the woman I had seen that morning through the window was taking coats and welcoming people. She had to be the housekeeper. On a sofa near the bar, I saw the woman with whom Antonetti had attended the ballet. She was wearing a long white gown with a ruched Queen Anne neckline and a vexed expression which creased her face as she eyed Antonetti and Gabrielle. The same necklace I had seen her wearing at the ballet rested against her pale, spare décolletage.

She tapped the yellow jewel pendant lightly with an immaculately manicured fingernail, mouth drawing into a frown. I passed her by, hands clasped behind my back, perusing.

There was plenty of art on the walls. Some old, age-darkened paintings of landscapes and hunting scenes and people in archaic costumes, some modern pieces. It was all nice stuff. I saw a couple of works by semi-famous contemporary artists. There were no big money pieces, though—no Matisse, Manet, Johns, Renoir, Pollack, Cézanne, or any of the multitude of others whose work sold for a premium at the auction houses. If Antonetti collected the kind of art I suspected he did, then he had to have a private gallery somewhere in the house. Unless it was all locked up in a vault at the Geneva Freeport. I couldn't imagine Antonetti as that kind of collector, though. He seemed like a guy who would want to look at and show off his collection. Also, Legere would not have flown into Milan if he was going to take the painting to Geneva.

I passed by a grand piano then a fireplace with stone caryatids on either side of the massive inner hearth and an ornately carved wooden mantle. Three giant logs were burning in the hearth, crackling and sending waves of heat out into the room. As I approached a couple standing on the far side of the fireplace, I could hear that they were conversing in English, so I lingered a bit. The man was tall and white haired and spoke with an upper-class English accent. The woman was younger, wiry, rail thin, and blonde. She spoke flat, west coast American English. The man turned toward me. "Good evening."

"Good evening. Sorry, I didn't mean to disturb you."

"Not at all. I'm Cedric Bond. This is my wife, Elizabeth."

I stepped forward and shook hands with them both. "Dustin Cruz," I said. "I'm visiting from the US."

"Wonderful. Where do you live?" Elizabeth Bond asked.

"San Francisco. And you?"

"Half the year here and half in Los Angeles."

"That sounds like a good way to live. How do you know Patrice?" I used Antonetti's first name intentionally, hoping to confuse them.

"My firm does some consulting for him. We've known each other for a long time," Cedric answered. "And you?"

I gestured back the direction I had come from. "My friend Gabrielle."

"Ah, you know Ms. Cartini?" Elizabeth, said, smiling and peeking around me. Something in her manner was off. I couldn't tell at first if she was awkward or condescending but then I saw her sway to the side and decided she must be a bit drunk. "You must be in the art business."

"Yes. In a way," I replied. "I'm actually an international art thief. I'm heading straight up to Paris to plunder the Louvre and the Musée D'Orsay after my visit with Gabrielle."

I watched them closely. If they knew who Gabrielle was, they probably knew about Antonetti's affiliations and history as well as hers. My answer was flip but could be construed as a way of sidestepping an explanation of my real relationship with Antonetti and Gabrielle, leaving open the possibility that I was involved with the Corsican mafia in some way.

"Very interesting," said Cedric, laughing. "I hope you get something good. Please pick me up a Van Gogh while you are there."

Another young woman in the same gray dress as the bartender passed by with a tray of hors d'oeuvres. Cedric took some sort of olive and cheese and toasted bread stack. I selected a stuffed mushroom.

"Of course," I replied. "Patrice has already requested a Cézanne."

"An early Cézanne, no doubt," Elizabeth said.

Cedric gave her a stern look.

"Yes. An early work," I replied, raising an eyebrow. "I'm off to find a bathroom. It was a pleasure meeting both of you. I hope we get a chance to talk more."

They both smiled. We shook hands again, and I continued on through the room. I was pretty sure Cedric and Elizabeth had seen Antonetti's private collection. Maybe a collection of early works by important artists if I could trust Elizabeth's slip of the tongue.

I headed straight through an arched doorway and into the ballroom which was similar to the drawing room but a bit larger and, like the entry hall, had a vaulted ceiling that rose a full two stories. To my right were big double doors leading out to the loggia I had seen that morning. There were casement windows on either side of the doors. I wandered to the window on the right and looked out over the terrace, the pool, the dark woods beyond. Two men with rocks glasses and cigars were out on the terrace, facing away from me. I turned my head. The room behind me was empty. I turned back and examined the windows. There was no wiring or contacts for an alarm system. I hadn't thought there would be. I lifted the handle on one of the windows and pushed it open a tiny amount, just enough so that it could be pulled open from the outside, then turned and traversed the room, passing through the doorway into the entry hall.

The housekeeper was still there, standing by the door. She turned toward me. "*Monsieur, cherchez vous quelque chose?*"

"*La salle de bain s'il vous plait.*"

She pointed to a doorway beneath the stairs, and I continued walking that direction. The doorway led into a

smaller living room with a fire burning in the fireplace, a
sectional sofa and side chairs upholstered in medium
gray, and windows overlooking the circular drive. At the
far side of the room was an open door leading to a luxuri-
ously appointed bathroom and another, closed door which
piqued my interest. It had to lead farther back to the
kitchen I had seen through the window.

I continued walking straight across the room, pulled
the second door open, and stepped through, closing it behind me. I was in a narrow hallway with dark wainscoting. About twenty feet down the hallway I could see what
was unmistakably the kitchen through an open doorway.
There were also doors on both left and right sides of the
hall. I walked down and pulled the door on the left open a
crack. It led to a formal dining room. The more I saw of
Antonetti's chateau, the more I liked it. The architecture
was decidedly old, perhaps from the 1500s, but the furnishings were modern and chosen with exquisite taste to
work with the architecture but also give the place an
open, chic, and minimalist feel. I continued on and
peaked through the door on the right. It led into a pantry.
There were wire shelves lining the walls holding cans,
bottles, canisters, boxes, and jars. In the far-right corner
was a giant, double-doored freezer. On the left was a
doorway that looked like it led into the kitchen and, catty-
corner to that, another door surrounded by a stone archway. The door was obviously not original to the house. It
was stainless steel and had a hefty looking latch style
handle with an electronic keypad. The wall I was facing
had to be very near the front of the house, so the door almost certainly gave access to a stairway leading down to
the cellars. My intuition told me this was it. Why else
would there be such a solid door with a keypad?

I was crossing the room for a closer look when I
heard footsteps approaching from the kitchen. I ducked

into a small space between the wall and the edge of one of the metal shelves just as the woman who had been serving hors-d'oeuvres entered, walking briskly. She grabbed something from one of the shelves and turned on her heel. As soon as she was gone, I went back out through the door I had entered from. I didn't want to be discovered wandering around the private areas of the house. Rather than going back through the entry hall, I used the opposite door to let myself into the dining room and from there back through to the library where guests were mingling and drinking.

I saw Gabrielle across the room, seated on a pale green velvet covered divan, conversing with Elizabeth Bond. I approached and sat next to Gabrielle. Mrs. Bond was clearly drunk now. She was in the middle of a long, rambling story involving the perceived misdeeds of somebody I didn't know. I looked around for Cedric but couldn't see him nearby. I leaned over and whispered to Gabrielle.

"We can leave anytime."

She nodded. "Let's give it half an hour, so we don't seem rude or arouse suspicion."

"Agreed."

Half an hour later, we said our thank yous and parted from Antonetti at the door. As we walked to the car, Gabrielle shuddered.

"I need a shower," she announced, sniffing herself. "I smell like Antonetti's cologne. He had his arm around my waist half the night. His girlfriend wasn't happy about it."

"I don't imagine she was," I replied as we climbed into the car and she started it up. "Thanks again for taking me to his house. I know it must have been unpleasant."

She waved a hand dismissively. "It was a trifle. Elizabeth Bond, as drunk as she was, gave me some inside information on an artist I've been trying to get for my gallery. So, it was worth it."

I nodded, thinking as we drove through the dark forest. I had made up my mind to go back that night and try to get in to Antonetti's cellar. I had no idea how I would accomplish it. I would have to improvise. "How late do you think the party will continue?"

"Not late. The previous and only time I attended one of his parties before, I left at eleven, and I was one of the last to go. It's not a late-night crowd. You're not going back tonight to try for the painting, are you?"

"Yes. I think so. It's as good a time as any."

She shook her head, eyes on the road. "I think you are a fool to try this. If he has the painting there, it will be well secured."

"If I can't get to it, I'll gather the information I need and then come back with the proper tools."

"If anything happens, if you are caught, I won't be able to help. I will have to deny any knowledge."

"Yes. That's exactly what I would want you to do. There's no reason for you to get caught up."

"I'm not afraid of Antonetti. He would never retaliate against me. He knows my family would crush him. Nonetheless, I don't want any kind of gossip or news coverage."

"Understood. Neither do I."

"Very well. I would appreciate it if you would call me to let me know you are all right, though. If I don't hear from you by morning, I will be worried."

"I'll certainly get in touch."

CHAPTER 11

December 18 ~ 19:

We drove in silence back to where my rental car was parked. As she pulled over and stopped the car, Gabrielle looked over, her pale eyes catching the light from the instrument panel. "I meant it when I asked you to get in touch. Leo will be worrying. He has taken a liking to you."

"I will," I replied.

She nodded, not letting go of my eyes. I broke away from her gaze, opened the door, and climbed out. A moment later, I watched her taillights fade away, lost in the silence and darkness of the forest. I felt even lonelier than I had earlier that evening, waiting to be picked up for the party. Now, I had nothing to look forward to but a dangerous, uncertain mission: gain entry to the house, somehow get through the door to the cellar, hope I would find what I was looking for there. What if I was wrong, if Antonetti's secret gallery wasn't there, or if he didn't even have the painting in his house? I didn't know. I had to act on my instincts and intuition.

In his autobiography, Bill Mason wrote about a fairly routine theft of jewelry from a condo in a fancy Florida high-rise. He was out the door and walking down the hall with the spoils in his pocket when a security guard appeared out of nowhere and yelled at him to stop. He ran. The security guard pulled out a gun and shot at him. A bullet passed through his side between two ribs and out his stomach, but he didn't realize right away that he'd been shot. The adrenaline kept him moving. He managed to get away. Later though, the untreated wound became septic, and he almost died. I often thought about that chapter when I was about to execute a job. It was a great example of how planning and preparation would not guarantee success. There were always random factors that could not be known beforehand.

In this case, I was walking into Antonetti's house with almost no plan and no preparation, aside from my years of experience. I would have to be ready to abort my mission and get out if things were not going my way. I didn't want to miss the chance by delaying, though. I was pretty sure Legere had delivered the painting only a couple of days before. If Antonetti was planning on moving the painting elsewhere, it would not stay in his house for long. It might already be gone. If he was planning to keep it at his house, the security would only get tighter. He might have a safe or vault of some kind. Now, though, unless I had misread him, he would have it out somewhere so he could look at it.

I unlocked the little Fiat and opened the hatchback. I had packed my backpack and brought it with me just in case. I changed out of my party clothes and put on black cargo pants, T-shirt, hoodie, and sneakers, shivering a bit in the cool air. I left my wallet in the car and, after locking the doors, hid the keys under a pile of dry leaves amongst the roots of a tree. Ready to go, I shouldered my pack and headed out. The moon had just risen, and the cold white light shone on branches and leaves before filtering down to dapple the trail, allowing me to pick my way along. I managed to find the path and stay on it, more or less, stumbling a few times over rocks and roots. Only ten days before I had been hiking through the Marin redwoods at night. Now I was six thousand miles away, on another night hike. It felt like fate, like another loop in the trajectory.

It took me significantly longer than it had when the sun was up, but I reached the promontory again and looked down on the chateau. The first floor was still lit up and the lights along the drive still burned too. I watched a couple say their goodbyes and walk to their car. So the party was still going but probably winding down. I needed to hurry. I wanted to be in place before all the guests left. The air became cooler and damper as I moved downhill along the trail and back into the trees. I jogged the half mile to the connecting path, turned, and continued, slowing as I reached the edge of the property. I could see the house now and hear sounds of conversation and laughter.

As I crouched just inside the tree line, I saw Antonetti's lady friend walk briskly out the front door, heading for a white sports car parked in the drive, the hem of her dress and her long blonde hair trailing behind. Antonetti also came out of the house, following her a few steps. I could hear his voice, placating. She answered without turning to look at him, gesturing over her shoulder, then hopped in and started the car. The lights came on, and she peeled off at great speed, taking out one of the cone-shaped topiary shrubs with a rear wheel and accelerating down the drive. Antonetti stood for a moment, watching her go, then shrugged and turned, heading back into the house.

I continued around toward the rear as I had earlier in the day. This time, though, I did not go so far into the woods, sticking instead to the edge of the tree line. The lights were still on in the library, the ballroom, and the kitchen. One dormer window on the top floor was lit up, but I could only see a patch of ceiling from my position. It could be the housekeeper's room. Or maybe the man servant's. The carriage house had a second floor, though, and my guess was that the man servant's quarters would be there. I situated myself with a good view of the library.

The party appeared to have dwindled to a group of five, seated by the fireplace. I recognized Cedric and Elizabeth. There was another couple, both on the young side of middle age. They looked like the same people I had seen in Antonetti's box at the ballet. The woman was dressed in a simple green sheath dress, and the man wore a black turtleneck and gray jacket. They were talking, laughing, and sipping wine.

I left the edge of the woods, walking as silently as possible, skirted the pool, and entered the loggia via an archway. Hurrying to the window I had left open, I felt around the edge, trying to get the tips of my fingers into the small crack and pull it open. It was shut tight, though. Somebody had noticed. I cursed under my breath, imagining the housekeeper walking past, feeling a draft, and pulling the window closed. I tried the doors, but they were locked too as I had suspected.

My next, less optimal option was entry via one of the second story windows. I crept to the edge of the loggia and looked up. The window I had seen earlier was still open, and there was a ledge below it. The room beyond the window was dark, and the window itself was above the dining room, which was also dark. *Go for it*, I decided. It was no time for second guessing myself.

I crept along the terrace, ducking below the windows of the library as I passed them. The sounds of indistinct conversation, the muffled tinkling of ice in a glass, and soft music playing wafted out, then I was past. Standing under a dining room window, I gazed up toward the open one and plotted my course. Both first and second floor windows had exterior sills, and there was an ornamental ledge at the level of the floor of the second story. I placed a foot on the sill, reached up, grasped the protruding bit that framed the top, and began climbing. It went about as I imagined until I was standing on the ledge and wrapping my hand around the top of the second story window to pull it open farther.

Suddenly, the stone crumbled under my right foot, and I nearly fell. Only my grip on the window itself saved me from plummeting to the terrace below. Luckily, the window was sturdy and held my weight. I heard bits of stone patter on the terrace and held still, frozen for several long moments. No one seemed to have heard the noise, though, so I pulled my body back toward the wall, lifted my right leg through the opening, and stepped as softly as I could into the room, pushing the curtain aside.

I crouched there for a moment, feeling sweat prickle my forehead and the backs of my hands. The near fall had raised my heart rate. Gradually, I became aware of a low, rattling breathing sound. I turned toward the sound and, as my eyes adjusted to the darkness, I made out a tall bed and a blanket-shrouded form, chest rising and falling rhythmically. I rose quietly and padded to the bedside. The sleeper was an old woman. Very old, judging by the fine network of wrinkles that creased her slack face. Antonetti's mother, I surmised. Gabrielle had told me she lived with him. I pulled the window back in, leaving it ajar a few inches as it had been. I didn't want her to get a chill. The room was large with soft carpets on the floor. I saw doors leading to a bathroom with a nightlight glowing, a shadowy closet, and a closed one that I guessed led out into a central hallway. The hinges creaked softly as I

opened the door a crack and peered out. It was, as I suspected, a hallway. There was a carpet runner down the
center and oil paintings, mounted antlers, and sconces
with dimly glowing bulbs lining the walls. To the right
were more doors, leading most likely to similar rooms.
To the left I saw the top of the staircase I had seen from
below, climbing up from the entry hall. Closing Antonetti's mother's door behind me, I walked softly down the
hallway then crouched down and peered over the edge of
the gallery, surveying the entry hall. It was currently
empty. The marble floor shone, reflecting the light of the
candles. To my right, where the railing ended, and the
hallway started again, was a pedestal holding a carved
stone head that looked early medieval—some ancient
king or duke whose name had been forgotten hundreds of
years ago. I moved around the pedestal and crouched in
the shadows on the other side of it. There was a small gap
there, through which I could still see down into the entry
hall.

I waited there for perhaps five minutes before I heard
a rattling sound, growing gradually louder. One of the
young women who had been working the party came into
the hall, pushing a cart laden with trays. The other woman followed close behind. They pushed the cart through
the front door and lifted it down the steps. They were
speaking softly to each other in French. I heard the sound
of a sliding door opening, the cart loading into the van,
doors closing, opening, closing. Then the engine started,
and the van drove off, gravel crunching under the tires.
After another couple of minutes, I saw the housekeeper.
She walked across from the direction of the kitchen,
heading toward the library. She seemed tired, her gait
heavy. A moment later, she reappeared with Antonetti.

"*Bonne nuit. Aller au lit,*" he said, waving her up the
stairs. She bowed her head, turned, and headed up. Hop-

ing she wouldn't come down the hall toward my hiding place, I readied myself to make a break down the stairs and out the front door, which still stood open, if she did. She turned the other direction, though, walked to the end of the hall, and opened a door that revealed a worn, bare wooden staircase leading upward. She pulled the door softly closed behind her as she mounted the first step. My guess about the room upstairs with the lighted window must have been correct.

Now I needed to wait some more and see what would happen. It didn't take long, maybe another five minutes. Antonetti and company all entered the hall, headed in the direction of the kitchen with the master of the house in the lead.

"*Vous avez une nouvelle peinture?*" Elizabeth said, following.

"*Oui...*" answered Antonetti, glancing back, the rest of his reply lost as they passed into the sitting room off the hall. My French was just good enough to understand that they might be headed off to see a new painting in Antonetti's collection. I had to follow.

Stealthily, I descended the stairs and crept to the door of the sitting room. The last of them, the man from the box at the ballet, was just passing through the door to the hallway leading toward the kitchen. I waited until he was through then followed across the sitting room. At the door, I paused, opened it a crack, and watched them move down the hall. They turned and all filed into the pantry. I heard Antonetti speaking to them but couldn't understand. I crept down the hall and ducked low, peering around the edge of the doorjamb. Antonetti was just turning to the door I had seen earlier. All his guests were gathered to his left, and he positioned himself between them and the keypad. From where I crouched, though, I could see it clearly. I watched him enter a five-digit code, memorizing it as he did, then ducked back, the numbers running through my head: two, four, seven, nine, nine. Crouched down, back to the wall, I heard him turn the handle, pull the door open. Hushed, the guests filed though, and the door closed behind them.

My luck was uncanny this night. I had what I needed now. Quickly, I crossed the hall and passed through the opposite door into the dining room. Beside the door to the left was an ornate buffet, moonlight from the windows gleaming on the polished wood. I lay down under it, the door open a crack so I could see back into the pantry. I had more waiting to do now. How long would Antonetti spend showing his guests the painting? Maybe twenty or thirty minutes? I would wait until they came back out then wait some more to make sure Antonetti was retired for the night before I made my move.

Time passed, and my mind wandered. The waiting seemed interminable. The shadows and silence felt like a weight on my chest. Through the dining room windows, I could see the silhouette of the tree line against the sky. Above that, stars. I watched them, imagining that I could see them tracing paths across the sky as the earth spun. Somewhere, in another room close by, a clock was ticking off the seconds. I listened to the dull thock, thock, thock until suddenly the clock began striking the hour with a low, echoing bong, bong. I counted, Eleven o'clock.

My watch agreed. I had been waiting now for twenty-seven minutes. Finally, a couple of minutes later, I heard the door in the pantry open and the sound of voices. The door closed and the lock engaged with a beep. The group walked into the hall and away, footsteps and the low murmur of conversation receding as they passed into the sitting room. I was fairly certain I would hear the sound of cars starting up and driving off very soon. My guess was correct. Antonetti had shown off his new treasure and now the guests, after oohing and aahing with the proper reverence, were dismissed. A dull thunk reverberated through the floorboards. I guessed it was the front door closing. Now I needed to wait some more, to make sure Antonetti was retired for the evening, in his chambers and, hopefully, asleep. I decided an hour would be safe and set a silent alarm on my watch. Propping my back against the wall, I leaned my head back and closed my eyes. I would spend the hour meditating and be ready when the time came.

An hour later, my watch began to vibrate, and I started. I had actually drifted off into a fitful doze. I pressed the button to turn off the alarm and looked around. Same dining room, same stars outside. I stood and stretched. Time to go get that painting.

I tiptoed to the double pocket doors that separated the dining room from the library and slid one open enough to peek through. The room was dark, quiet, and devoid of life. The fire was out. Back across the dining room, I opened the door into the hallway and walked across, into the pantry. Quickly, I entered the code, turned the handle, and pulled the door open. It was heavy and opened on precision hinges without a sound. Inside was a small landing with walls and floor of rough-hewn stone blocks.

A dim light set in the ceiling glowed yellow. To the right, steps led down. I entered and pulled the door closed behind me, leaving it open just a crack. I didn't want to get stuck in that dungeon. Carefully, I crept down the stairs, descending perhaps twenty feet before I reached the bottom. I expected a damp, musty basement smell but there was none. The atmosphere was climate controlled, cool but not cold, neither damp nor dry. At the bottom of the stairs was a ninety degree turn to the right and an arch

roofed hallway leading back under the house. There were
sconces in recessed niches, retrofitted with incandescent
bulbs, casting a murky light. A few paces and I came to a
heavy wooden door on the left side. I pushed and it
swung inward, revealing a barrel vaulted room full of
wine bottles on their sides in specially built racks, a narrow aisle down the center. There were no other entrances
or exits, so I pulled the door closed and continued down
the hallway. Ahead, I saw a blank wall and, just before it,
another door on the right. This door was modern but carefully crafted to look like the other one. It had a heavy-
duty bolt lock and also a locking knob set. When I
grasped the knob and turned, though, the door swung
open easily. Antonetti had not locked it.

Inside was another barrel vaulted cellar but much
larger than the first. It was about twenty feet wide and
fifty feet deep. Two tracks hung from the ceiling with
lamps bolted to them, trained on the stone walls which
had been painted stark white. In each pool of light, a
painting hung. There were a couple focused toward the
center of the space too where sculptural pieces rested on
pedestals. I entered, turned to the left and began making
my way down the gallery. The first piece I came to took
me a moment to place, but then it hit me: Cortege aux
Environs de Florence by Degas. It was one of the pieces
stolen from the Isabella Stewart Gardner Museum in
1990. The biggest heist in history. Five Hundred million
dollars' worth of art stolen.

I continued down the row, recognizing a Gauguin, a
Matisse, a Pollack, a Warhol. The collection was
astounding. I was used to seeing rare, expensive art hanging in fancy houses but not like this. It was more like a
private museum. I turned to the center of the room then to
look at one of the sculptures. It was a statue fragment
about fifteen inches tall, a male torso elegantly carved out

of solid alabaster, bearded, with arms held close to the body and staring forward with a solemn expression. I knew it immediately. I had paid attention to the news during the looting of the National Museum of Iraq. This was one of the better-known pieces—an ancient King of Uruk. It was about five thousand years old—an early work indeed.

I tore myself away from the King of Uruk and walked toward the back of the room where there was a large wooden table and several locking flat file cabinets. As I approached the table, I could see that there was something laid out there. From ten feet away I knew what it was. Any doubts I had harbored were erased. I closed the distance and stood staring down at Valerie's Heidrich. The corners were weighted down with pyramid shaped crystal paperweights. There was a border of raw canvas, creased where it had been wrapped around the stretcher bars. Inside that, Heidrich's composition—deceptively simple. The entire picture plane covered by a deep wash of crimson but with a dark, ghostly framework showing through suggesting girders, ground, pipe works, ruins. The painting looked like it had handled being rolled up and transported without damage. I bent closer to look at it, peering at the tiny cracks in the oil paint. Just then, though, I sensed something. A draft? A sound?

I didn't know what it was, but I wheeled around and there, half way across the room stood Antonetti, a look of astonishment growing over his features. We stood staring at each other for several heartbeats, then, all at once, he turned and ran. I followed immediately. He was wearing slippers, pajamas, and a robe of dark silk that billowed out behind him. He was faster than I expected, through the door by the time I was halfway across the room. The door slammed shut. Just as I reached it, grasped the handle, and turned, I heard a thunk of the bolt lock engaging.

He had locked it from the other side with a key. I threw my shoulder against the door, but it was like trying to knock down an ancient oak tree. There was no thumb turn on my side of the door. It could only be opened with a key from the outside. I stepped back and cursed, rubbing my shoulder, suddenly terrified. I was in deep trouble.

CHAPTER 12

December 19:

I stepped forward and considered the door, running my fingers over the top hinge which was cold and smooth to the touch. It was a fixed pin hinge—impossible to remove with the door closed. I quickly walked a circuit of the room, observing everything. There was no other way out. Looking up, I saw a couple of vents—probably for the temperature and humidity control system—but they were fifteen feet above the floor at the apex of the barrel vault and didn't look big enough to crawl through anyway. My next thought was holding a painting hostage. I could take one off the wall, threaten to slash it if Antonetti didn't let me walk out. That got me thinking about who he would bring with him when he came back. Probably his hired man. Or would he call the police? No—very little chance of that.

He wouldn't want any police in his private gallery. Maybe he wouldn't come back himself at all. He might just send some hired goons to collect me. What would happen then? A beating? Torture? Or would they just kill me? I didn't like that line of thought, so I turned back to my options. I could break all the lights. Maybe if the room was dark, I could slip out and have a chance of outrunning them. I had a knife—a wickedly sharp four-inch blade on my multi tool. I had never attacked anyone with a weapon, but I knew I could do it if I had to. I sat down beneath the Degas and leaned back, the stone cold against my spine.

I dwelled on my situation for a few more minutes but nothing else came to me. My options were (a) take a painting hostage and hope Antonetti came back and was willing to let me go to save it or (b) darken all the lights and hope I could slip out and have a running chance. I had always been a fast runner and knew I could run for many miles at a good pace. The knife would increase my chances of getting past whoever came to get me. I weighed the options, and my gut said, *Go with darkness.* I didn't know Antonetti, but my intuition told me he would rather lose a work of art than let a thief go.

I got up and looked at the nearest light. It was about ten feet above the floor. I could reach it by using one of the pedestals. How long did I have, though? Antonetti would not be in a hurry but neither would he wait all night. He wouldn't want to leave me alone with all his treasures for too long. I decided I probably had time, though.

The second pedestal held a large bronze urn that looked Chinese and probably weighed a ton. The ancient King of Uruk looked lighter so, very carefully, I lifted him off his pedestal and placed him on the table beside the Heidrich painting. I hesitated then because I realized that I needed to try to take the painting with me if I was going to make a break for it. The plastic tube the name-less thief had used and handed off to Booth and in which Legere had then transported the stolen work half way across the earth was leaned up in the V formed by the wall and one of the rear table legs. I could see the thief in my mind's eye meticulously disassembling the frame, tossing the pieces under the bed, rolling the painting up and stowing it in the tube—an act that set off a long chain of dominoes leading me to this moment. No time to ponder fate—I quickly removed the paperweights, rolled the canvas, slid it into the tube, and screwed the cap on. Now I could focus on the lights. The pedestal was a hollow wooden box, painted white. I moved it from spot to spot, unscrewing each light bulb enough to cut the current to it then moving on. I watched the light go out on each painting as I did so.

The pieces were all by famous artists. All early works. None of them painted before about 1850. The Warhol was the most recent. I left the Degas for last, watched it fade away to black, then hopped down off the pedestal and, using the light from my watch face, dragged the pedestal over to a position against the wall and about four feet to the right of the door. I would hide behind the pedestal, wait until whoever came was inside the room, probably shining a flashlight back and forth, then run for the door. I had no idea how long I would have to wait, but I needed to be ready so I put my backpack on and crouched down, back to the wall and knife in my hand.

It wasn't a short wait but not terribly long either. About an hour after Antonetti had caught me in the room, I heard what I thought was movement in the hallway outside. A scrape of metal against the door. The lock turned, and the door opened a few inches. Someone cursed. A man's voice. Deep. I couldn't understand the words, but it was clearly a curse. The door slammed shut, and the lock turned again. There was some coming and going in the hall and, five minutes later the door opened again. This time, a flashlight beam cut through the darkness. I calmed myself, took a deep breath, and held as still as possible. The man entered the room, shining the light back and forth, pointing it into the far corners. He took a step, another, his work boots heavy on the stone floor. One more step and it seemed like he was far enough away from the open door. I pushed the pedestal out away from the wall, knocking it over and darting from behind it toward the doorway.

The man turned toward the sound, flashlight on the pedestal, then toward me as he caught my movement in the corner of his eye. I was out the door and turning down the hallway when I suddenly ran into what felt like a mountain. The collision was hard enough to momentarily daze me. Almost immediately the mountain wrapped me up and fell on me, grasping my wrist and squeezing until the knife fell from my hand. After a moment, my head began to clea,r and I realized that the mountain was another man who had me pinned face down, my left arm behind my back and my right cheek pressed painfully against the stone. He called in Corsican to his buddy, who came and grabbed my other arm, yanked it behind my back, and tied my wrists together tightly with cord or rope. They both patted me down, checking all my pockets, then each grabbed an arm and lifted me to my feet. I was still wearing my backpack.

One of the men tried to take it off me, realized that it wasn't possible with my wrists tied and used my own knife to cut the straps. He threw the backpack into the gallery room, placed the painting in its tube just inside, then pulled the door shut. I got a good look at him while he was doing this. It was Antonetti's man. I had a sick feeling I knew, based on the wrestling move, who the other guy was but he was standing behind me, holding my upper arm in an iron grip. Neither of them seemed like they wanted to talk, and I didn't feel any compulsion either.

They led me down the hall and up the stairs, each holding an arm as before. We paused in the pantry and

Legere stepped out from behind me to close the door. I had known it was him, but it still made me feel a little sick to my stomach. There was something of the psychopath about his face—especially in the harsh overhead light of the pantry. Dead eyes. Lack of affect. He was dressed in black jeans and a gray T-shirt. Antonetti must have called him, and he must have driven out at once.

Hands on my arms again, guiding me, they led me down the hall, through the sitting room, out into the entry hall. The hall was dark. The moon must have set by then. The only illumination was pale starlight filtering in through the high windows. Antonetti was nowhere to be seen. He was probably in his bed asleep, confident that his hired men would take care of this issue. Legere opened the front door, and the other man pushed me through.

"*Marches*," he said, pointing toward the carriage house. I started walking. The night air was cool. I felt my brain calm and begin to work again. I was scared, of course, but I pushed the fear back with a fierce effort and forced myself to think. Gabrielle had warned me. I knew who Antonetti was. I had to expect the worst. I wasn't going to go down without a fight, but I needed a bit more luck. Some small opportunity. I didn't know what it would be, but I did know I needed to keep my eyes open and my brain alert.

"*Arettes*," Legere said.

I stopped about ten feet from the carriage house. Legere held my arms while the other man stepped forward, fumbling in his pocket. He was big and slow—one of those men who look like they were born to plow fields and scythe wheat. I didn't have any worry about being able to outrun him. I was pretty sure I could outrun Legere, too. If it came to any kind of strength contest, though, I would lose.

The workman found his keys and unlocked the set of big double doors we had stopped at. He pulled them open with a creaking of old hinges. It was dark inside but I could see, gleaming in the starlight, the unmistakable double Rs of the Rolls Royce logo on the grill of the car and the hood ornament standing above, wings or billows of fabric receding into the shadows. The man stepped inside, slid into the car, and started it up with a dull roar. Legere pulled me aside, and the car eased out of the carriage house, coming to a stop just after passing the spot where we stood. I don't know anything about cars, but I could tell it was vintage, maybe from the seventies. It was fussy looking but beautiful in its own way. There was a loud click, and the trunk popped open. Legere gave me a shove.

"*Montes*," he said.

I turned my head. He was standing now about five feet from me and held a small handgun in his right hand. He gestured to the open trunk with an impatient jab of the gun barrel. I stood looking at him for a moment then turned and tumbled myself awkwardly into the trunk. *No point in resisting right now*, I thought, *my opportunity has not presented itself yet*. The interior of the trunk was massive. They could have fit five of me in there. I turned on my back and almost immediately the lid slammed down, cutting out all light. I heard the passenger door open and close and the car started moving, slowly rolling down the gravel drive.

When I was a kid, around age four, I was taken away from my mother and placed with a foster family. I don't really know why. I could find out but I hadn't ever bothered. I hadn't seen her since, and I didn't really remember much about her. The people I was placed with had a farm. They didn't have any kids of their own. I was one of a rotating cast of foster children. There were normally three or four of us, and we did a lot of work on the farm. It was hard work. There was one other kid, Malena. who came to live there a couple of years after me who was still living there when I left. We were pretty good friends. I guessed she was the closest thing to a sibling I had, but I lost touch with her.

Our foster parents were big, quiet, potato-like people. They fed us, clothed us, sent us to a school run by their obscure religious sect, and took us to church every Sunday. Aside from that, they didn't do much parenting. There was a bedroom for the boys and a bedroom for the girls. I always had one or two roommates. Aside from me, boys didn't last long. Like I said, the work was hard, and the other boys who came to live there usually didn't have any experience being supervised and having to work. They also usually had emotional and mental issues. There was one place in the house where I could be alone. It was a hall closet on the second floor where the bedrooms were. Sometimes I would slip into that closet and close the door. It was dark and quiet there and smelled like old wood and mothballs. I would never stay in there for more than about five minutes for fear of being missed and getting in trouble, but when I thought back on my childhood it seemed like those five-minute escapes, every few days, might have been a large part of what kept me sane.

The darkness and warmth and smell of the Rolls Royce trunk somehow brought me back to that closet. I hadn't thought about it for a long time, but now it came back and I lay there, feeling the car bump along, accelerate, slow down, thinking about that closet and my childhood in general. I wondered what ever happened to Malena? It was crazy. There were a hundred other things I should have been thinking about instead: Where were they taking me? What was going to happen? What would

Valerie do if she never heard from me again? What about Gabrielle? Somehow, in that moment, it didn't seem important, though. I knew I would act when my opportunity arose, and I was confident that it would.

After a while, the sound of the wheels on the ground shifted, and it seemed we were on a dirt road. We traveled along slowly for about ten minutes then slowed, reversed, backed up a few feet, and came to a halt. I heard the two men exchange a few words then both doors opened and closed with the heavy, solid sound of precision engineering. I had to admit it was a nice car.

A key slid into the lock and the trunk opened silently a few inches. I saw a hand raise it farther then disappear as the owner stepped back. Legere came into view, rolled me onto my side with one hand, and cut the cord binding my wrists with the other. I felt the cool metal of the knife against my wrist and flinched before I realized what he was doing. Why free me? Maybe he didn't want to shoot a man with his hands tied.

I sat up and looked out. The workman was standing back and off to my right about ten feet away. Legere was closer, also to my right, a few feet from the car. A dim light shone on him and his shadow stretched back in the pool of light which lay across the dirt and branches and duff of a forest clearing. It looked like one of them had placed a flashlight on the roof of the car to provide some light for my execution. Legere held the gun in his hand and the light glinted on the round, precision-milled opening at the end of the barrel. He made a strange tic-like motion with his head, which I gathered meant that he wanted me to climb out.

He seemed on edge, amped up and impatient. I decided to take it slow and see if I could get him to come closer. My brain was working, and a desperate plan was coming together in my head. I lifted one leg over and placed my foot on the bumper, feigning awkwardness. I lifted my other leg, pretended to slip and fall, just catching myself with my hands and now laying across the rear of the car, half in and half out of the trunk. I looked up at Legere helplessly and he stepped forward, his face an angry mask, grabbing my shoulder and pulling me up. This was my moment. A week before, I had been in Krav class practicing wrist manipulations and disarming techniques over and over for an hour. Now, I suppressed my conscious mind and let my muscle memory handle things. As soon as both my feet hit the ground, I moved with all the speed I could muster. He was holding the gun high, his right arm raised from bending sideways to pull me out with his left. I clapped both my hands over his gun hand and bent his wrist upward so that the gun pointed toward the night sky. Simultaneously, I raised a knee and kicked him in the crotch with a low, powerful blow.

He bent forward involuntarily, the gun came free in my hands, and I swiveled it as I brought it down and drove it barrel first into his solar plexus. As Legere fell to the ground, I jumped back but he caught me with a flailing kick to my calf. I toppled, off balance, and rolled out of the way just in time to avoid the workman who lunged forward, grasping with his arms. I continued rolling through the damp leaves and dirt then sprang to my feet, brought the gun up, and fired into the air. Both men froze, and I lowered the barrel, training it on them. The workman rose and raised his hands, eyeing me with surprise that slowly morphed into a malevolent glare. Time seemed slow, and everything seemed to be happening in a cone of eerie silence, like a weird ritual.

Legere didn't stay down for long. After only a few seconds, he got up on one knee, then raised himself to his feet.

"I'm not much of a gun person," I said to Legere,

"but I know how to aim, and I know how to fire. I need to you to follow my instructions exactly. I don't want to kill you, but if you approach me, I will shoot. Understand?"

He nodded slowly, eyeing me. "Who are you?" he asked.

"No questions. Both of you side by side and strip down. Throw your clothes there." I pointed to a spot in front of them.

The workman looked at Legere, who nodded and said a few words in Corsican. I didn't want to find out about any hidden weapons the hard way, and I didn't want to try to pat them down either. I was sure Legere's brain was working just as mine had been when our positions were reversed, looking for an opportunity. They both stripped down to their underwear. Legere was wearing briefs and the workman wore boxers. I decided it was unlikely they were hiding anything in their underwear so I told them to stop.

"Now, climb into the trunk. You first," I said to Legere. He climbed in and the workman followed. The car keys were still in the lock. I stepped up, slammed the lid down, and locked it.

As soon as the trunk was closed, I took a step back, took a deep breath, and realized my entire body had been tensed up, ready for split-section action. I gathered their clothing and went through the pockets, reclaiming my multitool. What now? As soon as I asked myself the question, I knew the answer. I was going to go back and get the goddamned painting. I hadn't thought to ask Legere the way back to the house. No matter—it couldn't be far. I would find it.

CHAPTER 13

I put the gun in my pocket then walked around to the driver's side of the car. The flashlight on the roof was still casting a pool of light in the clearing. I took a moment to look over the piece of ground where I might easily be lying dead now, if not for a bit of luck, then reached up and thumbed the button to turn the light off. My quest to retrieve Valerie's stolen painting had suddenly taken on a different character.

I turned and opened the car door, tossing the flashlight onto the passenger seat as I climbed in. It was a very strange moment. I was sitting behind the wheel of a Rolls Royce with two people who wanted to kill me locked in the trunk. Sometimes life's trajectory looped and cycled, but sometimes it also brought us into situations so far outside our normal reality that we just had to keep moving by willpower alone, navigating the surreal.

I started the car. I was glad to see it had an automatic transmission. It had been a while since I'd driven a manual. I turned on the headlights, shifted to drive, and eased off the brake. The car began rumbling solidly down the dirt road. I saw the bright eyes of some creature frozen for a moment up ahead then disappearing quickly into the underbrush, moths dancing in the headlight beams, low branches hanging down. I drove slowly. After about ten minutes, I came to a paved road. I felt like we had gone uphill on the way to the clearing so I turned right and headed downward at a gentle grade.

After another ten minutes or so, I saw the gate to Antonetti's drive coming up on the right. We hadn't gone far. I shut off the lights, slowed, and pulled to the shoulder. If Antonetti was waiting up for the duo to return and report, I didn't want him to see me pull up in the Rolls. I killed the engine and got out, taking the keys and flashlight with me. It was a cool evening but the two men in the trunk would be fine. Maybe a little chilled but not dangerously. I locked the car and paused for a moment, standing by the rear door on the driver side. It felt weird to leave them there but, at that moment, something caught my eye inside the car. I could just make out the ghostly form of a shovel laid across the back seat. Now I had no doubt that they had planned to kill me. The sight made me shudder. Maybe that was why Legere freed my hands. They might have been planning on making me dig the grave. I steeled myself and headed back down the road on foot, backtracking, not giving the two killers another thought.

I walked until I gauged I was close to the position of the chateau then turned and hopped over the ditch that separated the road from the copse of trees just on the other side. The trees were tall and sparse, and the ground was level. It didn't take me long before I came to the edge of the copse and saw the backside of the carriage house fifteen feet away, looming up black against the slightly brighter sky. I didn't like the idea of going back into the house empty handed so I crept around the carriage house on the side facing away from the chateau and peeked around the corner.

The double doors were still open. It was dark out and I was wearing black so I took a chance and darted around the corner and through the doors. Once inside, I turned on the flashlight at its lowest setting and set about inspecting the place. The interior was tidy and smelled of oil, wood, and fertilizer. The other two parking spaces were occupied by a boxy Mercedes SUV and a sleek Porsche two seater. At the back of the building was a long workbench and wooden cabinets holding tools and landscaping supplies.

I combed through the tools quickly, pocketing a few things I might need—screwdriver, tape, pliers. On a shelf in one of the cabinets, I found a collection of bottles— motor oil, paint thinner, glue, epoxy, various lubricants. Among the bottles, one caught my eye. It was something I hadn't seen for a long time but remembered well: ether. The bottle was brown glass with a white label. There had always been some around the farm when I was a kid. It was useful for getting engines started when it was cold out and also worked as a very effective solvent. Seeing it triggered a memory and gave me an idea. I took the bottle and a rag I found nearby and put them both in one of my cargo pockets.

Equipped now as well as possible under the circumstances, I rounded the Mercedes, passed a staircase heading up to the second floor where the workman's quarters presumably were, and found a door leading to the outside. It let out into a cobbled pathway running between the carriage house and the stable. Even if it wasn't locked, I couldn't very well walk in through the front door of the house. My only option was to go back around and climb in the second story window again. I didn't really want to do it but couldn't think of a better plan, so I crept around the back of the stable where I stumbled on a stone in the tall grass and almost sprained my ankle. An injury was the last thing I needed right then, so I continued with caution. I passed a window and heard a horse

snort in its sleep. The sound seemed incredibly loud, echoing through the dark and quiet stable. My footsteps in
the grass seemed loud, too, but soon I was around the
building, out of the grass, and working my way along the
back wall of the house. As I passed the kitchen windows,
I looked up and saw Antonetti's mother's window still
open as I had left it. The two windows to the left of hers
were lit. It had to be Antonetti's master suite. It made
sense for it to be next to his mother's room. I wondered if
he was still awake, sitting up. I imagined he would be. I
needed to deal with him. I wasn't getting locked in the
dungeon again. My luck definitely would not be as good
the second time.

Having made the climb before, I didn't need to scope
it out. I knew I needed to be very quiet, though, since Antonetti's window was nearby. Out of habit, I started the
timer on my watch then began climbing. The stone was
cool and damp with dew under my fingers. I made my
way swiftly but cautiously up to the ledge and stopped for
a moment, steadying myself with a hand on the open
window.

It occurred to me that it might be a good idea to peek
in Antonetti's window and see where he was and what he
was doing. It didn't seem like a big risk. A person in a lit
room at night didn't see much through a window unless
they walked right up to it and peered out. I could take a
quick peek. Mindful of the crumbling stone of the ledge, I
slid my feet along as silently as possible until I was just
to the right of the next window over. Then, crouching
down and holding onto the exterior sill, I leaned over and
looked in through a gap in the curtains. It was a small sitting room with a desk against the far wall, sofa, and
bookshelf. The floor was wood with a carpet in the center
and the walls were hung with large medieval tapestries.
Antonetti was seated at the desk, his back to me, bent

over as if writing but I could see his shoulders rising and falling rhythmically. I watched him for about twenty seconds until I was sure he was asleep, slumped over the desk. He must have sat up, waiting, but succumbed to sleep. He was still wearing the robe and pajamas I had seen when he caught me in the gallery.

I made my way back along the ledge to the mother's window and climbed in, trying to be as silent as possible this time. She had not moved since I visited her room before. Her chest still rose and fell as she took long, rattling breaths. I pulled the window back in, leaving it open a crack as I had before, and exited. Back in the hallway, I made my way quickly to Antonetti's door and tried the doorknob. It was not locked. Now, what to do?

I had the ether in my pocket still. One of my roommates at the farm had been a boy named Steven, a couple of years older than me. He was tall and very skinny with a wry smile and a lazy, lethargic bearing. One day, I had gone into the workshop, which was built off the side of the barn, and found him slumped on the floor, a rag in one hand and a bottle of ether in the other. I still remembered his face, illuminated by a pale beam of winter sunlight from the window, mouth curled up into a peaceful smile. Later, I asked him about it, and he told me—just a few drops on a rag, breath in the fumes and fade away into a blissful sleep. He didn't last long at the farm.

Now, remembering Steven's calm, quiet voice as he told me about his experiments with ether, I took the bottle and rag out of my pocket, dribbled a bit on the rag, and, averting my face from the fumes while carrying it at arm's length, I turned the knob and entered Antonetti's sitting room. He hadn't moved. I tiptoed over to the desk. His head was laid down on his crossed arms and turned to the right. In one hand, he gripped a rocks glass with a gold rim and a small amount of some golden liquor just covering the bottom. I placed the rag on the desk, close to his nose, and drew back. His shoulders kept rising and falling but the breaths came slower, and his body seemed to relax. There was a low table by the door which held a squat whiskey bottle and a tray of glasses like the one in Antonetti's hand. I looked more closely. It was Hibiki twenty-one year. I poured myself half a finger and sipped it while I waited. The ultra-smooth liquor slid down my throat, coating it with a glowing warmth. After a couple more minutes, I stepped forward and shook him by the shoulder. Nothing. I shook him more violently. Still nothing. I set my glass down, took his out of his hand, then pulled him up to a sitting position, and tipped him sideways. He was heavy, but I managed to let him down fairly softly on the floor.

I moved the chair away and straightened his body, placing his arms at his sides. Quickly then, I went through a half open door into his bedroom, straight to his bed where I tore off the heavy, brocade duvet and grabbed the top sheet, wadding it up. I carried it through another door that I assumed led to a bathroom. I was right. It was a luxurious room with plenty of marble and gold fixtures, but I didn't have time to gawk. I put the top sheet in the tub and quickly soaked it with warm water, then wrung it out, so it was damp but not dripping profusely. I took the sheet back into the sitting room, laid it out on the floor, then rolled Antonetti up in it like a mummy with only his head poking out the top. I rolled it as tight as I could. I had read about this trick somewhere, but I couldn't remember where.

While wet, the sheet would be impossible to break out of. As it dried, it would become easier until, finally, he would be able to wriggle free. I figured I had a couple of hours, minimum, but I would only need twenty minutes. I found a sock in his bedroom, shoved it into his mouth, then placed a piece of duct tape from a roll I had lifted in the garage over his lips. That would, hopefully, keep him quiet once he woke. I stood and stared down at him. He didn't look peaceful the way Steven had. Not much I could do about that.

I glanced at my watch—sixteen minutes gone since I climbed up the wall outside. I needed to get the painting and get out. Before I left, I took a last sip of my whiskey and placed the keys to the Rolls and the gun on the desk. I was glad to have the gun out of my pocket.

By now, I was pretty familiar with the layout of the house. I made it downstairs, through the entry hall, sitting room, and into the hallway leading down to the kitchen without incident. In the pantry, I entered the code on the keypad once again, pulled the door open, and entered Antonetti's secret world for the second time. There was a feeling of timelessness and an eerie silence down in that subterranean crypt, broken only by the soft sound of my footsteps. I hurried, wanting to get out fast. The door to the gallery was unlocked still. Antonetti probably did not make a habit of locking it, trusting instead to the door at the top of the stairs. I turned the knob and opened the door.

Two of the lights were on—both of them at the rear of the gallery. Antonetti must have come back down while I was away with his goons. One of the lights shone down on the table, and the Heidrich painting had been laid back out, paperweights holding the corners, just like it had been. The ancient King of Uruk had also been put back on his pedestal, and the pedestal moved to its proper place. I walked briskly to the far end of the gallery and removed the paperweights. Immediately, the corners of the canvas began to curl up.

As I stood looking down at the painting, an odd feeling crept over me that something was off or out of place.

It was like walking into a friend's house and knowing that something is different but not being sure what it is. Was the couch over there before? Was that a new lamp? I stared at the painting for a moment longer then shrugged my shoulders and began carefully rolling it. As I rolled it I watched the raw canvas curl up under my fingers. It was high quality stuff—soft and tightly woven. When I was almost done, though, something struck me, and I stopped abruptly.

I hadn't seen a signature on the back. Valerie had told me very clearly that the painting was signed on the back. I unrolled it and examined the rear. No mark broke the plain of raw canvas. What the hell was going on? I turned it over again and looked hard at the brushwork, the lines, the washes. My feeling of something being off did not go away. It was very well done, but the longer I looked at it, the more my sense of unease grew. I had spent a fair amount of time looking at Heidrich's paintings recently, and I had seen the one in Valerie's bedroom a hundred times, even if I hadn't paid much attention to it. I wouldn't have been able to explain it verbally, but I had a gut feeling: It was a fake. I looked at the back again—still no signature.

That asshole Booth had double-crossed Legere. Something else struck me at that moment. The night of the Heidrich opening at the SFMOMA I had been talking to Roberto. He told me that his opinion of Heidrich had changed, that he had been studying Heidrich's technique, even painting some studies. Maybe it was a coincidence, or maybe he painted more than a few studies. Maybe he made a copy of Valerie's painting for Booth. I knew he had been stressed about money.

He would have assumed the painting was unsigned since Heidrich was famous for that. Shit. It all came together. I couldn't very well blame him—I had done a similar job once. He wouldn't have known the painting belonged to Valerie. So, the painting I held in my hands was a fake. What to do now? Where was the real one? It must be back in San Francisco. Booth must have it. He would probably unload it as soon as possible to whatever buyer he could find who could be trusted to stay quiet. It was a risky game Booth was playing. I knew well what kind of retribution Antonetti would seek if he found out he had been duped.

Enough—I could think through the details later. I needed to decide what to do. Take the painting? It could be useful—I might be able to swap it out for the real one without anyone noticing. Or leave it? Did I want to sign Booth's death warrant? If I left it and Antonetti discovered the double cross, I was sure Booth would not live long. Antonetti might go after Booth either way. He might assume Booth had bragged to someone about selling the piece and who the buyer was. How else would a thief know about the painting? That was Booth's problem, though, and I didn't want to have to take it through customs if I didn't have to. I would leave it. I rolled it back out, weighted down the corners, and turned to go.

Crouching there on his pedestal, the King of Uruk stared at me balefully. "What about me?" he seemed to be saying.

"What about you?" I said to the carved face, my voice echoing through the gallery. "You deserve to be repatriated, don't you?"

My backpack was in the corner near the door. The straps had been cut, but I could still use it. I took off my hoodie and wrapped the King of Uruk in it carefully before placing him in the open backpack and zipping it up. Antonetti would be plenty confused when he finally got free and found the Heidrich and all of his other paintings untouched but the ancient statue gone. The thought made me smile.

It was time to get the hell out of that house. I went straight out through the front door, placed the dangling backpack straps over my shoulders and, holding them tightly to keep it from falling off my back, set off jogging toward the tree line, the trail, and my rental car.

At the crest of the hill where I had picnicked with Gabrielle, I stopped and looked back. The house seemed to have shrunken, become part of the darkness, like an empty can tossed in the woods. I could just make out the roof line, the outbuildings, the circular drive. I turned and continued on, the king bouncing heavily against my lower back with every stride, hoping I wouldn't trip over a branch and break my neck.

CHAPTER 14

I had a lot to think about on the drive back into Nice. My trip had turned into a fool's errand that almost got me killed. Furthermore, I had lost valuable time. If Booth still had the Heidrich, I needed to get back to San Francisco as soon as possible and start figuring things out. I was going to get it back, I knew that much. How I was going to do it would be a mystery to unravel.

It was early morning when I arrived back to my hotel. There was a night bellman in the lobby staring at his phone and trying not to nod off. I gave him my car keys and went up to my room. I was exhausted, but I needed to do two things before I fell asleep. Sitting on the edge of the bed with my laptop, I composed an email to Ashna:

> Hi Ashna,
> I know I already owe you all kinds of explanations, and I promise to tell you everything as soon as I get back to SF. Right now, though, I need another favor. I need to get access to Booth's email and also any saved footage from the security cameras in his house. Is that possible?
> Thanks. Talk to you soon.
> Justin

I hit send and turned my attention to finding a flight

back to San Francisco. There happened to be a direct flight out of Milan the morning of the twentieth. I could get a few hours of sleep, drive back to Milan and return the car, stay over, and fly out early in the a.m. I booked it. Not first class this time. Just a regular seat. I would probably survive. With that business done, I remembered one more thing I needed to do. I pulled up my email again and wrote a quick note to Gabrielle, thanking her for her help and letting her know I was headed back to Milan in a few hours.

Now, all business done for the moment, I could lay back and rest. I was exhausted, but still, it took me a while to fall asleep. I kept rewinding and dwelling on the scene in the clearing. It had been very close. I could easily have been laying in a shallow grave among the trees rather than a hotel bed. I vowed to not get myself into that kind of situation again. Finally, I drifted off, but my sleep was restive, full of dreams where I found myself lost in a dark wood, pursued by unseen predators.

ꝋꝋꝋ

At eight a.m., the strident beeping of my alarm woke me with a start. I turned it off and sat up, rubbing my eyes. As the haze in my brain cleared, my thoughts drifted to Antonetti and Legere and the workman. I wondered what kind of scenes had unfolded at the chateau. I wasn't worried about them tracking me down. I had checked into the hotel under my real name, not Dustin Cruz which was the name I had given to Antonetti. Gabrielle had assured me that Antonetti would stay away from her, fearing her father's retribution. Even if he did contact her, she would merely say I was an acquaintance, an American she didn't know well, and that I had disappeared without telling her where I was going.

Whatever happened at the chateau, I was sure it wouldn't be good for Legere or the workman. Antonetti would not be pleased with their failure. There was no way for me to know or find out what had happened, so I put it aside and rose from the bed, heading for the shower.

After my shower, I dressed and grabbed my backpack to start packing. As soon as I lifted it though I remembered—the King of Uruk and the cut straps. I needed a new backpack and something to put the statue in. I called down to the concierge, who mercifully spoke strongly accented but serviceable English, and arranged to have a box and some packing material sent up to my room. When I asked where to find a backpack, he told me there was a luggage shop close by and offered to send the bellman to purchase one for me which I could pay for when I checked out. While I waited, I opened my email on my phone and saw several new messages—one was from Ashna, and one was from Gabrielle. Ashna's simply said: *Working on it. Details soon.* I turned to Gabrielle's reply:

Justin,
I'm spending the weekend at my house outside the city. Please stop by on your way out of town. It's just off A8 near Mont Agel. I would like to hear the details.
Gabrielle

The address of the house followed with some directions. I considered for a moment. In reality, I was not in a hurry. The drive to Milan would only take four hours and I wasn't flying out until the following morning. Furthermore, I did owe her the details. I wrote back, letting her know I would be there around ten a.m.

While I waited, I scrolled through a few more emails,

deleting spam, and giving quick replies to some less important ones. Soon, I heard a knock and went to open the
door. A young man in a valet uniform stood there with a
brand-new backpack in one hand and a cardboard box
full of bubble wrap in the other. I took the items, gave
him a good tip, and let him know I would be down to
check out in ten minutes. My old backpack went into the
garbage can, and I packed my things in the new one. It
wasn't what I would have chosen, but it was at least an
anonymous dark gray, not some crazy array of bright colors, and it had enough pockets.

Next, I carefully wrapped the king in a towel from
the bathroom, then encased him in bubblewrap, and put
him in the box. The suit I had purchased for the ballet
was still hanging in the closet. I hesitated for a moment
but decided to leave it. I had nicer suits back home and
damned few opportunities to wear them.

Downstairs, I tipped the concierge and checked out.
My car was waiting out front with the keys in the ignition. I hopped in and started it up. The weather had
turned chilly, and the sky was a mottled gray of low
clouds, bellies full of rain. I mapped Gabrielle's house on
my phone and eased out into the traffic, allowing the
pleasant robotic voice to guide me.

Soon I was out of the stop and start traffic of Nice
and onto the A8 freeway. Rolling green hills thick with
trees marched by under the ash colored sky which still
seemed poised to unloose a downpour at any moment.
After about twenty minutes, my phone alerted me to take
the next exit, and I did so. This put me on a two-lane road
that crossed under the freeway and snaked up into the
hills.

I passed through a small town called La Turbie, driving down the main street, then continued on up into the
hills on a narrow road lined by rock walls overhung with

bougainvillea. As I rose higher in elevation, a dense fog began to form and, before long, I had to slow down considerably as the road switched back and forth in tight curves. I passed through a golf course, which I only recognized because I happened to see a sand trap just to the side of the road. After that, the way became even narrower and the fog even thicker. Another five minutes of crawling along, cursing myself for telling Gabrielle I would come, and the phone suddenly informed me that my destination was coming up on the right. I slowed even more and saw, looming out of the fog, a two-story stone house surrounded by enormous trees and looking much the same as it probably had two hundred years ago. I pulled into the gravel drive in front of the house and shut off the engine.

As soon as I opened the door, I heard barking, and Leo rounded the left side of the house, bounded over the stone wall separating the drive from the front yard, and ran up to me. His fur was damp with beads of fog. I offered a hand, which he licked with gusto, then we both made our way toward the house, passing through an arched gateway. A light turned on above the front door, and I saw Gabrielle emerge. She waited as we walked up the path and then beckoned me in.

"It's cold out there today. I have a fire going in the living room. Let me take your coat. This way." She gestured for me to continue through the entry hall and down a short hallway. Leo trotted ahead of me, and we emerged into a large, comfortable room with roughly plastered walls and exposed beams. A fire was burning in a huge stone hearth with a grouping of sleek, low, modern furniture in a close semi-circle around it. One whole wall of the room was dark wood framed windows looking out on a large courtyard with an ancient oak tree in one corner.

"This room used to be the stable," Gabrielle said,

seeing me looking out into the courtyard. "I had it converted into the main sitting room."

I nodded, appreciating the furnishings which were tasteful and minimalist.

"Please sit. Would you like coffee, maybe something to eat?"

As soon as she asked I realized I hadn't eaten breakfast and my stomach was grumbling. "Coffee would be great," I answered, "and I wouldn't mind something to eat if it isn't any trouble."

"Of course not. I'll be right back."

Leo curled up by the fire with a grunt, and I sat, stretching my feet out. It was a nice room. It felt comfortable but impactful at the same time, not an easy accomplishment. Gabrielle returned a couple of minutes later with a tray which she set down on a low table next to my chair then seated herself on the couch opposite. There was a big, earthenware mug of steaming coffee and a cut baguette with ramekins of butter and jam.

I helped myself and sipped my coffee while she waited patiently, smiling at me. She was dressed in riding pants and a black turtleneck sweater.

"Have you been out riding?" I asked.

She shook her head. "Not yet. I'll go a bit later if the fog clears. Tell me what happened at Antonetti's house."

I leaned back in my chair, holding my coffee mug and staring into the fire. "Okay," I said. "I guess I'll start with when I got back to the house after you dropped me off." I related the whole sequence of events. Gabrielle did not react when I got to the point where Antonetti locked me in the gallery. She just nodded her head and gestured for me to continue. I obliged, describing my gambit with the lights, the trip out to the woods in the trunk of the Rolls, disarming Legere, and locking the two men in the trunk I had occupied only minutes before.

"You were lucky," she commented.

"Yes," I agreed and continued. Finally, I got the part of the story where I discovered the painting was a forgery.

"A fake!" she exclaimed, "I didn't see that coming. How was Legere fooled? Didn't he have the painting appraised?"

"Yes—at least, I overheard him discussing it with Booth. I don't know how it happened. That's something I need to figure out when I get back to San Francisco."

"He was careless. So you left the painting?"

"Yes. But I did take something else. A small statue I recognized from news coverage when the Iraqi National Museum was looted. It's from the ancient city of Uruk. Priceless. I need to get a crate so I can ship it back to the museum."

"That will sting. Antonetti will not be happy." She sat for a moment then exclaimed, "I might have a crate you can use. I bought this place two years ago, and the remodeling was only finished a year ago. I had some art shipped here from storage when I furnished the house. In fact, if you leave the piece with me, I can take care of it for you."

I considered for a moment. "No," I said. "I should do it. I don't want to leave even the tiniest opening for Antonetti to discover that you helped me. I'll take some packing supplies if you have something that will work, though."

We walked out through the house to her garage—an outbuilding connected to the main house by a breezeway. Leo trotted along with us. Her BMW took up most of the space in the garage, but there was a ladder leading up to a loft which held an array of boxes. In one corner was a stack of wooden crates. I looked through them and selected one that seemed about the right size.

Gabrielle and Leo walked me out to my car. I put the crate in the trunk then turned to her.

She stepped forward, and we embraced briefly before she pulled away and, hands on my shoulders, held my eyes with hers. "I'm glad you didn't die, Justin. Come visit again sometime."

"So am I. I will. Thanks again for all your help."

She nodded, and Leo yelped and whined. I gave him a pat on the head and got into the car. They both stood in the driveway, and Gabrielle waved as I backed out. I watched the house disappear quickly into the fog in the rearview mirror, wishing I could have stayed longer. I liked Gabrielle. She managed to be hard and solitary but simultaneously warm and inviting. Like her sitting room, she blended contradictions and made it seem natural.

The fog was, if anything, even denser than it had been when I came up. There was a steady wind from the sea that sent the murky vapor rolling in billows across the road. I drove along slowly, wary of meeting any cars coming up the road. About five minutes after I left Gabrielle's house, I noticed headlights in the rearview mirror. Another car was coming up behind me, driving fast. The driver braked and then stayed with me, tailgating. I resisted speeding up. He could pass me if he wanted to. The headlights were bright in my mirrors, but I ignored it. The occasional glimpses I got through the fog to my left showed a narrow shoulder edged by a steep hillside covered with trees. On my right was the stone wall and the bougainvillea.

A sudden, loud crack from behind made me jump. It was hard to see much in my rear-view mirror between the headlights of the other car and the fog, but it seemed like the driver had his window down and his arm hanging out. I saw a flash, heard another loud crack and, all at once my car began to pull left, bumping along. It took me a second, but then it dawned on me that the driver was shooting at me and must have hit the left rear tire. Reflexively, I braked, pulled to the left shoulder, and slammed the transmission into park as I simultaneously opened the door, rolled out, and continuing to roll down the steep hill. As I rolled, I saw the bright headlights of the other car, pulling in behind my rental and heard another crack.

I rolled over a big rock which tore at my parka then came up against a tree trunk with a bump. Hurriedly, I rose to a crouch and got behind the tree. As I did so, I heard another shot and pieces of bark showered my left cheek. I kept moving, dodging between trees, heading downhill. I heard several more shots as I ran, but none seemed to come as close as the one that had struck the tree. I didn't dare look back, but I had a good guess as to the identity of my pursuer.

How the hell did he find me? I wondered. Then it struck me: he must have been waiting for me. He had taken a chance on me visiting Gabrielle, had seen me go by on my way there, then had waited for me to pass on my way back. Smart. I should have considered the possibility. I wondered how many bullets Legere's gun held. I didn't know anything about guns, but I had held it in my hand, and I knew it was not full size. I had a notion that a full-size handgun might hold about twenty rounds. I knew a compact handgun would hold more than six but less than twenty. Maybe twelve? I would not have bet my life on it. He had fired about seven or eight rounds so far. Did he have an extra clip?

I kept moving down the hill. I could hear him following, bounding down the hill after me, his feet sliding in the leaves and dirt with every step. Two more shots rang out and, with the second one, I felt a tug at my sleeve as if a child was trying to get my attention. I felt the spot with my opposite hand, and there was a tear where the bullet had grazed my jacket. Was Legere a bad shot or were the fog and the wind making it difficult to aim? I wondered. Maybe a combination of all three plus my constant motion.

I heard a yelp then a sound of something heavy crashing through the underbrush. I turned for an instant and, through a break in the fog, saw Legere sliding down the hill on his butt. He tumbled once, nearly ran into a tree, then regained his footing. I kept moving. Dodging this way and that, trying not to be predictable. Another shot, and another, and another. I heard the first thunk into a tree trunk two feet above my head. The second went whining off into the distance. How many bullets was that now? Maybe twelve or thirteen.

The hill began to flatten and, for a moment, I was running full out on level ground but then, up ahead, I saw that it dropped off again. I slowed and stopped myself just in time, wrapping my arms around a tree to halt my momentum. The drop off was not a hill like before. It was a sheer cliff about twenty feet high. At the bottom, wispy sheets of fog blew across scattered boulders then the trees started again, marching down the hill. I hesitated for a moment, looking down, then turned to my left to continue running along the edge of the cliff. My hair and face were soaked from the fog and water ran into my eyes.

"Stop!" yelled Legere from behind me, much closer than I had thought he was. "I have a clear shot. I won't miss this time."

I slowed, stopped, and turned, holding my hands up and taking a ragged, shuddering breath. He was standing fifteen feet away, the gun pointed at me. He was soaked too, and dirt and leaves clung to his jacket and pants.

"Why don't you just shoot me?" I asked.

"I want to ask you a question first."

"Go ahead."

"Who are you? How did you get into Antonetti's house? What did you come to steal?"

"That's three questions," I said. "Why would I answer you?"

"It never hurts to ask. Shall I say, pretty please?"

I thought for a moment. There was no harm in talking. I could buy some time, maybe think of a plan.

"I came for the Heidrich."

"Why didn't you take it when you went back?"

"It's a forgery. Didn't you have it appraised?"

"Impossible," he sputtered. "I had an expert check it out."

"I would love to know the expert's name. If you tell me, I'll tell you how I got into the secret gallery."

He stood still, considering for a few seconds. The gun, pointed at my chest, did not waver. "You will die here, thief. I don't see why it matters. His name was Christoph Mather." I had heard that name before. It took me a moment, but I remembered. It was the name of Valerie's appraiser. I nodded.

"I don't know the name," I lied.

"How did you gain entry to the basement at the chateau? Did the Cartini woman help you somehow?"

"Gabrielle?" I laughed. "No. She had no idea. I fooled her into taking me to that party. She barely even knows me. It's quite simple. I hid in the house. I followed Antonetti. I watched him open the door and memorized the code."

While we were talking, I had been glancing around at my surroundings. There was a tree next to me I could try to dodge behind. There was a sturdy branch above my head I could jump up and grab. It was pretty high, but I thought I could get to it. There was also the cliff behind me. I could always jump over and hope for the best.

"How did you know about the Heidrich?"

"Enough questions," I said, my voice low. I was trying to stay under control, but that gun pointing at me was making me swing back and forth between anger and fear. My whole body was prickling with a barely suppressed fight or flight reaction. "How many bullets do you have left? I thought I counted twelve or thirteen shots."

"Let's find out," Legere said, and as he said it, he squeezed the trigger. I had no time to try to jump or dodge. I just stood there stupidly. The gun clicked, and nothing happened. Legere let out a bark of laughter.

"You were correct. No matter. I have another clip." He reached into his pocket and, as he did so, I considered rushing him. He would kill me with his hands as easily as with a gun, but it was my only option. Just as I tensed my body though his face changed, and he pulled his hand out of his pocket empty.

"Lose your extra clip?" I asked. "Maybe it fell out of your pocket when you took that tumble."

Legere's hand balled into a fist, and his face turned red. He clearly had an anger management problem. "Try kicking me in the balls this time. I'm ready for your tricks," he yelled and threw the gun at my head as he ran forward, arms held out to tackle me.

I dropped into a crouch, and the gun sailed over my head, over the edge of the cliff. As he approached, I jumped up with every bit of strength I had. My leap was fueled by adrenaline. I reached the branch easily, wrapped my fingers around it, and swung my legs forward, lifting them up. Legere jumped, too, but he was a moment too late, and his momentum carried him forward, making it hard for him to jump straight up. He just missed me and, as he passed below, I swung my legs back down and kicked him in the back of the head with my heels, letting go of the branch as I did so. The kick sent him staggering. I turned as I fell, landed almost on top of him, and pushed him with both hands in the center of his back. One of his hands shot backward, grasping for my wrist. He got a hold of it and held on as he stumbled forward, but the fog and dirt had combined into a kind of slurry on my skin and, as he floundered and fell, my hand slipped through his fingers. I watched him fling his arms up as he went over the cliff, grasping in the air for anything that might stop his fall. Then he was gone and, a moment later, I heard a thump as he landed on the rocks below followed by the sound of some smaller rocks and pebbles rolling and clattering down the hill.

I collapsed and lay there for a time, my cheek pressed into the dirt, then pushed myself up and crawled to the edge. I saw his body below, twisted around a boulder. He wasn't moving. I let my eyes unfocus, watching the fog swirl. Finally, I didn't know how much later, I rose to my feet. The bruises and abrasions I had collected on my way down the hill were aching, and I was shivering with cold, but I had to be certain. I moved along the cliff until I found a place where I could climb down safely. When I reached the bottom, I worked my way along the cliff edge, scrabbling in the loose dirt and stones, until I came to the spot where Legere had fallen. He was not moving. I approached, rolled him onto his back, and felt for a pulse. His skin was clammy and cold. He was dead. I thought about how he had cut the cord around my wrists in the forest. Why had he done that? I should have asked him. Now I would never know. If he hadn't, it would be me who was dead, Legere still alive.

I went through his pockets quickly and found his phone and a handwritten slip of paper with Gabrielle's address. He was not carrying anything else. I took both items. There was nothing else that could tie him to Gabrielle.

Slowly, I picked my way back up the hill in a daze.

When I finally reached the top, I found the Fiat and Legere's car both still running, lights on. I wondered if anybody had driven by while we were in the woods. What
might they have thought?

I got a bandana out of my backpack then wrapped
my hand in it so I wouldn't leave fingerprints. With my
wrapped hand, I opened the door and turned the key to
shut off Legere's car. I pushed the button to turn on the
hazard lights, quickly searched the vehicle, but came up
with nothing, then closed it up, and walked back to my
rental.

Though my fingers were numb and stiff, I changed
my tire in record time, not wanting to be there a moment
longer than necessary. I was happy to find that the spare
was full size and was actually inflated. As soon as the
spare was on, I put the bullet punctured tire in the trunk.
It had an entry and exit hole, so I was pretty sure there
was no bullet stuck inside. Back in the car I cranked the
heat up, shifted to drive, and got the hell out of there.

Somewhere just before I crossed the border into Italy, I exited the freeway at a combination truck stop and
rest area. I pulled into a parking spot and turned the car
off. My hands were shaking. I got out of the car and went
inside, heading straight for the bathroom. As I passed
down an aisle of junk food, a woman shopping for candy
glanced at me. Her expression turned blank, and she
looked away quickly. In the restroom, I saw that my
clothes were stained with mud. A few dead leaves still
clung to my parka which was torn at the arm and abraded
where I had rolled over rocks. My face and hands were
dirty, too, and I had a cut on my eyebrow which had clot-
ted. I went into a stall and changed into clean clothes. My
body was mottled with bruises. I put my dirty clothes in a
dry-cleaning bag I had taken from the hotel to keep my
laundry separated, then went out and washed my face and

hands in the sink. Dirt and dried blood swirled together and ran down the drain. I got a Band-Aid out of the small first aid kit I kept in my pack and covered the cut on my eyebrow. My hands were shaking badly now, and it was difficult to place the bandage. I decided I was presentable enough and went out into the diner, where I sat at the counter and ordered a café creme and a petit déjeuner Américain.

I wondered if anyone had passed by yet, seen Legere's car empty, and investigated or called the authorities. What would they think? They would probably find the gun and the bullet casings, see the bullet holes in the trees. Maybe they would think he had been chasing a deer and had fallen over the cliff. Hunting deer with handguns was not normal, but I couldn't imagine what else they would come up with. I thought about Legere. He was a psychopath who had tried twice to kill me, but still I was sorry he was dead.

Before I got back on the freeway, I drove around to the back of the cinderblock building and found an open dumpster. I got out and heaved the ruined tire in, my body aching with the effort. I used the tire iron to smash Legere's phone open. I found the flash storage and pulled it out. I also pulled out the SIM card. The rest of the phone I dumped in the trash. Back in the car, I turned on the radio and found a station playing classical music then shifted to drive and headed for the freeway and Milan.

CHAPTER 15

December 19 ~ 20:

Rain began falling from the dreary, gray sky short-ly after I crossed the border into Italy and contin-ued for the rest of the drive. I felt physically and emotionally exhausted. I wanted to pull off the highway, find an anonymous hotel in some small seaside town, and spend a week or possibly the rest of my life just staring out at the sea all day. My quest had gone sideways and was slipping out of control. There was a famous crusader I had read about named Robert of St. Albans, a member of the Knights Templar, who converted to Islam and stayed in the Middle East. He eventually became a com-mander of an army for Saladin and married Saladin's niece. I wasn't interested in leading any armies. I wasn't really interested in getting married to anybody's niece either. This thought struck me, just as I was leaving the outskirts of Genoa, heading into the rain dampened coun-tryside.

I had often mused on the insubstantiality of my rela-tionship with Valerie. I had thought it suited us both. I wasn't so sure anymore. We would need to talk when I got back to San Francisco. I remembered Gabrielle ask-ing me whether or not I was in love with Valerie. She was right—I should have been able to say yes without qualifying it. My project to recover the Heidrich painting had started out as a favor to Valerie, but I had to admit that it had quickly become a kind of obsession. I wasn't doing it for Valerie. I was doing it for myself. There was some kind of need I was fulfilling.

Maybe what I saw in this quest was a way out of the life I had chosen for myself. A life that had started to feel like a sort of trap. Maybe being literally trapped in Antonetti's dungeon then in the trunk of his Rolls Royce had shaken me enough to admit that to myself. My mind was confused and wandering along circular paths, coming back to the same conclusions then starting off again like a Templar knight pacing the halls of his fortress in his white mantle with the red cross, waiting for the attack to come.

The countryside passed in a blur until finally the farmhouses and fields began to give way to warehouses and office parks. I realized I hadn't thought about where I would go when I arrived. I had no better ideas so I decided to return to the hotel I had stayed in before while following Legere. Before I did that, though, I had one unfinished piece of business to take care of. About twenty kilometers from the city center, I saw what looked like a fair-sized town so I pulled off the highway. The place was called Trivolzio. I drove until I found a hardware store, where I purchased screws and a screwdriver, bubble wrap, and a newspaper.

Standing on the street with the hatchback of the Fiat open I packed the ancient King of Uruk into the crate as best I could, surrounding him with bubble wrap and wadded newspaper, then screwed the lid on using the holes where the previous screws had been removed. It seemed pretty secure. There was a Poste Italiane just down the street so I carried the crate there and filled out a shipping

label with the address of the National Museum of Iraq.
The clerk did not seem curious. He just weighed the crate
and pointed to the readout showing the cost. I didn't want
to use a credit card because it would allow me to be
tracked so I held up a hand in the universal "please wait"
gesture, crossed the lobby, withdrew some Euros from an
ATM, then returned to the counter, and paid cash. The
clerk took the crate and placed it next to a pile of boxes
behind the counter. *Goodbye, King*, I thought as I turned
away, *have a good trip home.*

Walking back to the car, I crossed a culvert where
water from the recent rain was flowing swiftly. I pulled
the remaining pieces of Legere's phone from my pocket
and tossed them in. The SIM card floated on the surface,
quickly swept away. The flash memory sank.

The rental car return lot was easy to find. I pulled in
and parked the Fiat then gathered my things and headed
for the counter. I had prepaid the gas so I just left the
keys on the counter, nodded to the desk attendant who
was helping another customer, and kept walking. I hoped
they wouldn't notice the missing spare tire and charge me
for it, although it would be fair if they did.

Back in the intergalactic spaceship hotel lobby, I
stepped up to the registration desk and asked for whatever room they had that was cheap. The desk clerk nodded
and, her fingers moving with practiced competence,
found a room for me, swiped my credit card, and handed
me keys while I was still staring stupidly around the lobby.

"Signore?" she said.

I started and focused on her, realizing that she had
been speaking but I hadn't heard a word. "*Mi dispiace*," I
said, struggling to focus.

She started over, telling me how to get to my room
and explaining the hotel amenities. I thanked her and

walked away. Eventually, I found myself standing in an elevator and, a short time later, in my room, staring out the window. In the distance, another wing of the hotel rose up—cyclopean in its raw bulk. Another room just like mine was there, directly across, but the window looked like the tiniest letter on the eye exam chart. I imagined another person, standing and staring out. The thought made me turn away. I needed to get some food and a drink.

I wended my way through the alien corridors until I finally emerged into the bar where I had seen Legere seated at the long counter, drinking his glass of wine. For a moment in my mind's eye, I saw him seated there but then also broken and twisted at the bottom of the cliff—two images superimposed. *Forget it*, I told myself and sat down at a table.

Before long, a server came by. I ordered a beer and a pizza. While I waited, I scrolled through the photos on my phone until I came to the ones of Legere's passport, his business card, and the invoice he had submitted to Antonetti. His younger face stared out at me from the passport photo. Knowing more about him now, I could see—or at least I convinced myself I could see—a certain hard, psychopathic distance in his eyes. I deleted the photos, one by one, then turned back to my food which had just arrived. I followed the pizza up with a whiskey, then another, possibly a couple more. Later, I woke, fully dressed, lying diagonally across the bed in my room. I had no memory of how I got back there. My head felt like it was going to split open every time my heart beat. I rose and went to the bathroom where I drank two large glasses of water, stripped, and took a shower with the water as cold as I could stand it.

The clock radio on the bedside table said it was two-seventeen a.m. when I emerged from the bathroom. I put on a complimentary robe I found in the closet, took some ibuprofen, and lay back down. Twenty minutes later, my head felt better but I was wide awake, so I rose, dug my laptop out of my new backpack, and booted it up. I logged in to the computer then to my Protonmail account where a new message from Ashna was waiting for me.

Bingo. Got Booth with a phishing attack. The old fake shared google doc exploit. You will need to install a mail client that can open the archive. You can also log in to his account but be careful since he will be able to see that someone else is in there if he cares to check (which he won't). Getting the video feeds from his sec system was easy since I already "pwned" that. Only two cameras: one at the front door and one in the entry hall. Motion activated. I looked at a couple and just about decided to kill myself. Booth walks this way. Booth staggers that way. Full bottle in this one. Empty bottle in the next one. There is sound too, but I had to turn it off. I was afraid the sound of Booth's footsteps going back and forth would drive me insane. Footage is kept for a week then recorded over. I uploaded the videos and the mail archive.

She had appended Booth's email address and password at the end and also a link to a shared folder containing the video files and email archive. I clicked through and started downloading the email. A quick search told me I could open it with any mail app that could handle mbox format, so I downloaded one and installed it. When the installer was done, I went through the initial configuration then opened the email archive so I could start digging. Everything was in the inbox. Booth was not one for filing his email in folders. There were thousands of emails, and the video was calling to me, so I switched over and started going through it. It was just as Ashna had said. There were thirty-four segments in all. None of them were very long—the camera turned on when activated by something moving then turned off thirty seconds later unless more movement was registered. The indoor camera was placed at the back of the entry hall, high up with a wide angle lens. The outdoor one was over the entry. The first segment was from the evening of December twelfth. I worked my way through them all. I saw Booth come home that evening. I saw him go out for wine. I saw myself creep up and try the front door. I knew it was me but I was wearing a hood, and the camera could not see my face. Still. I should have noticed the camera. I made a note to look more carefully in the future. Ashna must have disabled the alarm but missed the video cameras. I didn't blame her. She had been working under suboptimal conditions. I saw Legere arrive then leave. After Booth closed the door on Legere, though, the video kept going. He stood there at the door, looking through the peephole for a few seconds, then pulled his phone out of his pocket and made a call. I turned the sound up.

"It's me. He's on his way…good…Okay…tomorrow morning."

Interesting, I thought. Who had he called? It had to be Christoph Mather. That's who Legere had gone to see when he left Booth's house with the painting. Legere had told me as much just before he tried to kill me for the last time. I kept going. I saw Booth leave the next morning with a tube identical to the one he had given Legere. Several days of footage passed by then with nothing interesting. Finally, on the morning of the nineteenth, Booth was heading out the door when his phone rang, and he paused to answer it.

"Booth here." A long pause ensued while the caller spoke and Booth listened. "I see," he said, "on the twenty-third?…very well…" At this point, he continued walking out the front door and pulled it closed. It could be anything, but one of the possibilities was Mather calling to let Booth know that he had found a buyer. The exchange to be made on the twenty-third. Two days before Christmas. It didn't seem like Booth talked to other people on the phone much. There were only two more videos after that, and neither of them was useful. I turned to the email. My first thought was to run a search on my friend Roberto's name. Three emails contained the term. I clicked to open the oldest one.

Mr. Olivera,

I was referred to you by a mutual acquaintance. I am in need of a painter who is very discreet and can work on a special project involving the duplication of an existing painting. There will be a substantial payment. Please reply if you would like to meet to discuss.

Jenkins Booth

I read through the next two emails. Roberto had replied and had offered a time to meet with Booth. Booth had confirmed. I wasn't shocked. I had already suspected it. Someday, I would tell Roberto the whole story and ask him about it. I would have to wait for the right moment, though.

Next, I searched for Christoph Mather's name. There were two results. I started with the second one which was nearly a year old.

Jenkins,

It was a pleasure meeting you at the Renton opening. You mentioned a client with a specific need. I believe I may have found a possible lead. Please let me know when you would be available to meet with me.

Christoph

Booth had replied suggesting a meeting at a bar in SOMA the next evening. So, as I had suspected, the two had conspired to steal Valerie's painting and sell it to Antonetti. At some point, they must have decided selling to one buyer was boring when they could sell the same painting to two different people and make twice as much money. The greed felt palpable to me. Reading their emails gave me a hollow feeling. I thought of T. S. Elliott. Hollow Men, indeed. I switched back to my email account and replied to Ashna.

You are amazing. This was very useful. Thanks. Booth is up to some evil shit. With the time difference, I will be back in San Francisco by 2 p.m. I'll get in touch. Can we meet at my place early evening? I wish there was some way we could bug Booth's phone.

I hit send then shut the laptop and lay back on the bed. I was tired now. Before I fell asleep, I sent a quick text to Valerie, asking if she could pick me up from the airport, then set an alarm. As I put my phone down on the bedside table, a humming filled my ears, my eyes closed, and I fell slowly down into the dark well of sleep.

⋐⋑⋐⋑

After checking in for my flight and waiting in the long security line, I stopped at a food counter and got some coffee and a pastry. My eyes still felt bleary, and I knew I probably looked like hell.

I could sleep on the plane, though, and, hopefully, arrive in San Francisco refreshed. I was still wearing the clothes I had slept in, all my other clothes being dirty, so I stopped next at an Armani Jeans shop near my gate and purchased the least gaudy things I could find: a pair of gray jogging pants that looked like they would not be out of place at a resort on the French Riviera and a black T-shirt. The prices were ridiculous but I was getting used to it. I changed in the men's room.

My soiled and torn clothes were still at the bottom of my backpack. I loitered by the sink, washing my hands, until the restroom was empty then stuffed them in the garbage can and walked out. Back at the seating area by my gate, I sipped coffee until the boarding announcement crackled over the PA system.

Shortly after takeoff, I drifted off and spent the next eight hours waking periodically, glancing around the cabin, then falling back into my fitful sleep. Economy class was definitely not as nice as first class. Eventually, I woke and could not fall back to sleep, so I decided to check in on how things were going outside the gates of Troy. Several armed clashes and an airplane meal later, the captain told us to put our tray tables up and turn off our electronic devices.

I gazed out the window, watching the little whitecaps on the bay, seeing the Oakland hills, then the San Francisco skyline. It felt good to be home. We landed gently and rolled up to our gate. I hadn't heard back from Valerie before we took off. I hoped she would be there. As soon as I took my phone off airplane mode, though, a text message from Valerie popped up.

>*Text me when you land. I'll be waiting.*

I responded to let her know we were on the ground and then gathered my things and got ready to deboard. Outside the terminal, I looked for her fancy vehicle and spotted it after a minute. She popped the trunk when she saw me coming, and I tossed my backpack in. Her door opened, and she stepped out of the car, looking elegant and beautiful as ever. I wrapped her up in a hug.

"Justin. Where the hell have you been and what have you been doing? I called Gabrielle and she wouldn't tell me anything. Nice outfit by the way. I would never have suspected Armani."

"I'll tell you everything, but I don't want to say it all twice, and I need to tell Ashna, too. Can you wait a little longer?"

"Yes, but what does Ashna have to do with it? Just tell me whether or not you tracked down the painting."

"I have a very good idea of where it is and who has it. I'll need help from both you and Ashna to get it back. She's been helping me with some extra-legal research."

"Okay. Where to?"

"My place. I'm going to text Ashna now and see if she can meet us there."

Valerie piloted us out of the airport traffic and onto the 101, heading north while I got in touch with Ashna. She replied that she was taking the day off work and could meet us. Valerie told me about happenings at the gallery and about a dinner party she had attended at a mutual friend's house while we drove, but the conversation was strained, hampered by the knowledge that there were more important things to talk about. Soon we were exiting at Caesar Chavez and not long after pulled up outside my building.

It was a clear, chilly day in San Francisco. Some of the ladies from the sweatshop downstairs were outside on their break, drinking tea from thermoses and chatting. I waved hello as we entered and they smiled and waved back. Mr. Lee was in his office at the back. He ignored us as we climbed the stairs. I had emailed Roberto before visiting Gabrielle to let him know when I would be back. He was in Oakland staying with another friend now, but his paints, brushes, and canvasses were still in the corner of my workshop. He had left a note thanking me for letting him stay and a nice-looking bottle of wine on the kitchen counter.

"Open the wine if you want," I said to Valerie. "I need to take a quick shower. Ashna should be here in a minute."

I spent ten minutes under the hot water. The bruises and scrapes from my run in with Legere were still painful but beginning to heal. When I came out of the bathroom, I found them both on the couch in my sitting area with glasses of wine. Ashna was telling Valerie about something deeply technical she was working on, and Val was nodding politely. They both turned to me expectantly.

"Okay, Justin," Ashna intoned, "time to spill it all. We've decided you have no excuse for the secretiveness."

I got a glass from the cupboard and joined them, dropping into my faux Eames lounge, glad to feel the familiar leather and hear the squeak of the springs. "All right," I said, looking first Val then Ashna in the eyes, "Where should I start? After I left Val's apartment on the morning of the twelfth, I got in touch with some people I know..."

It took me about twenty minutes to tell the full story. They both listened attentively without asking questions until I was done. I left out the part where I was apprehended and taken to the clearing in the woods. I also left out the part where Legere tracked me down and tried to kill me. I didn't feel like talking about those events, and it didn't seem like they needed to know. I told them everything else, though.

"Jenkins Booth!" Valerie exclaimed when I was done. "And Mather. Assholes. I had Mather do the appraisal. He's the only real expert on twentieth-century non-figurative paintings in the Bay Area."

"Yes," I said. "And he told Booth about the painting. Booth is an antiques dealer. The antiquities scene is knee deep in the corrupt auction house system—just like the art market. Booth must have heard through a contact that Antonetti was looking for early Heidrich works. He might not actually know Antonetti's name, though, since all his dealings went through Legere."

"So where's the painting?" asked Ashna.

"It could be in a safe at Mather's office," I replied. "He might also have it at his home, but there would be no more protected place for them to store it than his office or maybe a safe deposit box. We have access to Booth's email account, but I doubt they'll discuss the location over email. It would be really nice if we could figure out exactly where the painting is stored."

"I think I might be able to help with that," Ashna said, a devilish smile spreading over her face.

"What? How?" I asked.

"Remember your email? When you said it would be nice if we could bug Booth's phone?"

"No, you didn't!"

"I did. It wasn't easy, though. He didn't have cloud backup enabled on his phone, so I needed physical access to turn that on. I went over to his shop in North Beach earlier today. Nice place. Classy. I stopped in Chinatown and bought a bunch of chicken feet and fish heads on my way there. I dumped them all over the sidewalk outside, then I went in and pretended to be shopping for a Louis the Sixteenth armoire. I looked that up before I went. He has a big old roll-top desk at the front of the store and his phone was sitting right there.

I casually let it drop that someone's shopping bag must have broken open, and there were animal parts all over the sidewalk outside.

He ran outside, and I picked up the phone and

changed the setting. He got an email alerting him, of course, but I deleted it before he saw it. I had to wait a bit for the backup to run, but now I can use his app store password—same as his email account password—and some third-party software to monitor his text messages, phone logs, and GPS logs."

Valerie and I stared at Ashna in amazement.

"Fish heads," I said, stunned. "You're a genius."

"I know. Here." She handed me her phone. "Everything gets uploaded and is accessible from this app. You can view his text messages. Any phone calls he makes will be logged but not recorded, unfortunately—you have to jailbreak the phone and install an app for that. I didn't have time." She crouched beside my chair and scrolled through the messages. "These two," she said, pointing, "are relevant, I think."

The first was from Mather to Booth, followed by a reply from Booth.

>*Exchange set for 10 a.m. Thursday morning. My office.*

>*I'll be there.*

I read the messages aloud for Valerie.

"Assholes," she repeated.

"So," I said, looking up. "The painting is either there now or will be on Thursday morning. I can try for it. If it's not there or I can't get in, we'll have to figure out a way to intercept it Thursday morning. They store high value art there all the time, though. The security has got to be good."

Ashna snorted. "The security probably sucks, actually," she said. "Corporate banks and securities trading firms have good security. Very few other businesses do.

They usually put on a good show, but their systems are rarely patched. Sys Admins are lazy."

I nodded. "Good," I said, "because I'm going to need to get in there tomorrow night."

CHAPTER 16

December 20 ~ 21:

Valerie and Ashna both stared at me for a moment then Val spoke. "I want to get these fuckers. What do we need to do?"

I took a deep breath. "Here's my plan," I said. "First, we're going to need to do some reconnaissance. We need to know what kind of security they have there, where they keep the art, the layout of the offices, etcetera. Val, can you call Mather and tell him you have a piece of art that needs to be appraised ASAP? It's an emergency. You're willing to pay extra. The client has to fly out tomorrow. Something like that? We need to get you in there today or tomorrow morning at the latest."

Valerie nodded. "No problem. I can do it right now. I have a painting at the gallery that will do." She dug her phone out of her handbag, looked up Mather's number, and placed the call. There was a pause while she waited for an answer.

"This is Valerie Walker calling for Christoph Mather...Nonsense. Tell him it's an emergency, and I need to speak to him immediately." She held the phone away from her face and stage whispered to us, "He was just leaving for the day." She turned her attention back to the call. "Christoph. Wonderful to hear your voice. Thanks for taking my call on your way out...Yes—absolutely an emergency. My customer is leaving tomorrow for Hvar and needs the piece authenticated before he leaves. He is price insensitive. You know the type. He can pay double if necessary...It's a Hammons. Recent...Half an hour?...Excellent. I'll see you then." She hung up the phone and looked at me triumphantly. "I can drop it off now, and he will take a look. He said he could go in early tomorrow to finish the appraisal if needed," she said. "I need to leave immediately if I'm going to pick up the painting from the gallery and get over to the Chatham's office in time."

"Okay," I said, jumping up. "Go. Ashna and I will meet you there. While you're getting the painting, we'll figure out a way for you to shoot some sneaky interior footage of the place."

Val nodded, leaned in for a quick kiss, then headed out the door without looking back, digging for her keys as she went.

"Be right back," I said to Ashna and dashed into my bedroom where I hurriedly retrieved the box of stuff I had packed and put on the top shelf of the closet before I left for Milan.

I brought it out and set it on the coffee table. Ashna scooted to the edge of her seat and looked on with interest while I dug through the jumbled equipment and wires until I found what I was looking for. It was a tiny camera with a lens that could be covered by a button. The camera part went behind the wearer's shirt, the lens poked through a buttonhole, and then the button covering was screwed on to hold it in place and hide it.

The camera was wired to a small DVR which could be carried in a pocket or tucked into a waist band. I had purchased it for scoping out a place I was considering for a job but had decided my visual memory was just as good after only using it once. I showed it to Ashna. "I think this will work," I said, "but we need to get something she can wear that has buttons."

"She wouldn't wear any of my clothes," Ahsna said, arching an eyebrow, "not classy enough."

"I know. We'll have to stop on the way."

"Is it charged?" she asked.

I turned it on and checked. "Forty percent. That should do."

Ashna looked at me quizzically. "Why do you have this thing?"

"Long story. I owe you that one too but it will have to wait."

"Okay. Let's go."

We took Ashna's car and made a quick stop at a fancy women's clothing boutique on the way. Chatham's was in SOMA. There were not a lot of boutiques in that area, but I happened to know of a place that had just opened because it was owned by a friend of a friend. Ashna double parked while I ran in and quickly sifted through the racks. Valerie had been wearing a gray blazer with a black linen slub weave T-shirt underneath and indigo jeans. She was picky about her clothes so I needed something that would look right.

After a couple of minutes of fruitless searching, I found an ivory crepe de chine blouse in Val's size with a three-button half placket and black buttons about the right size. The camera came with several button covers so I was pretty sure one of them would work. I held it up, scrutinized it for a moment, and decided it would do. The shop girl wanted to wrap it in black tissue and tie a purple bow around it.

The corners of her mouth crumpled into a dissatisfied pout when I refused, and she insisted on at least putting it in a fancy bag with braided cord handles and the logo of the shop hand stamped on the outside. I accepted and ran back out to the car. While Ashna drove, I got out my multi tool and carefully cut the thread to remove the lowest button.

Chatham's was on the second floor of a three story, non-descript concrete box that housed some sort of tech start-up on the ground floor and a law office on the third. A couple of tech bros were standing outside vaping. One of them exhaled and a cloud of swirling vapor blew away on the afternoon wind. The building was on a corner and had an alley on the back side. Ashna drove past, turned left down the alley, and stopped with her passenger side wheels on the sidewalk so other vehicles could get by if necessary. I texted Valerie to let her know where we were. A couple of minutes later, I saw her car turn the corner, and she pulled in behind us.

"Here we go," I said and climbed out of the car.

Outside, I was immediately hit with the stench of human shit and decomposing garbage but the cold wind whipping down the alley helped dissipate the odor.

"Sorry about the smell," I said, walking up to Valerie's car. She had just stepped out and was wrinkling her nose up as she slammed the car door. I held up the blouse for her. "You'll need to change into this. I have a little camera that will look like a button here." I pointed out the missing button. "This will tuck into your waistband to record the video."

She nodded, looked around, stepped behind me for cover, and quickly changed into the shirt. I turned the DVR on and tucked it into the back of her jeans where it was held solidly against the small of her back by the slightly stretchy denim. I then threaded the camera up under her blouse, poked it through the buttonhole, and screwed on the button cover I had selected.

"How much video can it record?" she asked.

"About forty-five minutes, I think."

"Then let's start it now and leave it running. I don't want to have to turn it on and off."

"Sounds good," I said and swiveled her around so I could press the button to start it.

She got the painting out of the trunk of her car. It was wrapped in brown paper and blue masking tape. I placed my hands gently on her shoulders. She seemed small at that moment, even though she was only half an inch short of my height in flats. The close, sheer brick and concrete walls rising up on either side of us skewed my sense of perspective. "You look nice in that blouse. You need to get a look at the place where the painting will be stored if possible. Good luck."

She smiled at me and nodded. "Thanks. I'll do my best," she said then turned and walked away.

I watched her until she rounded the building and disappeared from sight. Ashna had gotten out of her car and was standing next to me.

"She has solid abs. Expensive bra too. Not that I would have expected anything less."

"Jealous?" I asked.

"Never," she replied and walked back to her car.

I sat in the driver's seat of Valerie's car, in case we needed to move. A delivery van squeezed by and stopped farther down the alley. The driver got out and started unloading boxes of produce into the back door of a restaurant. I watched him load them on a dolly, wheel them in, return with the empty dolly. A marginal-looking guy in soiled clothes wandered by. A lean, dirty cat crept out from under a dumpster, ran under the delivery van, sat for a minute, then darted out and away. I looked at my watch. Eighteen minutes had passed. It was another five minutes before I saw Valerie in the rear-view mirror, turning the corner and walking briskly. She opened the passenger door and got in.

"Let's go," she said as she pulled the DVR out of her jeans and pushed a button to turn the camera off. I flashed the headlights at Ashna. We both pulled out and headed back to my place.

Back in my apartment, we resumed our seats, and Valerie and Ashna waited patiently while I transferred the video to my laptop so we could watch it.

"I tried to walk slowly and not bounce too much," Valerie said as I opened the video file.

I fast forwarded to the spot where Valerie was entering the building. We saw a grainy image of the lobby. A young man in a black hoodie zoomed by on a hover board, head bent down, staring at his phone. We clearly heard Valerie's mumbled "Moron," as she crossed to the elevator and pushed the up button. The doors slid open at the second floor, and Valerie walked up to a reception desk where a woman in a severe suit and tight bun was seated between two large flower arrangements.

"Valerie Walker here for Christoph Mather. I called half an hour ago," Valerie said.

"Oh yes," the receptionist answered, "I'll call him."

She picked up the phone and dialed an extension. Soon, a man emerged from a hallway behind the desk. He was middle aged, tall and slim with a high forehead and short blond hair. "Valerie!" he called, "A pleasure to see you. This is the painting, I presume," he said, gesturing.

"Yes. This is it."

"I can just run it back to my office. Cheryl has the paperwork for you to sign."

"If you don't mind, I'd like to go with you and see it safely secured," Valerie said. "I had a painting stolen from my home very recently, and it has made me nervous. I'm sure you are very careful with all the work you keep here, but it would ease my mind."

Mather hesitated for a moment, face blank. "Of course," he said. "No problem. Please come with me. You can sign the papers after we stow the painting."

Valerie followed him down a hallway, passing a couple of heavy wooden doors before he opened the door to his office and they entered. His desk was dark wood, scattered with papers. Behind the desk were a couple of large, deep, flat file cabinets. He produced a set of keys from his pocket and inserted one into a lock at the top corner of the left cabinet then pulled one of the drawers out. The painting fit with room to spare in the drawer.

After he slid the drawer closed and relocked the cabinet, he turned back to Valerie. "Voila," he said, throwing his hands up. "The cabinet is locked. My office door is also locked at night, the elevator is disabled to this floor, and we have an alarm which rings to a twenty-four-hour security service."

"Great," Valerie said. "Thanks for humoring me."

We watched Mather's back precede Valerie down the hallway. Valerie signed some papers, got a receipt, and they parted in the lobby when the elevator arrived.

"Thanks again," Valerie called as she entered the elevator.

"Of course," Mather answered. "I should have the certification ready for you by nine a.m. tomorrow."

"Nice work, Val!" I said, shutting off the video. "I'm glad you got us footage of his office. Did you see that camera in the corner of the lobby?" I asked. "They have a surveillance system. I didn't see any cameras in his office, though. There's a door in the lobby next to the elevator. It probably leads to a stairwell. It had an emergency exit sign over it. There was a door in the alley too. That's probably where the emergency exit lets out."

"It took a lot of control not to ring that asshole's neck," Valerie said, sitting back in her chair.

Ashna sat back too and picked up her laptop. "I'm going to see what I can do about getting into their network," she said, fingers already typing something into a terminal window.

"Listen, Ashna, you've helped a lot already with this. I appreciate it, but I don't want you to do anything you're uncomfortable with or that could get you in trouble."

She looked at me searchingly. "You're not the only one with a secret identity, Justin. This is minor league shit compared to some of the stuff I handle." She held my gaze, unblinking.

"Okay," I said, nodding, "let's see what you've got."

"I have a dinner appointment with a customer," Valerie said, checking the time on her phone. "I can come back later this evening."

"That's fine." I rose, and we embraced. "I'll fill you in when you get back."

"Thanks for helping with this, Ashna," Valerie said. "That painting is important to me."

"I know," Ashna replied, smiling. "Booth and Mather are dicks. We'll get it back."

I sat down next to Ashna and watched as she got to work. Her laptop screen was a tiled array of terminal windows with different colored backgrounds and contrasting text. I watched her type a command and a block of output scrolled by.

"Can you tell me what you're doing or does it break your concentration?" I asked.

"I can talk and hack," she said. "Right now, I'm gathering information. Studying the attack surface. Penetration testing. The wankers have various fancy names for it. Basically, we're just rattling doors. A network is like a building. There are multiple virtual points of entry. All of them are like locked doors. Some of the doors might have old locks, though, with known exploits. I start by finding subdomains that point to internal servers. Nobody hosts their own website internally anymore, but there are usually subdomains that lead to internal services like FTP, SSH, VPN, etcetera. Chatham's has several. I run a reverse lookup like this and get the IP addresses associated with those services." She typed a command into another terminal window, then another. "That just gets me to the door, though. Once I know how to get to the door, I have to figure out the vulnerabilities. I'm going to do a little googling and see what I can find out about their IT. They probably outsource."

She opened a browser and started searching. After a few minutes, she pointed to the screen. "Bingo. This is a local outsourced IT company I've run into before. These guys are bargain basement, so I figured it would either be them or their competitor. They list Chatham's as a client on their site. I don't know why these people are so stupid. Of course, I'm going to try to find out who does their IT if I'm trying to hack them." She clicked a link and a page full of logos loaded. "And here they are telling me exactly what vendors and systems they like to use. Certified partner!"

She laughed. "Okay. So, the VPN is probably running off one of these." She pulled up another webpage showing a fancy rack mounted box with lots of LEDs and ports. "I can probably verify by port scanning it. That model opens some non-standard ports for remote management." She switched back to a terminal window and started typing more commands.

"Something to drink?" I asked, standing up.

"Coffee."

"Okay."

I went to the kitchen and filled the kettle. A few

minutes later, the rumbling turned into a whistle, and I poured the water over freshly ground coffee I had prepared in the meantime. I brought the coffee to the sitting area and dropped back onto the couch.

"Mmm. Good. Coffee," Ashna said, sipping it, then turned back to her screen. "The firewall is the model I thought it was. I'm searching for a zero day."

"What's that?"

"Unpublished vulnerability the vendor doesn't know about. Hackers pass them around the darknet. Sometimes you have to pay for them." She was chatting with somebody in a small window. The text was in a Middle Eastern script I didn't recognize. "I'm asking a friend in Pakistan."

She was quiet for a few minutes, typing questions and replies. A URL popped up in the chat window, and she clicked it, opening a browser window. "Bingo again," she said. "This is what I need. My friend came through. I'm going to need some quiet time to get this script ready."

"Okay. I'm going to go check on my garden," I said, rising.

Ashna nodded without looking up.

Up on the roof, it was cold and windy, but Roberto had done a good job taking care of things. I had carrots and beets that were almost ready to harvest. I watered them, checked my solar panels and other systems, then went back down. Ashna was right where I had left her, still bent over her laptop.

"Exploit worked," she reported, looking up. "I'm in their network. They have a NAS that their workstations and servers back up to. I'm downloading a backup from their file server now."

There was a progress bar made up of plain text hyphens advancing in the active terminal window. The download finished, and Ashna ran a couple of commands.

"Unbelievable. It's not encrypted. It's just a tar file. Let's see what we've got in here." She was typing and lists of files in directories were scrolling past. "There are a lot of people's files here. Everybody's favorite professional social networking site might be our friend here." She opened a browser window, logged in to the site, and searched on the name of the IT company. There were about ten people listed as current employees. Ashna made a note of their names then switched back to her terminal. "Aha!" she said, pointing. One of the top-level directories was named "sjohnson." This was the first initial and last name of one of the employees of the IT firm. She opened the directory and listed the files. Dug deeper and listed again then pointed at the screen, smiling. The document she was pointing at was called "passwd.txt."

"Nice," I said.

"Beyond nice," she replied, typing a command. The contents of the file scrolled up the screen. There were five lines. The third line in the file was:

secdvr | admin | P@ssword | 192.168.101.10

"Nice password. That's going to get me into the security system," Ashna said, still smiling.

I watched as she opened another tab, in her browser, and pasted the IP Address in. A login page appeared. She entered the username and password, hit enter, and the homepage of the security system control panel opened. She poked around for a while, looking at various settings, switching between pages. She ran an internet search and opened a technical manual from the vendor's site.

After several minutes of reading, she looked up. "Problem," she said. "If I turn the cameras and alarms off, the security company is going to be alerted. It looks like they are alerted any time the system is disabled outside of business hours. It's not something I can edit in the config."

"What do we do?"

"Simple. We DDOS the security company."

"What does that mean?"

"Distributed denial of service. We hit their network with a huge amount of traffic from a botnet. They will be too tied up to receive the alert from the security system."

"And you just happen to have access to a botnet?"

"Sure. Of course, I do. Don't you? I thought everybody had one." The devilish smile was back. "I don't know how long it will give us. If they respond appropriately, at least ten or fifteen minutes. If they're idiots, it will keep them busy for as long as we want. And it will take time for somebody to respond, once they get the signal. They'll call somebody from Chatham's first. Whoever the designated contact is. Then they'll send somebody out."

"Good," I said. "That will be enough time."

"How are you going to get in?"

"Good question. I'm hungry, though. Let's discuss over dinner."

I found enough ingredients in my refrigerator and cupboards to throw together a passable dinner, and we talked while we ate. It was almost nine p.m. when Valerie returned. I buzzed her through the downstairs door, and she entered a few moments later. She was still wearing the white blouse.

"Shit! Sorry. I forgot about your shirt."

"So did I. I spent the whole dinner with this fucking camera inside my shirt." She seated herself and dropped the camera on the table. "Well," she asked, looking from me to Ashna, "what's the plan?"

"I have one important task for you when you go back

to collect the painting tomorrow," I said. "Ashna found some building plans in Chatham's files. The door in the lobby leads to a stairwell that exits to the alley as I suspected. I'm going to need you to take the elevator down, exit through the emergency door in the ground floor lobby, then disable the lock on the alley door on your way out."

"How do I do that?"

"Super glue. You'll have to hold the handle down until the glue dries. About ten seconds. Then the latch bolt will be stuck inside the door and won't engage. You'll put a couple of spots of glue on the door frame itself to hold the door closed in case anybody randomly tries to open it from the outside. A good hard yank will open it up, and I'll be in that much faster. Time is going to be important."

Valerie nodded. "Okay. Let's get it done. One thing though—I want to go in with you."

"What? No. I don't think that's a good idea—"

Valerie cut me off. "It's my painting. If you are going to risk yourself again, I'm going with you." Her expression was fierce.

"Okay," I said, nodding. "All right. We'll go in together."

CHAPTER 17

December 21 ~ 22:

A shna had to go to work in the morning, so she left shortly after we finished our planning. Valerie stayed over. We woke early and sat on the roof deck in silence, drinking coffee and watching the pelicans catch their breakfasts out in the bay. The sky was clear, and the water was still. After a while, we both drifted downstairs, took showers, and dressed for our days.

"After I pick up the painting, I'll be at the gallery all day," Valerie said, gathering her things and getting ready to leave. "I'll go home after then come meet you here. I'll let you know if I have any trouble with the super glue trick."

"Take a nap before you come if you can," I said. "Try to get here around one thirty. We're going to go in at two a.m. It's not good to sit around getting anxious for too long before."

Valerie nodded. "Justin," she said, looking into my eyes. "I wanted to thank you for all of this. You flew to Europe, broke into a chateau owned by a mobster—I didn't expect you to go to these lengths."

"I know," I answered. "It's complicated. I've felt sort of obsessed or driven since that morning when I left your condo. I can't really explain why, but getting this painting back has turned into a kind of personal quest for me."

"We'll get it back tonight. If it's there."

"I have a feeling it will be. Where else would he keep it?"

Valerie squeezed my shoulder then turned. At the door, she looked back. "See you at one thirty," she said.

I nodded, and she left.

I spent the day working on the sculpture I had left behind when I flew off to Milan. I had wasted several days on that wild goose chase, and now my deadline was approaching. The work went well and kept me from thinking too much about what I would be doing that night. I got a text from Valerie about an hour after she left.

>*Super glue worked. Door is ready for us.*

Roberto showed up around ten in the morning, and we both worked in silence until early evening. Dust from the welding and grinding was getting into his paint. I offered to help him put up some plastic sheeting, but he declined. He said he liked the texture it was giving the piece he was working on. I resisted asking him about the Heidrich forgery. It wasn't the right time yet.

When we were both done working for the day, I suggested a trip to a taqueria close by. We got caught up while eating. He asked where I had been, and I told him I had gone to LA to meet with a gallery about an upcoming show.

We parted at the door, and he headed off to catch the BART back to the East Bay where he was staying. I took my own advice and had a nap.

With the jet lag, it was easy to fall asleep, but I was restless and didn't get much out of it. I woke around eleven p.m. and started getting the things I would need together. Ashna texted me shortly after I woke.

>*Still on? The botnet is ready. I'll flip the switch when I get your call.*

>*Shooting for 2 a.m. still. I'll get in touch.*

I was ready by midnight. Cursing myself for being ready too early, I tried to think of something I could do then remembered my bike which I had abandoned at Syn Bar. As soon as I thought of it, I pulled on a jacket and ran out. I managed to hail a cab on Third Street and asked the driver to take me to the bar. The usual crowd of smokers and vapers was gathered outside. Inside, throbbing industrial noise assaulted my ears while I searched through the bikes. Magically, mine was still there right where I'd left it.

A bearded bartender wandered over while I was unlocking it. "Glad to see you came back for that. I've been wondering whose it was for days."

"Sorry," I said. "I had to take an unexpected trip out of the country."

I was still a little stiff and sore from rolling down the hillside in France and running for my life through the forest, but I wheeled the bike out and hopped on, jumping off the curb.

The cool, damp night air didn't help my stiffness at first, but I felt good by the time I pulled up outside my front door. I had worked out some of the kinks and was feeling more like myself. While I waited for Valerie, I made coffee and drank it. It never hurt to have a little artificial alertness. Finally, she texted me.

>*outside*

Go time. I hefted my backpack which was quite heavy with all the equipment I had packed, checked my pockets, grabbed my keys, and left. Valerie was parked right out front. I put my pack in the back seat and climbed in. It felt strange to be in Valerie's car and not on the way to some party or opening. I wasn't sure what to say. She was wearing black jeans, dark gray sneakers, and a black sweater.

I gave her the once over then nodded. "Acceptable. Barely."

Valerie laughed and stepped on the accelerator. The drive was quick, and we found parking on the street a couple of blocks away from the Chathams building. It was a Wednesday night, so the streets were mostly deserted. We passed a couple of homeless guys in a doorway drinking forties in paper bags. We saw a woman staring at her phone at Sixth and Howard, waiting for a cab or a ride share. Billows of fog blew by her and were momentarily illuminated by the blue light from her screen. She gave us a nervous smile as we passed.

"How are we going to get through the interior doors?" Valerie asked, shivering.

"I have a plan. I brought some tools."

"Okay. Am I just going to be in the way?"

"No. The only drawback is that two of us will be arrested for breaking and entering if we get caught."

"I can accept that. But I can't let you do this alone after everything you've done already."

"I understand."

We came to the intersection, continued past the building, and turned down the alley. It was dark in the alley with just indirect moonlight shining on the side of the building up above. When we got out of the car, Valerie hunched her shoulders, shivering. I put my finger to my lips then, and we stood quietly for a few moments. A car passed out on the street, then another. I listened but didn't hear any more cars coming, just the distant sound of traffic flowing on Market Street, horns honking.

"Let's go," I said and pushed send on the text message to Ashna I had prepared earlier. Her replies came in quick succession almost immediately.

>*releasing the botnet*
>*shutting off security system*
>*feel free to break and enter*

I handed Valerie a pair of gloves then started the timer on my watch and pulled my own pair on. When she was ready, I turned around and grabbed the door handle. I gave it a hard pull, but it didn't badge. I pulled again, harder, and it came open with a cracking sound.

"You first," I whispered, and Valerie hurried in. I followed, dabbed some more super glue on the frame and closed the door, holding it for several seconds until the glue was tacky enough to stick. "Okay. Up the stairs."

The stairway was metal and lit by buzzing fluorescent lamps that cast a harsh yellow light on us as we climbed. There were three steps up to the first-floor landing then two flights with an intermediary landing to get to the second floor. We stopped outside the door that led into the Chatham's lobby. Valerie looked at me expectantly, her eyes nearly hidden by the shadows from the overhead lights.

I took off my backpack and crouched down, opening it. "The door has a latch handle instead of a knob," I said, digging in my bag for the case that held the toolset I needed. "It's pretty standard for this type of door but highly insecure."

I found the case and pulled it out. It was a custom tool I had made myself by following instructions I found in a book on lock bypass methods. I crouched and slid the device, which was made of rigid steel holding a thin wire, into the gap between the bottom of the door and the concrete floor. Carefully then I lifted it up and hooked the wire over the handle on the other side of the door. As I moved the wire into place, I thought about the hours I had spent practicing on the door of my own building until I could do it effortlessly. Once I was good at it, I replaced the latch with a knob. Focusing back on the present, I slid the metal piece to the opposite side and pulled the end of the wire toward me, rotating the handle down and disengaging the latch.

"Push the door," I said.

Valerie reached out and gave it a shove and the door swung open. "Magic," she whispered, peering into the dark lobby.

"And a little bit of skill," I answered. "Let's go."

We hurried across the lobby. The red glow from the emergency exit sign above the door gave us enough light to see by. Valerie led the way, around the reception desk and into the hallway. It was dark there, so I took out my LED flashlight and aimed it down the hall.

Valerie stopped in front of the third door. "This is Mather's office."

I knelt down and examined the lock, shining the light on it. As I had thought, based on the quick look I had gotten on the video, it was a simple tumbler lock. It was a good one but not immune to what Ashna would call a brute force attack.

"Okay, I'm not going to bother with finesse here," I said, digging in my pack again. I pulled out a heavy duty cordless drill motor, a box of bits, and a hammer and hole punch. "Hold the light," I said, handing her the flashlight.

Quickly, I pounded an indentation just above the keyhole with the punch, fitted a bit into the drill, and started drilling. After ten seconds, the bit slowed and stopped so I reversed it out with a cascade of metal shavings that glinted in the flashlight beam. I went in again. Another five seconds and I felt the last pin give way. I pulled the drill out and stowed it quickly then used a flat-head screwdriver to turn the lock. It rotated easily, and I pushed the door open.

"We're in," I said.

"Magic again," Valerie replied.

We both stepped in to the office. The blinds were drawn, so I went ahead and turned the light on. My watch said eight minutes twenty-three seconds. We were making good time. I repeated the drill trick with the flimsy lock on the flat file. I was through in no time and opened it with the screwdriver.

With the lock open, I turned to Valerie. "You do the honors," I said.

She stepped forward and started pulling drawers open. I watched over her shoulder. Most of the drawers were empty. She opened another. Empty. The next one held an abstract painting in whites and greens. She wrinkled her nose. "Godawful," she whispered and slammed the drawer closed. I had to agree.

She made it to the last drawer and hesitated, looking at me, her face blank, then pulled it open. It was empty. Valerie slumped down to her knees. "Shit," she said.

I stood for a moment, not sure what to do. It had to be there somewhere. "Wait a minute," I answered, looking across the room.

There was a safe on the floor next to a file cabinet. It seemed deep enough to hold the rolled-up painting. I pointed to it.

Valerie's face brightened for a moment, then turned sarcastic. "I suppose you can just drill that too."

"No. But I can probably open it." I said, walking over to the safe for a closer look.

It was what I expected it to be: a mid-range model probably purchased at one of the big box office supply stores. I had just the thing. "Hand me my backpack please."

"Damn, Justin. Why is this thing so heavy?" she said, lugging it over to me.

I smiled, opened it, and pulled out a yellow plastic case. "Stand back," I said, opening the case and pulling out my rare earth magnet. It was wrapped in an old sock.

"What's that?" Valerie asked.

She looked truly perplexed. Just as she spoke, though, my phone buzzed in my pocket. I put the magnet down, holding up a finger and checked my phone. It was a text from Ashna.

>*Get out asap. Their network guys are good. Circumventing my DDOS. Security will be alerted. Might be there very soon.*

"We need to get out soon. I'm just going to try this," I said, glancing at Valerie.

She nodded. I picked up the magnet and placed it on the upper left side of the safe door then moved it carefully down and to the right. I was pretty sure the solenoid was located in the upper left of the door somewhere. As I slid the magnet, I tried the handle of the safe. Suddenly, after I had dragged it perhaps an inch and a half, the handle gave way and the safe door opened as I pulled back on it.

"What the hell, Justin!" Valerie called out.

"Simple. I can explain later."

I pulled the door open the rest of the way, and there it was. The black tube whose doppelganger I had pursued across Europe. The last time I had truly been in its presence was when I watched the unnamed thief hand it off to Booth at the cafe in North Beach. I felt prickles of sweat on my forehead, and my breathing quickened. No time for panic now. I took a deep breath and shut my eyes for a moment, calming down, then reached in and grabbed it. I handed the tube to Valerie, slid the magnet off the safe, and stowed everything back in my pack.

"Let's go," I said.

We both hurried back down the hall and out into the dark lobby. I held up a hand, and Valerie stopped. I pointed to the windows to the left of the reception desk, and we both walked over. The blinds were closed here too. I pried two slats apart and looked through just in time to see a marked security vehicle pull up at the curb outside. Another vehicle was already there. Big guys in paramilitary garb started climbing out of the cars.

"Crap. Let's hurry," I said, grabbing Valerie's hand and pulling her across the lobby.

I opened the emergency door quietly, we both stepped through, then I closed it again carefully, not making any noise. I led the way, creeping softly down the stairs. After only three steps, though, I heard a noise below—a door opening and the squawk of a walkie talkie.

I turned and motioned to Valerie. "Back up. Keep going."

I had taken a good look at the neighboring building when we were parked in the alley, and I had a feeling we could get to it from the roof, so I grabbed Valerie's hand again, and we both ran silently up the stairs. We went up four flights, passing the third floor and continuing up. At the top, we opened the door as quietly as possible and passed through onto a tar and gravel roof lit by a bright moon overhead. I pulled the door closed behind us, found the tube of superglue in my pocket, and squeezed as much as I could between the door and jamb, working it up and down, then tossed away the empty tube. Valerie was looking to me for the next move, her face fearful.

"It's okay," I said. "We're almost home free. Let's go. This way."

I took her hand again, and we fled across the roof, the cool night air on our faces. I led her to the edge. The building next door was close. The gap was about five feet, and the roof was slightly lower than ours.

Valerie stopped at the edge and turned to me, her face silver in the moonlight. "I can't."

"Yes, you can. Come on. I know you ran track at that fancy boarding school. Gabrielle told me. You can jump that. I'll go first." I tossed my backpack across, and it landed with a thump. I backed up then and took a running jump, clearing the gap and landing hard on the other side. "Toss me the painting," I said, turning back to face Valerie.

She underhanded the tube to me and I caught it.

"I didn't realize you were going to make me jump off buildings."

"You'd better hurry if you don't want to spend the night in jail."

She backed up about fifteen feet, took off running, and sailed over the gap. Her leap was much more graceful than mine, and she landed a good five feet from the edge, beating my distance by several feet.

"One of my events was the long jump," she said, straightening up.

"Clearly. Let's get out of here."

The roof we were on now was white thermoplastic. I felt exposed in my dark clothes on the white roof. We hurried toward the far end where I saw the top of a fire escape ladder poking up. When we reached, it I looked down. It went all the way down the side of the building, with landings at each floor, and stopped about ten feet from street level in a narrow walkway between the building we were on top of and its next-door neighbor.

"Ladies first," I said, and Valerie snorted.

She went over the edge, and I followed her. I paused at the top of the ladder, just my head above the edge of the roof, and looked back. I could hear a pounding sound coming from the building we had just exited. Suddenly, the roof door flew open, and one of the security response team guys came tumbling out. He had broken through the super glue. I quickly ducked and moved down the ladder. The rungs were cold and damp. Valerie was at the bottom.

"You'll have to hang and drop," I said. "It's not far. Hurry, they're on the roof."

She climbed down farther, hung from the lowest rung, and dropped. I followed and felt the impact in my fillings when I landed.

"Okay," I said. "We're going to walk out of this alley. We're two tech workers who just worked until two-thirty a.m. on a project, and we're laughing and happy to be leaving."

Valerie nodded, and we headed down the walkway to the street, where we turned away from the Chatham's building and headed the other direction. Behind us, there were flashing lights, and I could hear radios crackling with anxious commands. We reached the end of the block just as a police car pulled up. An officer jumped out of the car, gave us a once over, then headed up the street, talking into his radio. His partner followed with a flashlight which he shone into windows and doorways. We turned and kept walking.

"I would have been arrested right there if I was by myself," I said.

"Yes. But you would have been out sooner without me."

"Maybe. All the same, I'm glad you're here."

"Me too. Let's go look at my painting."

"Good idea."

I felt exhilarated, and Valerie clearly did too. We walked fast, holding hands and striding along, back to Valerie's car. When we reached the car, she slid into the driver's seat immediately and started the engine with a muffled roar. I threw the painting and my backpack in the back seat, climbed in, and shut the door just as she put it in gear and stepped on the accelerator. Soon, we were blocks away, crossing Market Street, out of danger. On our way back to Valerie's condo, I took deep breaths and tried to quiet the racing of my heart.

"That was fun, but I'm glad I never have to do it again," Valerie said.

I was trembling with the adrenaline and starting to feel like a crash was coming on. By myself, I would have been calm. Having Valerie with me, being responsible for her, had made me nervous. Remembering Ashna, I got out my phone and texted her.

>*Made it out. Got the painting (I hope—haven't unrolled it yet). Dinner tomorrow?*

She replied a moment later. >*Phew! Yes. I want the story.*

>*OK. Tell me where you want to eat and when and I'll meet you there.*

We drove through the deserted streets of North Beach. In the garage, I closed the car door and the sound seemed crazily loud. I was still hopped up on adrenaline.

We rode the elevator up in silence. Inside, Valerie turned on the light over the kitchen table and put down the tube.

"You open it," she said.

I unscrewed the cap on the end, turned it upside down, and shook it. The rolled canvas slid out into my other hand. I placed it on the table and carefully unrolled it. Heidrich's composition lay there before us. I found it beautiful now. Somehow, I had developed a taste for his work. I stared down at the thin red glaze, the black lines ghostly and receding into the background. Unlike the forgery, it felt right, harmonious. I turned to Valerie. Her hand was covering her mouth and tears were sliding down her cheeks. I put my arm around her.

"We got it back."

"Yes, we did."

CHAPTER 18

December 22 ~ May 24:

I woke before Valerie the next morning and extracted myself from the bed, careful not to wake her. I set a kettle of water boiling in the kitchen and stood staring stupidly into space until the whistle of the kettle roused me. The hot water soaked into the coffee grounds I had prepared in a pour-over basket and began dribbling down into the cup below. When it was ready, I shuffled into the home office in Valerie's second bedroom, clutching the steaming mug.

The computer was asleep, so I tapped the spacebar and logged in. I had installed the Tor browser on Valerie's computer a few months before, so I started it up then typed the URL of an anonymous email service into the address bar. The site opened, and I typed in Booth's and Mather's email addresses, referring to a note I had made on my phone. I hesitated for a moment, thinking and sipping coffee, then typed into the subject line:

Your missing Heidrich :(

I tabbed to the body of the email, took another sip of coffee, and began typing:

Dear Booth and Mather,

You have been pretty stupid, but greed does that to people. Do you realize who you sold the Heidrich forgery to? His name is Patrice Antonetti. You may not be aware of this since you went through a middleman named Legere. Legere is dead now, but Antonetti is very much alive. Look Antonetti up. He is a member of the Corsican mafia. I can personally attest to the fact that he is not a nice guy. If he finds out about the forgery, I guarantee that he will arrange to have you both killed in unpleasant ways. I hope I don't have to send an anonymous email like this one to Antonetti, letting him know that the painting is a fake and who is responsible. What will keep me from sending that email? First, no harm will come to Valerie Walker, and no attempt will be made to steal this painting from her again. I hope for your sakes that no other thief unconnected to you tries to steal it because I will not know the difference, and I will have to notify Antonetti. I also hope Valerie does not get into a random automobile accident or fall a cliff because that too will trigger an email to Antonetti. Do you get the picture? You need to pray that nothing happens to Valerie or this painting.

What else? Oh yeah—the money. You will take the money you received from Legere for the forgery, and you will put it in a black backpack. Make it a Patagonia Refugio 28L. I need a new one of those. You will leave the backpack at the pier 52 boat launch on the bench closest to the 25 MPH speed limit sign at precisely 12 p.m. on December 24th. After you place the backpack on the bench, you will get back in your car and drive away. Failure to follow these instructions exactly will also trigger an email to Antonetti. I have devised a system that will automatically notify Antonetti if I do not manually stop it by a certain time every day. So, please don't think you can get out of this by trying to harm me.

One more thing: Legere is dead because of me. If Antonetti doesn't kill you, I will. Don't fuck around. Get this done.

I hit the send button and closed the browser. I did not actually intend to notify Antonetti if they didn't follow through, but I had a feeling the threat would work. They had no idea who they were dealing with. The sender of the email could be a psychopath who meant every word. I didn't think they would take the chance.

I stood and went back to the kitchen to rinse my cup. The Heidrich was still spread out on the kitchen table. Mason jars of homemade apricot jam held down the corners. Few people knew, or would have believed, that Valerie made jam every summer. She had told me it was a family tradition. Slanting, golden morning light was throwing the surface of the painting into relief, and the shadow of one of the jars stretched across the painting blending an apricot hued light into the red. I studied it again. It felt good to have it back where it belonged.

In the bedroom, Valerie was tangled in the sheet, the blanket thrown off onto the floor. A shaft of the same golden morning light lay across the foot of the bed, shining through the peaks of sheet, throwing the valleys into shadow. I picked up the blanket and laid it over Valerie, kissed her lightly on the cheek, and left.

လာလာလာ

That evening I met Ashna at her favorite restaurant in the Mission. It was a sushi place away from the main drags of Mission and Valencia, up a side street and around a corner—the kind of place that catered to locals, although the locals were a different crowd now. I got there early and procured a table in the back corner where it was dark and quiet. I sipped a soju cocktail while I waited for her. When she arrived, she swept in and dropped into the chair across from me, brushing her impressive mane of hair back from her forehead with one hand.

"Tell me everything. Now. This is the reckoning. All of the secrets you've been keeping and promising to tell me but putting off."

"All right," I said, looking her in the eyes. "Let's start with this—I'm a thief."

"I figured that out. Tell me about it," she demanded.

I nodded, took a sip of my drink, then started at the beginning. We ordered at some point, our food arrived, we ate. We were still talking when the check arrived. I paid, and we went to the bar across the street—a dark place with candles, white table cloths, and an old movie from the forties playing silently on a TV screen up in the corner behind the bar. We kept talking. Finally, I was done. It was an immense relief to have told somebody. I had given her the details of every theft I'd ever committed. I had never told these things to anyone else. Valerie knew I was a thief, but she didn't know details.

"Interesting," Ashna said, nodding her head and looking me over. "Very interesting. I want in."

"Ashna, come on."

"What? We work well together. Would you have been able to pull off the last one without me helping you?"

"Maybe. I probably would have figured it out. I've done it before. Mainly though, I don't really want to steal art from people anymore. Getting Valerie's painting back was an interesting job for me. I'm not sure how to go about it, but I think I want to start helping people get stuff back, instead of taking stuff from them."

"That's interesting too."

"Yeah. I think it could be lucrative as well. Which brings me to something else. I think I'm going to have a large amount of cash in the very near future, and I want to give some of it to you."

කෘෂ

The next day I was out on the pier with a fishing pole, a tackle box, and a white plastic bucket. That morning, I had ridden my bike around and observed the old men who fished from the piers then went to a thrift store and purchased some clothes that looked just like theirs— a flannel shirt, baggy, well-worn jeans, a green hoodie, and a wide brimmed straw hat. There was one other guy fishing but he was farther out, near the end of the pier. I checked my watch— eleven-fifty-seven a.m. The bay smelled fishy, and my thrift store clothes smelled musty. I watched the seaweed bob in the small waves.

At two minutes after noon, a green Jetta pulled up and stopped in the bike lane. I watched out of the corner of my eye, the brim of my hat pulled low. The emergency flashers turned on, and a tall blond man stepped out of the car. It was Mather. He glanced around nervously then opened the trunk and took out a backpack. I could tell it was heavy from the way he carried it.

He didn't look like he was used to carrying heavy things. He walked over to the bench, put the pack down, looked around nervously again, then went back to his car, and drove away toward the ball park. I watched until I could no longer see the car, then stood, leaving my brand-new fishing gear where it was, walked to the bench, and picked up the pack. I pulled the straps over my shoulders. It was the backpack I had specified, and it was really heavy. My bike was locked up across the street. I unlocked it, hopped on, and took off.

The route I took home was circuitous. I went down small alleys, side streets, through a park, and took shortcuts through a parking lot and a construction site. By the time I got to my building, I was certain that I had not been followed.

Upstairs, I dumped the contents of the pack out on my coffee table. It was one hundred-dollar bills in bundles of fifty, held together with red rubber bands. The money—all together like that—smelled terrible. The bills were different vintages, non-consecutive serial numbers, and were worn from use. I counted the haul. The total was five hundred and seventy-three thousand dollars. I had no idea how much Antonetti had paid for the painting. My guess was seven hundred thousand based on what Booth and Mather had put in the pack. They would have had to pay the thief. They had probably already spent some of the rest. I didn't really care about the money. I just didn't want them to have it. The amount was close enough to what I had expected. Now I needed to figure out how to convince Valerie to take a third of it. Ashna had already consented. Valerie would be the real test.

℘ↄ℘ↄ

Spring in San Francisco was treacherous. Some of the nicest weather all year happened in April and May. Then, all of a sudden, the fog rolled in, and you might not feel warm again until September. The easy solution was to head over to the East Bay, down the Peninsula, or up into Marin where it was almost always warm and sunny. Somehow, I almost never did that. I stuck with the city through the cold summer. This year though, I was planning a trip.

The day was warm—maybe one of the last warm

days before that fog came in. I was up on top of Bernal Hill again, looking out over the old gold mountain. I had promised Roberto that I would help him hang a show, so I got up off my hard-stone seat, stretched, and brushed the moss off the seat of my shorts. My trusty old Miata had been stolen a couple of weeks before when I left it outside the main library branch at civic center. I had a new bike—a matte black Trek commuter bike. I wasn't sure whether I liked it yet.

Passing by Precita Park, I saw the kids playing and the dogs running. I rode slowly through the Mission, through the edge of SOMA, and up into the bustling heart of downtown. When I reached the gallery, I went around to the back and brought my bike in through the rear door. Valerie and Emilio were there with several paintings leaned against the wall, planning which ones to hang and where they should go. Valerie broke away and gave me a quick embrace.

"Thanks for coming, Justin. Roberto needs your help. He can't decide which ones to hang and which ones to hold in reserve."

We were a little awkward with each other, having broken off our relationship by mutual consent shortly after Christmas. We had talked it out and agreed that we needed space to explore. She was dating a guy named Greg who did something with money. I had met him once at an opening. He seemed more her type—tall, patrician, well-bred. Truthfully, I wasn't sure what she had ever seen in me. I had succeeded in convincing her to take a third of the money I got from Booth and Mather, though. She used it to pay off the loan for expanding the gallery, and she was now in negotiations to open an extension in Los Angeles.

I had no doubt that it would be successful. Before long, she would be at the top of the art world food chain, commanding a string of galleries around the world in all the hottest markets.

"I'll go talk to him," I said.

In the main gallery space, I found Roberto striding back and forth, moving canvases around. His face was anxious as he turned to me. "Justin! I need your advice."

"Okay," I said, "let's get to work. First, though, here are the keys to my place. I'll forget if I don't give them to you now. Thanks again for housesitting."

ℯↄℯↄ

The plane touched down with a jolt that woke me from a deep sleep. I rubbed my eyes, rolled up the shade, and looked out the window. The runways of Charles de Gaulle airport were sun baked, and the saturated green of the grass between them was vibrant in the bright light. I wandered through the terminals in a daze until I finally came to the exit and the arrivals curb where I walked up and down, scanning the arriving vehicles. Suddenly, I saw Gabrielle's white SUV pull up to the curb fifty feet down the terminal. She jumped out and waved, smiling. Leo was jumping up and down in the back seat, banging his paws on the window.

ℯↄℯↄ

A week later, after a leisurely drive through the heartland of France and plenty of wine consumed in ancient vineyards, I found myself stretched out in the warm sun on the deck of a truly impressive yacht, somewhere off the coast of Corsica. My body felt relaxed to the point of near immobile languor. I opened my eyes a crack and saw Gabrielle stretched out nearby in a white bikini, a tall glass of something peach colored in her hand. An ice cube clinked in the glass, and the soft lapping of the Mediterranean waves on the hull lulled me back into a catatonic doze.

That evening, after a dinner of fresh fish caught that morning by the crew, we were sitting on the teak floored upper deck, a light breeze ruffling our hair and cooling our faces. Leo was stretched out asleep, his paws twitching. Gabrielle's father, on whose yacht we were guests, was sitting with us. He was a medium-sized man, dark, with strong hands. He lifted a glass of sparkling white wine and took a sip, then turned to me.

"Justin," he began, pronouncing my name with a fluid Corsican accent. "Gabrielle has told me a bit about your dealings with Antonetti and your eventual success recovering your friend's missing painting."

I nodded, glancing at Gabrielle who was smiling. "Yes," I answered. "It was an interesting adventure."

"I have a friend, a man of means, who has recently lost an item of great value and significance to his family. A piece of art." His eyes were boring into me with the same intense gaze I had seen in Gabrielle's the first time we met. "Perhaps you would be willing to consult with him? To see if there is something that can be done?"

I met his gaze, nodding and smiling. "That is a very interesting proposition, Signore Cartini," I replied. "I would certainly be happy to speak with him."

About the Author

Bradley W. Wright is a writer and educational technology professional. He lives in Los Angeles, California, with his family.